Risking it all for love and valor . . .

When Corporal Sean MacBranian awakens after being injured in battle, he is sure the luck o' the Irish has run out on him. Or that he's died and gone to Heaven. There can be no other explanation for the blonde-haired, blue-eyed angel standing before him. But his "angel" is a truehearted lass named Ashlinn, and she wears a nurse's uniform. Her tender ministrations have brought him back from the brink of death—and have given him a new reason for living.

Ashlinn knows their parting is inevitable; her handsome hero must return to the 69th infantry of the Union army, and there are no guarantees of his safe return. With most of her family already destroyed by the war ravaging America, she is sure she cannot survive another loss. Yet she feels powerless against the draw of Sean's strong and steady heart. Neither time nor distance nor the danger of battle seems to lessen their bond. But when their secret letters are intercepted, the devoted nurse's love will face the ultimate test . . .

Visit us at www.kensingtonbooks.com

Books by Heather McCorkle

Emerald Bells
Honor Before Heart

Published by Kensington Publishing Corporation

Honor Before Heart

Emerald Belles

Heather McCorkle

LYRICAL PRESS
Kensington Publishing Corp.
www.kensingtonbooks.com

First Electronic Edition: March 2017
eISBN-13: 978-1-5161-0286-0
eISBN-10: 1-5161-0286-X

First Print Edition: March 2017
ISBN-13: 978-1-5161-0289-1
ISBN-10: 1-5161-0289-4

For my heart, Edd McCorkle

Acknowledgements

There are so many people that helped get me here that I don't know where to start, so I suppose the beginning it is. I must thank the Dropkick Murphys, an American Irish punk band whose music has been paramount to my inspiration for this novel. It was their song The Fighting 69th that first made me want to know more about the 69th brigade, and thus, sparked the inspiration for this entire novel. Thank you to my husband, Edd, who put up with all the hours of writing, questions, and brainstorming sessions. Thank you to my mentors, William Bernhardt and Eldon Thompson. I would not be the author I am today without you two. Thank you to my writer tribe on Twitter and Facebook, my Seymour Family, my fans, family, and my good friend and fabulous author Scott Wilbanks. You all give me strength and inspiration. Last, but certainly not least—not ever least—I want to thank the good people of the 69th brigade, both those who serve it today and those Irish American's who originally served it so long ago.

Chapter 1

Not even the threat of rain heavy upon the Virginia air could banish the sickly sweet stench of death. The boom of cannons and rifle fire slowly trickled to a stop. That, or Sean's hearing was going. A quick glance around revealed bodies of the dead and dying strewn across Malvern Hill, turning its green grass a brilliant red. Relief churned with the ever-present guilt of all he had done in the name of country and freedom this day. Turning his head up to the cloud-choked evening sky, he said a silent prayer for the fallen on both sides of the conflict.

Only soldiers in blue coats were left standing and not many of them down near the river where Sean was. It made him wonder how many of the 69th regiment had perished this day. So many Irish brothers lost…no, American brothers, he had to remind himself. They were more than just Irish now. They were Americans, and had died as such.

The muzzle of his rifle drooped until the bayonet fixed upon the end of it touched the muddy bank of the James River. With General Lee's soldiers on the retreat, it seemed they had won the day. But at such a horrible cost.

A rustling in the brush along the river pulled Sean from his dark musings. In the fading light, he couldn't quite make out what moved within the tall brush. Whatever it was, it was close, no more than ten feet away. Though his heart hammered like a galloping horse, his hands were steady as he tossed his empty rifle aside and drew his saber.

"Damn beast!" a man cursed with a thick Southern drawl.

The voice came from much farther down the bank than the rustling brush. Sliding into a fighting stance, Sean split his attention between the direction of the voice and that of the rustling. From the brush emerged a furry shape that at first glance seemed the size of a bear. Wouldn't that just be his luck? To survive such a battle only to be mauled by a bear. Huge brown eyes gazed out of a gray face that was decidedly canine. While the creature was over three feet at the shoulder, it was most certainly a dog. And it was a breed Sean knew well: an Irish wolfhound. He began to wonder if perhaps he had been struck on the head. Such a dog didn't exist in America. He hadn't seen one since he'd left Ireland over three years ago. Mesmerized by the creature's curious eyes, he took a step toward it. Pink tongue lolling from the side of its grinning mouth, it moved toward him as well.

The click of a rifle hammer locking back froze Sean in mid-stride. From out of the brush, not five feet away stepped a soldier in a filthy gray uniform. Blood stained his left arm. His gap-toothed sneer inspired more contempt in Sean than it did fear. The end of the rifle barrel pointed at him was another matter altogether.

"Two fer one, must be my lucky day," the man said.

A low rumble like a distant train, only far more menacing, sounded from the dog beside Sean. Canine eyes filled with deadly intent fixed upon the Confederate soldier as her lips curled back from long, pointed teeth. The barrel of the gun swung from Sean to the dog. Overwhelmed by a powerful need to protect not only a creature his people treasured, but an innocent, he lunged for the gun with his saber. The explosion of the bullet exiting the barrel of his enemy's rifle reverberated through his saber and up into his arm. Followed by a trail of smoke, the Minie ball tore off through the brush, thankfully far wide of both Sean and the hound.

"Damn Yank!" the soldier cursed as he swung his rifle back toward Sean.

Sunlight shone in a bright line upon the bayonet fixed to the end of the rifle that thrust at him. Sean blocked the strike with his saber. Arms shaking from exhaustion, he shoved the bayonet away and stepped back.

"Your regiment is defeated this day. Retreat and be done with it. There's no need for more bloodshed," he said.

Snorting laughter erupted from the soldier. "Not a chance, Yank. I'll kill that hellhound if it's the last thing I do."

Brows pulling together, Sean shook his head. How anyone could stand amid so much death and wish for more, especially when it involved an innocent creature, he simply could not understand. But then, he expected no better from a man who fought to keep others as slaves. Men such as him were what kept Sean fighting when all seemed hopeless. Freedom was worth the cost, even if it wasn't his own and even if it cost his own life.

The Rebel soldier's eyes flicked to the dog and back again. His lip curled up from yellowed teeth, muscles tensing. Keeping his attention locked on the man's eyes, Sean noticed his gaze skitter to his midsection. Sean blocked the strike to his abdomen but he didn't see the Bowie knife coming at him until it was almost too late. Bringing his left arm forward, he tried to block the second strike. Breath stolen away by the pain that seared through his left bicep, he staggered back. Dark eyes filled with a terrible satisfaction, the soldier pulled his blade free of Sean's skin and came at him again. Sean blocked the thrusting bayonet and sidestepped the Bowie knife. The man growled in frustration.

Canine teeth snapped and snarling issued forth from the hound that moved up to Sean's side. Eyes dancing between the dog and him, the man raised both weapons and lunged. Diving in the way, Sean blocked the bayonet from the dog and brought his arm up to block the knife strike aimed at him. Instead of going for his chest like it appeared he would, the soldier stabbed the Bowie knife at his midsection. At the last moment, Sean was able to twist away enough that the blade pierced his side instead of his abdomen, but it still burned like the fires of hell. He shoved the man back with a strength born of fury.

Before the Rebel could recover, Sean swung for the arm that held the rifle, cleaving the limb off just below the elbow. Spurting blood and obscenities, the man stumbled backward, nearly tripping over his own feet in his haste to get away. The massive hound at Sean's side gave chase, barking with a ferocity that made him glad it wasn't directed at him. Screaming all the louder, the man turned tail and ran. The saber in Sean's hand slowly sagged toward the ground. That small movement made pain erupt through his wounded side. The sight of the battlefield before him swayed and suddenly he was on his knees in the mud and blood.

"Dog!" he called out as loud as he dared.

The idea of saving the poor creature only to have it meet its death from seeking revenge for his wounds sat wrong with him in so many ways. The two fleeing figures bounded out of sight over a hill. Again, Sean called out to the canine. An eerie quiet settled once the Rebel soldier's screams faded into the distance. With great reluctance, Sean looked down at the wound in his side. A crimson stain spread steadily across his blue uniform. The color wasn't dark enough to indicate arterial blood, but enough of it flowed from him as to be alarming.

Even though he was on his knees, the world still swayed. He toppled onto his side, the pain shooting through his wounded left arm snapping his eyes back open. For a fleeting moment, he worried about how he was going to hold a fiddle again if a doctor amputated that arm. But with the wound in his side, he realized it wasn't likely that he'd make it off this battlefield without help. At least he had saved the life of one innocent today, and while he had done terrible things in the course of this war, it had been in the name of freedom. Hopefully whatever lay in wait to judge him took that into account.

Big, fat drops of rain started to fall from the gray sky that loomed overhead. He turned his face up to it, trying to breathe in the clean scent of rain as opposed to the stench of the carnage around him. Were it not so warm, he could almost convince himself that it was the land of his birth he lay bleeding out upon instead of foreign soil thousands of miles away. If there were any mercy in the afterlife, he'd be allowed to return to Ireland, or better yet New York, and haunt its shores instead of this forsaken place.

A ridiculously big tongue slobbered across half his face, drawing him from his woeful musings. Soft whining sounded near his right ear. Warm fur brushed his right side, pressing against the entire length of his body. He had a moment to send up a prayer to whoever would listen that the hound at least waited for him to die before it tried to eat him. Then darkness swept him away.

Chapter 2

At the count of thirty, Ashlinn finally gave up on finding a pulse and removed her fingers from the doctor's neck. She pried the blood-splattered leather bag from his stiff fingers and marched on through the sea of corpses. Time was of the essence and sparing any for a prayer or kind word toward a man who had shown her nothing but contempt could cost another man his life. Steeling her heart against the carnage before her, she marched on, searching the field of corpses for anyone still breathing.

At least, that's what she told herself she searched for. The other medical personnel had long since pulled back with the union troops, returning to Harrison's Landing to regroup. But she refused to leave while daylight still set the cloudy sky aglow. Little danger remained since the Confederate soldiers had retreated hours ago. So she told herself.

Rain began to drip down the back of her exposed neck and run beneath the collar of her shirt. She longed to let her long hair free from her woolen forage cap to protect her neck, but she didn't dare. The long blond tresses would be a blazing fire that branded her a woman to any who may look across the field. It was one thing for her gender to be known at the ambulance wagons or field hospital, another entirely to be discovered out here amidst the carnage where civility had been abandoned completely.

Carefully inspecting the face of each corpse, she searched to find the one so familiar to her—and prayed not to at the same time. More than once she had to roll bodies over, wipe coagulating blood away, and even discern identity from only part of a face that was left. Each one made her heart ache for a family that would never again see their son, father, or brother. But it was a distant, dull ache from a heart that had hardened over the two years she had spent as a nurse in this war. Such curing was the only way for one's heart to survive the atrocities surrounding her.

On and on her search went and not a single survivor stirred amidst the carnage. Most had been picked up and hauled off, but she had already checked those. In the fading light it soon became difficult to make out the faces of the dead. Casting her gaze out across the blood-soaked field, she took in the dozens upon dozens of bodies strewn about that she still had to check. Today's casualties easily numbered in the hundreds on both sides. The cloud-choked sky deceptively hid the sun's march toward the horizon. It was nearly impossible to tell how late it was. She was too close to finishing to stop now, though. At least she had reached an area where the ground had leveled out now and would be easier going. The hillside didn't look like much, but it had been hell maneuvering through the bodies coming down it.

Roused from her searching by a soft woof, she instinctively clutched the doctor's medical bag to her and looked up. A long-legged gray dog that looked more like a monster out of an old myth than a canine came loping across the field toward her. At the size of a small pony, it leapt over the bodies it couldn't go around, clearing them with ease. Letting out a breath, Ashlinn relaxed.

"Cliste, what are you doin' out here, girl?" she whispered.

Again came the soft woof as Cliste bounded to her, licked her face, and turned to start back the other way. Knowing the dog's signs all too well, Ashlinn rose and followed like an obedient owner. Once upon a time Cliste's discoveries sent a thrill through her, a hope that the one her hound had found just might be the one she searched for. But that hope had died a long time ago. Still, a survivor was a good thing, regardless of whether or not it was the one she longed to find.

At the muddy bank of the James, Cliste darted into the brush.

Ashlinn shook her head. "Bloody hound, if you just have a rabbit in there..." she whispered as she followed slowly behind.

One hand strayed toward the knife belted at her waist. At least a rabbit would mean fresh meat for dinner. As much as she detested harming any living thing, she had learned to do what she had to so that she survived this damnable war. Careful of her footing on the slippery slope, she followed Cliste's wagging gray tail down the riverbank. The big hound began backing out of the bushes, the muscles along her neck and back flexing as she dragged a burden along with her. The sight of the collar of the blue uniform clenched between Cliste's teeth made Ashlinn's heart thump so hard in her chest that it hurt.

Or perhaps it was the thrill of hope that caused the pain. The loyal hound never touched the survivors she found, only stood over them. The soldier attached to the collar didn't so much as stir as Cliste dragged him through the mud. Blood stained the abdomen and left arm of his uniform a dark crimson. It was always hard to tell if the blood on a man was his own or another's, but this one's lack of movement did not bode well. One look at his face and the hope that had blossomed in her heart withered and died as if poisoned.

Clean-shaven as he was, she knew instantly that he wasn't the man she searched for. Swallowing back the tears that tried to choke her, she put her mind to the task at hand. At least she could save someone's brother, husband, or father this day. Slightly prominent cheekbones and a strong jawline framed a handsome face that tugged at something deep inside her. She found herself wishing his eyes were open so she could see what color they were. His forage cap had gotten lost sometime during either the battle or Cliste's handling of him, leaving his dark brown hair to tumble loose and drag in the mud. His chest rose and fell rhythmically, a good sign despite the blood covering him.

After a quick glance around the still battlefield, Ashlinn knelt beside the man. She undid the rain-slick buttons of his uniform, exposing his undershirt. Grabbing the collar of the threadbare beige garment, she tore it open easily.

"Sorry, soldier. I know you probably brought that from home," she murmured as she pushed it open wider.

Blood still oozed from a horrible gash in the man's left side about four inches wide and deep enough that Ashlinn could see muscle. A bayonet wound, which likely meant it was even deeper than it appeared. From the placement, the chances that the weapon had missed anything vital were good. Another glance at the lengthening shadows of twilight stealing over the land and she knew she wouldn't be moving him far. Her gaze methodically checked the landscape, looking for anywhere she could hide him away from prying eyes and the weather.

Most of the trees had been chopped down for one army or another's use, leaving nothing but open fields and brush along the river. A few abandoned cannons and broken-down wagons lay a good distance away back up on the hillside, but they weren't exactly a good option. Too obvious. A soft woof drew her attention back to Cliste, who stood wagging her tail so hard her entire rear end swayed. The moment Ashlinn looked at her the hound dashed off into the underbrush and disappeared. Another woof sounded, this one echoing.

Trusting her furred companion, Ashlinn grabbed hold of the soldier's collar with both hands and slowly began to drag him back the way Cliste had brought him. The tall bushes allowed her to duck beneath them, and the mud helped her pull the man along despite the fact that he probably weighed almost double what she did. Once she had him beneath the cover of the bushes, Ashlinn turned around to see where Cliste had disappeared to.

Between the leaves and the shadows of the rapidly approaching night, it took a moment for her eyes to adjust and realize what they beheld. Around the edge of this bush and down along the river a little was a dark spot on the bank that resembled a cave mouth. Like a gray ghost, Cliste bounded from the yawning darkness and reached Ashlinn's side in less than four steps. While Ashlinn stood catching her breath with her hands on her hips, Cliste took the soldier's collar in her teeth again and began to drag him toward the cave mouth. Shaking her head, Ashlinn crouched low to avoid the snarling branches and lifted the soldier's wounded arm out of the mud.

More than once the riverbank sucked at her calf-high boots, nearly making her slip. Only a few feet of rain-slickened plant life lay between her and the muddy waters of the James River. Warm though the evening was, this man had lost so much blood he was bound to get cold, and his battle to survive the night would be hard enough as it was without a plunge into the water. She had to be careful. The closer they got to the cave opening, the less it looked like a cave. It was more like a shelf of ground hollowed out by the river when it had been swollen with winter water. Regardless, it would have to do.

Finally, with Cliste's help, she was able to pull the soldier inside the makeshift cave. She suffered a few scratches shoving aside leafy branches of the bushes that were trying to overgrow the opening, but they made it inside. The earthen roof was almost high enough that she could stand up and wide enough for the three of them with room to spare. Sitting slightly above the water level, the alcove would keep them warm and dry, which was all she could have hoped for.

Outside, rain began to fall in great sheets, obscuring what little view of the river she had from between the leaves. A sigh of relief slid from her. She'd be able to start a fire without having to worry about the smoke being seen. She had to boil water and cleanse the dead doctor's medical instruments and stitching material. God knows he certainly hadn't done it. More than once she had tried to convince the doctors of the Union army that such precautions were necessary, but they always dismissed her ideas as the ramblings of an uneducated woman. All despite the fact that the hacks knew her father had been a forward-thinking doctor and her mother a midwife who fancied herself a scientist. In fact, she had often thought her lineage was part of why they seemed to despise her so. Softly chastising herself, she shook her head. To think ill of the dead invited nothing but trouble.

Like a massive sentinel, Cliste lay down close to the soldier's head. Again, Ashlinn puzzled over what could possibly make the hound so protective of a complete stranger.

She began to collect the few bits of driftwood that she could find in the dark alcove. She would need more, a lot more, but this would do for now. Several of the branches were dry enough that she was able to strip the bark from them with ease. She piled the strips beneath the wood. From within her frock coat she pulled a small box of lucifers, struck one, and touched the resulting flame to the pile of dry bark. In a few moments the tinder caught. When the tiny flame started to devour the driest bits of bark, she placed a few of the smaller branches over the orange flames. With a bit of coaxing a steady fire soon burned.

Removing her frock coat, she laid it aside, then removed the small satchel she kept hidden beneath it. She dug out a small pan from within the satchel and filled it with water from her canteen. Using a few rocks and larger branches she found near the entrance of the alcove, she made a place for the pan to sit over the fire. Upon her coat she laid out the contents of her satchel: clean linens for bandages, vials of morphine, a bottle of iodine, suture needles, and suture thread that had been boiled and stored carefully within a wax-sealed envelope.

Such items weren't customary and often got her laughed at by the other nurses and the few doctors who had ever seen them. But they were items vital to a patient's survival, according to her father. And considering the survival rate of his patients versus any other doctor she had ever known, she put her trust in his teachings. Morphine was the one thing that the hack doctors of this war used, but they did so sparingly and often only on officers. It was hard to come by, which was part of why she kept it hidden inside her coat with her other precious items.

Feeling as prepared as she was going to get, she set to the task of removing the soldier's coat and undershirt. Unable to move him much due to the wound in his side, she had to settle for removing his wounded arm from his coat and pushing his clothing away from his side wound as much as possible. Not an ounce of fat seemed to cling anywhere to his muscled frame. Though the sight of his mostly naked chest stirred her, it also saddened her. Lack of good food kept the poor man teetering on the edge of skinny, like so many of the soldiers in this war. That thought led down a slippery path of concern, hope, and despair, haunted by the ghostly images of her brothers.

More water from her canteen cleaned the blood away and revealed the wounds. Much like the wound in his side, the one on his arm was so deep that she could see the gleam of muscle. His arm was starting to swell, which would make it more difficult to sew the wound closed if she didn't hurry. Thankfully, the bayonet hadn't gone through the man's arm and didn't appear to have hit bone. Regardless, the three-inch or so wide laceration was nasty looking.

Brown eyes wide and trusting, Cliste watched every move she made. Ashlinn shook her head at her companion.

"Don't know what draws you to this one so much, but I'm curious to find out," she murmured.

Standing, she held a finger out to the hound. "No lickin'," she commanded in a soft whisper.

Eyes dropping in disappointment, Cliste lowered her head onto her huge, crossed front paws.

Though the water in the pan hadn't started to boil yet, she dropped the suturing needles and the end of the tongs in it as she moved to leave the alcove. Rain fell from the sky as if it wept over the atrocities of the day, turning the world into a dreary gray haze that was impossible to see through. Nevertheless, she scanned the area, listening hard as she did so. All she could hear was the splatter of thousands upon thousands of fat drops of rain. With the ghosts of her past waiting to haunt her, she didn't want to go out there, but she had to. The urge to return to the battlefield and continue searching pulled at her the moment her gaze drifted that direction. She fought it with every ounce of strength she had. This man needed her help. Returning to a fruitless search wasn't an option.

Careful of the slippery slope, she climbed down the last few feet to the mud-colored water and plunged her hands in. With a bit of soap she kept tucked into her pocket, she washed as thoroughly as she could with such water, scrubbing until even her nails shone clean. If only the "good doctor" of the regiment could see her now, he'd surely be cursing and shaking his head at her supposed foolishness. Washing one's hands was a waste of precious time he had always told her. Well, she would waste time so that this soldier didn't join the bastard in the afterlife.

Lips curving up into a smile, she glanced skyward.

By no small miracle, she made it back to the alcove with her hands held up and out before her without touching anything. The soldier's breathing had become slightly labored, his chest rising and falling too rapidly. She knelt beside him.

"Sir, can you hear me?"

His eyes fluttered beneath his lids. Cliste's tail thumped in the dirt.

"If you can hear me, sir, this is going to hurt."

Careful so as not to overuse the precious mixture, she poured the iodine tincture directly into the open wound on the soldier's arm. A colorful curse flew from his lips as his eyes shot open and he tried to sit up, getting only a few inches off the ground before collapsing back. Surprisingly, he did not scream as most soldiers did when exposed to the tincture. Those eyes she had wondered about were copper with sunbursts of darker brown coming out from the pupil. They fixed upon her, their pain and beauty ensnaring her so that she couldn't move, let alone look away.

Beside them, Cliste whined. The soldier's gaze shifted and the trap released, allowing Ashlinn to breathe again.

"Is the dog all right?" he asked.

The heavy Irish brogue coloring his voice sent a thrill into her that darted straight for her abdomen. She possessed a similar accent, but not nearly as strong since her family had been in America for two generations and had worked hard to get it out of her voice. It made her wonder if he were a new immigrant. When his words sank in, she smiled.

"Of course, she is just worried about you."

Hair so dark brown it was nearly black fell across those alluring eyes as his head turned to look at the hound. "The Reb didn't hurt her, did he? I tried to stop him, but when he wounded me, she ran after him."

Ashlinn sat up straighter, having to fight the impulse to cover her gaping mouth with her clean hand. "You saved my hound?"

A smile turned the man's rugged face handsome. "Aye. But she saved me as well."

Were he not bleeding and nearly mortally wounded, she would have hugged him, societal rules be dammed. "Thank you. She is all I have left," she whispered.

The man's gaze shifted back to her and it was as though the sun itself shone upon her again. "You are an angel hidin' in men's clothin', but an angel nonetheless for it." His voice began to drift, trailing with each word.

Smile turning crooked, she cocked her head. "You won't be thinking that for long. I've got to clean the wound in your side and it's going to hurt like hell. But I need you to hold as still as you can, understand?"

He turned his gaze to the roof of their little alcove and nodded. "Aye."

"Would you like some laudanum or morphine first?"

Closing his eyes, he shook his head. "No. That stuff's wicked addictive."

"All right then. Here we go."

She poured the tincture into the wound on his side. Lips closing tight over a groan, his back bowed. Using the clean cotton rags she had brought with her, she cleaned the area around the wounds after flushing them both with the iodine tincture.

"Bloody hell, 'tis not water you're cleanin' me wounds with, is it?" he asked when she retreated to get the needles and thread.

"No. It is an iodine tincture."

His labored breathes tugged at her heart. "Why?"

She looked deep into his pain-filled eyes. "Because it will save your arm and your life. You do want me to save your arm, do you not?"

"Aye. My soul would die if I could not hold me fiddle."

Shock raised her eyebrows. Few men she had used such methods on had ever acquiesced so easily. Most wanted the false comfort of their regiment doctor's usual practices, even if that was sawing off their limbs. She wasn't about to tell him that her methods included two sets of sutures, one inside the wound, and one outside. Some things were just best left unsaid.

While he wasn't looking, she dipped the little finger of her left hand in laudanum. Holding it up to his lips, she gave him her best casual smile.

"Here, suck on this."

His eyes widened and he grinned. "I would deny you nothin' me angel," he murmured.

"Delirium already, not a good sign," she said through a smile.

The tightness around his eyes and lips betrayed his pain despite his playful expression. Obedient as his word, he opened his mouth and closed his lips around her little finger. The warm wetness of his mouth made her skin tingle. The smooth, bumpy texture of his tongue running along her finger caused her to shiver in the most wonderful way. His brow furrowed deeper as she withdrew her finger, tongue darting out to touch his lips.

"You tricked me," he said.

"I am sorry, truly. But no worries, it was not enough to make your body want more. Just enough to take the edge off."

His head turned away from her. "Hope you're right, I'd rather be dead than addicted."

Respect for the man swelled within her. Not many would refuse laudanum or morphine, even knowing what it could do to them. All too often their fear and pain got the better of them until many begged for it.

"You are very brave, soldier. And smart," she said as she picked up the suture thread and the first needle she would use.

He opened his mouth but only a moan came out. Already the drug was taking effect. It took several tries before he could produce words. "Sean. My name...is Sean."

"'Tis a fine name. Now you just relax while I sew you up."

Eyes falling closed of their own accord, Sean's mouth worked wordlessly. She watched him for a few moments. The long lashes touching his cheekbones fluttered like moths against a flame as his eyes moved beneath his lids. When his breathing deepened and he went still, she set needle to flesh and began to mend his body.

Chapter 3

Pain lanced through his left side as he tried to roll over, pitching Sean from the arms of sleep. The muscles in his side and abdomen tightened until they were rock hard, catapulting the sensation from pain to agony. A groan worked its way up his throat but he closed his lips tight against it, not daring to make a sound.

Where was he? He remembered the fight with the Reb, getting stabbed twice, saving the dog—he hoped—then an angel. Surely he couldn't be dead, though. Death wouldn't hurt this much, would it? Perhaps. After all he had done in this war there was a strong chance he was not bound for anywhere good in the afterlife.

"Lie still, or else you are liable to tear your stitches," came a feminine voice with just a hint of an Irish accent to it. It certainly sounded heavenly.

The word *stitches* brought back the memory of a lovely woman dressed in men's clothing pouring something horrible onto his wounds. Not dead after all then. Slowly, he forced his sleep-gummed eyes open. The instant they set upon the beauty hovering over him, his pain faded into the background. Sunlight filtered through long golden tresses that framed a face with high cheekbones and stunning blue eyes filled with concern. A loose, button-up blue uniform shirt hid much of the outline of her upper body and breeches clung to legs that folded beneath her.

"An angel in wolf's clothing," he murmured.

Casting her gaze to the earthen roof above them, she shook her head. Not so much as a dab of rouge entered her cheeks at the comment. He would have to try harder.

"How are you feeling?" she asked.

He recalled her having more of an Irish accent. But then, she had an air of propriety to her now that she hadn't possessed when he'd been bleeding out. Like many of his kind, she likely hid her accent as best she could when in the company of others. It was what they were taught, after all. But it was one of the expected things of society that he had never likened to. The fact that she worked hard at it meant she was likely of at least the middle class and he would need to be on his best behavior.

"Like someone shoved a red-hot poker into my side and arm."

The fight replayed in his memory. His eyes shot to his arm. A long breath eased from him when he saw it was whole—swollen, but whole. Just to be sure, he flexed the fingers of his left hand. The movement hurt all the way up to the wound near his bicep, but each finger moved at his command. Again he sighed. The skin gleamed. It was so clean, a line of neat stitches cutting a red and black swath through it.

"Keep that up and you will pass out," the woman said.

"'Tis just…I cannot believe you saved it. The doctors would have cut it off."

An old anger that likely had nothing to do with his wounds filled her eyes. She shook her head. "'Tis because they are idiots. There was no need to take the arm. It will heal."

There was that lovely accent.

His head tilted and his brows rose. "But the risk of infection…"

She fussed with the dressing that covered the wound on his side as if she didn't want to meet his eyes. "Is far less because of the precautions I took." Her voice was guarded, defensive.

With his good hand, he reached over and touched her arm, drawing her gaze to him. Such a touch was completely inappropriate, he knew, but their situation was hardly normal. The heat in her crystal-blue eyes warmed him from the middle outward. "I did not mean to offend you. I'm grateful for what you did for me," he said.

The stiffness in her shoulders melted away a little. "I was happy to do it. You saved Cliste, after all."

A tail thumped to the left near his head. He turned to see the huge gray hound lying beside him, head upon its massive paws. "She belongs to you then? Quite an amazin' creature you have there."

The tail thumped harder.

Lips turning up into a smile that lit her radiant face, she patted the hound on the head. "Aye, that she is."

Reluctantly, he withdrew his hand from her arm. Tempting as she was, he couldn't allow a brush with death to compromise his sense of honor and propriety. "My apologies for being so forward. 'Tis just that I have never brushed shoulders with death so closely. Since we've no one to properly introduce us, I suppose I shall have to make due. I am Sean MacBranain, Corporal with the 69th regiment. And who do I have the pleasure of addressin'?"

Pink brightened her cheeks, taking a bit of the haunted look out of her eyes. "Ashlinn O'Brian, nurse of the 69th regiment."

"'Tis a pleasure to meet your acquaintance, Ms. O'Brian," he said.

"And yours, sir."

The moment her gaze dropped in a demur, ladylike fashion, he looked away as well. He had to, else he would run the risk of staring at her. She captivated him more than he wanted to admit. From the earthen ceiling and walls and the nearby rush of water, he guessed they were hidden away in a hollow somewhere very near the river. What a nurse was doing way out here amidst the battle, he couldn't fathom. Slowly, and with far more care this time, he started to sit up.

"We have got to get back to the regiment," he said through gritted teeth.

Hunger roiled through him at the movement, morphing quickly into pain, a lot of it.

"Easy, easy," the woman warned as she reached out to help him.

The hound whined and inched closer, crawling on her belly.

Once he achieved a sitting position, he had to stop. Struggling to draw breath through the haze of pain, he blinked and breathed deep until the darkness framing his vision went away. The woman's hands were like brands upon his arms, wonderfully hot, but almost too hot.

"Your hands are so hot."

He didn't realize he'd spoken the words aloud until she made a small sound between a grunt and a laugh. "'Tis warm out for sure, but my hands only feel that way because you lost so much blood."

The sunlight upon the ground behind her seemed to have retreated a bit since he'd first awoken. That or time was playing tricks on him. "How long was I out?"

Her head turned in the direction of the light. "Two nights and almost two days now."

Heart pounding out a rhythm a drummer boy would be hard pressed to keep up with, he pushed himself to a knee. "The regiment…"

Dipping under his good arm, she helped him stand. "Careful of your head; the roof is low."

Hunched from the pain twisting his guts, he had no need to worry about striking his head. He couldn't stand up straight if he wanted to, which he most certainly did not. One hand sliding around his waist, below his wound enough to make him blush had he more blood in him, the woman stabilized him. The touch was so inappropriate, so improperly familiar, that he started to draw away. The world swam. Moving faster than such a large creature should be able to, the hound was suddenly at his other side, pushing her muzzle beneath his hand.

"The 69th has withdrawn to Harrison's Landing," Ashlinn said.

His heart picked back up a frantic rhythm. "But it seemed we were winnin'."

"We did. They withdrew after the Rebels retreated."

Sean shook his head. "That makes little sense."

"True enough, but I am certain of it. I walked back through enough of the soldiers to know."

She let go of him long enough to put her satchel and coat on and grab a medical bag. When she supported him again he tried to think of her warmth, her nearness, for what it was—a nurse assisting a patient, nothing more. It helped clear his mind and sharpen his focus, which was a double-edged sword. Relief over their victory became eclipsed by the trepidation brought on from what he had to ask next.

"How many dead?"

Head dropping, she started to walk him toward the entrance to their little alcove. The way her shoulders stiffened beneath his arm told him he wasn't going to like her answer long before she spoke. For a while, though, all he could focus on was the lancing pain each step sent up into his side.

"A lot, Sean."

The familiarity with which she spoke to him, along with the sorrow darkening her voice, told him everything her hidden face wouldn't.

"So where is it you are from, Ms. O'Brian?" He had to say something to drown out the sound of his manic heart.

As if sensing his distress, Cliste pushed her huge head higher beneath his hand. Her soft gray fur caressed his rough fingers, soothing him in the way only an animal could.

"New York."

Thoughts torn between her and the battlefield they moved closer to, he had to force a smile. "Thought I recognized that accent. But for a moment there, I swear I almost heard a touch of Irish in it."

She made a sound that was close to a laugh. "Aye, but my family has not immigrated as recently as you, from the sounds of it. My teachers in New York insisted on weeding out the 'detestable brogue' in my voice, as they put it. But upon hearing you, I find I rather like it."

A true and easy smile came to his lips. "English bastards they must have been."

"Aye, they were. Careful of the brush now."

They left the small alcove behind and worked their way through the leafy green brush that choked the riverbank. His skin began to crawl and his muscles tightened with the desire to turn back to the safety of their hidden place. But he couldn't. He wouldn't. Swallowing hard, he pushed through the last of the brush and laid eyes on Malvern Hill. His breath sucked in hard.

Bodies numbering in the hundreds lay strewn across the small hill and the field before it, painting the once green landscape crimson with blood and gore. Of those close enough to him to make out, he didn't see any blue uniforms lying among the gray. A few living moved among the dead, gathering them up and hauling them off. In the fading light of dusk it was hard to tell, but Sean thought their uniforms were gray. Thankfully, none of them seemed close enough to see him and Ashlinn hovering by the river's edge.

"We collected the dead as we returned to Harrison's Landing, and as you can see, the Rebels have begun to collect theirs as well," Ashlinn whispered.

"Then that means…" He couldn't finish, couldn't force the words out his constricted throat.

From the amount of bodies still on the field and from what he remembered of the battle, there had to have been thousands dead on both sides. Thousands. The realization struck him with the force of a cannon.

So many of his men dead… His knees went weak, making him rely on Ashlinn to hold him upright. Whining, Cliste pressed close to his side and rubbed her head against his leg. Both the warm woman against him and the concerned dog at his side helped bring him back from the brink of a breakdown. Now wasn't the time to lose it, not when his life wasn't the only one at stake.

"We have to get out of here," he whispered, gaze darting about in search of the best route.

Plenty of brush grew along the river that they could dash into and hide if need be. Ashlinn nodded and started to move that direction as if reading his mind. Her arm was firm around his waist, offering as much support as her small frame could. Just enough of a drizzle came from the gray clouds above to leach the worst of the heat from the day. Unfortunately, it wasn't enough to obscure them. But, considering the closest living person Sean could make out was too far away to even shoot at, chances were good that he and Ashlinn would blend into the scenery. He hoped.

As if sensing what they were about, Cliste slinked along before them, tail low, head swinging back and forth, checking the scents in the air. Each step was like a fresh stab in the side, but Sean took the pain and buried it deep within, not letting out so much as a whimper. He didn't want to make Ashlinn worry. They couldn't stop, and he didn't want to risk her trying to talk him into it. By the time they reached the edge of the first forested area, he was gasping from the pain, unable to hide it any longer. Ashlinn pulled him into the cover of the trees and leaned him against the rough bark of a pine.

As she moved his coat aside to check his wound, his gaze traveled back to the field of battle. The hill still loomed in the distance like a nightmare that refused to be banished. They were far enough away now that he couldn't see or smell the bodies, but such things were etched upon his memory. From the looks of it, they had barely traveled over a mile and already darkness began to steal across the land. While night would bring much needed cover, it would also make traveling on unknown terrain more difficult. They could follow the swath the Union army had cut through the landscape, but then they risked discovery by Rebel troops.

Even alone Sean would be reluctant to take such a risk. Knowing what the soldiers would do to Ashlinn if they captured her, there was no way he would risk it. During the past week of fighting, he and his regiment had traveled around this area enough that he was confident he could find his way back to Harrison's Landing without the use of the marching road.

"You are bleeding again. We need to find somewhere to stop for the night," Ashlinn whispered.

"Aye, but we have to find a better place to hide."

She nodded and ducked under his arm again. Pausing only to relieve a dead soldier of his pack and gun, they traveled deeper into the forest. They communicated with gestures and looks instead of words whenever they could. The way she looked around, listened, and the ease with which she kept quiet impressed Sean. But it also made him wonder how often she traveled in enemy territory and why. Traveling with the medical wagons in the regiment surely wouldn't imbue her with such skills.

Soon the forest surrounded them, the river birches becoming so thick the rain scarcely fell upon them anymore. The patter of it upon the diamond-shaped leaves overhead began to lull Sean into a sleepy daze. His feet were soon stumbling along in the near dark. When one boot caught beneath a fallen branch, Ashlinn's strong hands were all that kept him from sprawling face first to the forest floor. Agony shot through his side as his muscles bunched in preparation for an impact that didn't come.

"'Tis enough; we have to stop. Your wound is bleeding again," she whispered as she inspected his side.

Out of breath as he was from the pain, he could hardly argue.

The panting of a dog preceded Cliste's emergence from the dense undergrowth that choked the tightly packed birch trees before them. Tail wagging, she dashed up to Ashlinn, licked her nose without so much as a foot leaving the ground, then dashed back the way she had come. The dog's antics were a stark reminder of her sheer size, which suddenly made Sean very grateful that she had taken to him. Ashlinn turned them to follow the hound.

Shrubs and ferns pulled at them from every direction as they plunged into the thick undergrowth. The deeper they went, the darker it became as the trees formed a complete canopy overhead. Even the small drizzle of rain that had been making it through ceased to fall upon them. Unfortunately, moisture was so thick upon the air that it coated everything and brushed off onto them. Despite the warm July evening, a chill began to creep across Sean's skin and into his bones.

They came upon the twisting branches of a sycamore tree, many of which were low enough that they nearly touched the ground. The tree was so choked in by birch that he didn't see it until they were nearly upon it. Leaving him to lean against one of the lowest branches, Ashlinn began digging in the pack they had picked up off the battlefield. Smooth bark supported him while the huge fanlike leaves with three points tickled his arms. Moisture transferred from the leaves to him, making him shiver when it touched his bare forearm. He drew his arm back into his coat as he watched Ashlinn.

She pulled out a small package of paper from which the strong scent of salted pork wafted, making his mouth water. Another larger package followed—hardtack, no doubt—then a folded bit of stiff material that had to be the dead soldier's dog tent. The sight of the tent brought Sean almost as much relief as the scent of the pork. Cold had seeped so deep into his bones that he began to shiver, which made his arm and side ache horribly. If he could just get dry, he might not be so bloody cold.

Like an experienced soldier, Ashlinn draped the tent—which was really no more than a large square of treated fabric—over one of the sycamore branches that hung nearly to the ground and staked out its four corners. Such skills were rare among the gentle ladies he had known in his life. A smile tried to turn up his lips but his muscles were so tired they refused to complete the action. She reached out to take the musket from his hands. He hesitated, but the stern look she gave him convinced him it was in his best interest not to argue.

To his relief, she placed the weapon inside the tent, then turned back to offer him her hands. Undignified though it was, he allowed her to help him to his knees and then into the tent. By the time he was laying on his back staring up at where the tent draped the branch, his chest heaved with each breath. Despite his exhaustion, he repositioned the musket so that it would be easy to access should he need it. Ashlinn crawled in beside him and Cliste lay down at his head. With the hound blocking the breeze and Ashlinn's warm legs against his, he instantly warmed a bit. It wasn't quite enough to make him stop shivering, but it helped.

"You are shivering in this awful heat. 'Tis not a good thing," Ashlinn said under her breath.

Drawing a knife from her belt, she cut the bandages around his midsection and peeled them away. Propped up on the pack, he watched mutely as she cleaned away the blood and checked his stitches. When she withdrew the bottle of iodine tincture from her satchel he took a deep breath.

"'Tis best to fight off infection. I will not use much this time."

Her whispering voice softened her hard edges, making her seem more human. The sound sent a thrill of heat through him, one that was almost enough to make him forget her words. Distracted as he was, he didn't have time to brace before she poured the scalding liquid onto his wound. Groaning, he sat up a bit more and looked closer at it. After she wiped away the liquid, he saw that no pus or drainage came from the wound. Concern gnawed at him.

"'Tis not infected, is it? Shouldn't there be pus?"

"No, there should not." The words sounded clipped and short, barely a whisper.

Her brows pulled together and her eyes narrowed to slits.

"But 'tis not that a good thing? 'Tis the bad humors comin' out, right?"

He didn't know much about medicine, wounds, and such, but he had heard more than one field doctor say that about pus.

"That is a load of shite as big as the doctors who spread it. Pus is a sign of infection. Think of how many soldiers you have seen lose more of a limb or scar terribly with wounds that had it."

For a moment he thought back and realized she was right.

"How do you know such things?"

"My da was a doctor who studied the forward-thinking teachings of the time. My mum was a nurse who studied science. I watched and learned alongside them." Her voice dropped lower as she spoke until Sean had to strain to hear her. Pain laced each word.

He laid a hand on her arm. "What happened to them?"

"Cholera," she said in a voice void of emotion.

Terrible as it was, it was a noble end compared to some. He didn't dare say that, though. His own shameful demons would remain just that, his own. Putting on a tight smile that didn't reach her eyes, she patted his hand where it sat upon her arm.

"I need you to sit up for a moment so I can rebandage the wound."

Dwarfed within his big hands, hers didn't look like they could lift a man such as himself, but they did so with ease. Though she may not look as stalwart as most of the nurses he had come across, she most certainly proved herself to be. She placed a piece of pristine white cotton cloth against his wound, then wrapped it, going completely around his waist.

"Will you not run out of wrap by usin' fresh material?" he asked.

She nodded. "Aye, but if I use the old material it could introduce contaminants to your wound."

Head cocking, he raised an eyebrow at her. "Most doctors would say they cannot waste material in the midst of war."

Copying his one eyebrow raise, she placed her wrist against his forehead. "Aye, and 'tis why most of their patients die. Hmmm, you have a bit of a fever. I think I saw some yarrow a ways back. You rest here while I go fetch it."

She started to rise and turn for the opening of the tent. One hand going to his side in anticipation of the pain, Sean sat up, grabbing her arm with his other hand. It felt wicked to touch her bare arm, wicked and wonderful.

"Don't, please, 'tis too dangerous."

The look she gave him reminded him of one his mum used to give him right before she chastised him. "I can take care of myself. I have been a nurse in this war for over two years now."

He tightened his grip when she tried to pull away. "I have no doubt you are quite capable, but we are far from the protection of the regiment."

Her eyes softened, her hand covering his. Warmth seeped from her skin into him, giving him an idea. "Please do not leave me. I am so cold."

Nodding, she sat down beside him. Heat poured into him from where her legs touched his, pulling a sigh of pleasure from him. He turned toward her until his wound pinched so much he had to stop, then curled around that warmth as much as he could. A resigned sounding sigh eased from her.

"All right, I will not leave you."

She opened her coat, snuggled intimately against him, and wrapped both her arms and her coat around him. Shock rendered him speechless. Such boldness was unheard of, forbidden. But then, he had nearly died and still might if fever took him. He supposed that must be enough motivation for her to break such codes of acceptable conduct. The men's clothing couldn't hide the press of her breasts against his chest, the wonderful curve of her hip as he snaked his arm around her. Best of all, this close, the medicine, wet wool, and blood scents faded, allowing him to catch a whiff of her feminine scent of vanilla and roses.

Had he his wits about him, he would have done the honorable thing and moved away. But he didn't. Or so he told himself. Sleep snuck over him like the mists of his old homeland. Suspicion stirred in him that she would not stay true to her word, but his thoughts became muddled and he grew unable to fight off unconsciousness. Soothed by the feel of her heart beating against his, he drifted off.

Chapter 4

Leaf-laden branches grabbed at Ashlinn's clothing and arms, some snagging material, others snagging flesh in their attempts to thwart her efforts to move along the riverbank. Clouds crowded the night sky, choking out both the moon and starlight. She had to walk slowly just as much because of lack of light as to ensure her footsteps remained quiet. More than once she was forced to backtrack and go around impassable bushes that she didn't recall being in the way.

But she had to do this. Sean had been burning with fever when she left, his skin so hot she became uncomfortable lying beside him. And not just because of the heat. She had never been so close to a man she wasn't related to before, and though he was wounded and sick, it still felt wonderfully intimate. If she didn't get something to help his fever break, she feared he might not make it. That bothered her more than she cared to admit. This soldier had a quality to him that was charming, unforgettable, and it had wormed its way into her somehow despite her reluctance to allow attachments to form.

What little light made it through the oppressive clouds shown upon the flowing water of the river on her right. It offered at least a bit of guidance so she didn't wander off and get completely lost. The temptation to do so, to continue searching for someone she would likely never find, tugged at her, as always. This time, having a purpose, she fought it off. That light soon reflected on a towering tree that tugged at her memory. She recalled a big old oak near where she had seen the yarrow growing. Stopping, she drew in a deep breath through her nose. Even beyond the wet plant life, dirt, and brackish river, the overly sweet scent of yarrow drifted to her.

Following her nose, she let her hands trail along the tall grass, feeling for the flowering plant. The smell grew particularly strong and she stopped, concentrating on the area. At last, her fingers brushed across a head of flowers. Even in the dim light, she could tell the tiny flowers were those she needed. She picked several and tucked them into the pockets of her coat. Dried, they would have been much better in tea, but at least this way they'd be more potent. Just as she was about to rise from her crouch, footsteps rustled through the tall grass nearby. Hand going to the knife at her waist, she turned to look over her shoulder. A figure approached from not more than twenty feet away.

Dim light shone off the long barrel of a musket pointed in her direction. Halfway up from her crouch, she froze.

"Be you Reb or Yank?" called a gruff voice. The thick, Southern accent marked the man more clearly than a look at his uniform would.

Doing her best to deepen her voice, she answered, "Reb."

The barrel of the gun lowered a bit but didn't point away. "What are you doing out here, soldier?"

She had to bite back the temptation to ask him the same thing. Again she tried her best to sound like a man. "Doctor, not a soldier. Gathering herbs." Deepening her voice and throwing a Southern drawl into it proved incredibly hard.

"What's wrong with your voice?"

The rough knife handle dug into her hand as she gripped it tighter and stood. "Soldier with a fever."

Head cocking to one side, the Reb moved closer. "No, that ain't it."

Fast as a snake, he lunged in and knocked the cap from her head. Her blond tresses tumbled free, falling down past her shoulders to shine like beacons that betrayed her. In her haste to leave, she hadn't bound her hair up, just stuffed it under the cap. A rather feminine gasp slipped from her as her hand dashed out to catch her cap.

The soldier let out a whoop. "A woman! Well then, I think it's time for some healing, little miss."

She took another step back as he moved another closer. Thrusting her head up high, she poured on the Southern accent. "You would not dare violate the person who may one day save your life." The ruse of being a man may no longer save her, but she hoped that of being a Reb nurse might.

Laughter hiccupped from the soldier. "Of course not, I'm no idiot. But yah see, your accent keeps slipping from Georgia to Virginia, putting me of a mind that maybe you ain't Southern at all."

Eyes scanning the darkness, she swallowed hard and looked for any avenue of escape. Would he use the musket on her? Doubtless. The real question was, would he use it before or after he raped her?

"That is ridiculous. I am from Georgia but have just been in Virginia long enough to pick up the accent," she attempted.

He shook his head. "Naw, that ain't it at all."

Again and again he stepped forward, forcing her back farther and farther. Something soft brushed her arm. Her back struck the rough bark of a tree. Heart racing like a wild horse, she clutched her knife tighter, holding it to her side so he couldn't see it. The last thing she wanted to do was use it on him. After all the death she had seen, the lives she struggled to save every day, it went against everything she stood for. The twisted grin on his bristly face revealed crooked teeth that he kept running his tongue over. His beady eyes crawled over her with a hunger that made her cringe.

"You do not want to do this," she tried one last time.

The barrel of the musket finally lowered as he tucked it under his arm and reached for his belt. "Oh, I most certainly do. Ain't never had me a Yankee woman. Reckon they's a bit different." Each word was rushed and a bit breathless, as if the idea of violating her had him worked into a frenzy. Her repulsion to use the knife on him began to fade.

His belt buckle jingled and she was suddenly quite glad for the darkness. She did not want to see what was coming at her.

"Now you be real nice and I won't kill you," he said.

Another step and his tobacco rank breath panted against her face. Hands grabbed for her, fists burying in her coat, yanking her from the tree. She slipped, stumbled, and fell sprawling on her back. Wet grass cooled her sweating palms.

The knife!

Oh God, where had it gone? Panic prickled through her like a porcupine's quills. Fingers scrambling around in the grass, she began to turn. A rifle butt collided with her shoulder hard enough to throw her onto her back again. Pain exploded out from the point of impact. Her physician's mind analyzed the injury on instinct. Nothing felt broken, but damn it hurt. The man was suddenly upon her, his knees forcing her legs apart.

Reaching up as high as she could, she wrapped her legs around his midsection, bowed her back, and thrust down and to the side with her hips. The soldier grunted as he slammed into the ground. For a blessed moment, she was free. Her left hand came across a cold, metal object. After a moment of fumbling with it, she found the hilt of the knife and grabbed it. The back of a hand slapped her hard across the face, leaving her right cheek stinging. Not caring about the small indignity, she slid the knife beneath the man's beard and pressed ever so slightly against his throat. The man froze.

All that wrestling with her brothers when she was young suddenly didn't seem like child's play, and she was more than thankful that they hadn't been easy on her.

"I will kill you if you do not get off me," she said.

A low growl rumbled nearby, soft and threatening. In the darkness behind the soldier, a figure approached. So intent was the soldier on her that he didn't even seem to hear the shuffling gait. A rifle rose behind him. Ashlinn moved the knife away from the soldier's throat just before the butt of that rifle came slamming down on the back of her assailant's head. The man collapsed onto her, going limp. His rancid breath brushed her cheek. With a mighty shove, she pushed him off her and scrambled up. Swaying on his feet, face pale as moonlight, stood Sean, the hulking shadow of Cliste at his side.

Shame burned through Ashlinn. Though she knew it was undeserved, she couldn't banish it. She scrambled to her feet. Her head dropped and she fussed with her clothing, trying to straighten and smooth the material. Before she could finish drawing in a ragged breath, Cliste reached her side and began nudging her hand. Sean approached, moved past her toward the downed Rebel, and a moment later, she heard a blade enter flesh. She spun around to face him, all concern over herself banishing.

"Did you really have to kill him?"

Sean nodded as he stumbled back over to her side. "Aye. He would have searched for us, told others about us. And if he found us, I'm not sure I could protect you in my state. And o' course there's the fact that he would later kill my brothers-in-arms."

It was such an impossible thing to argue with, but she found herself wanting to nonetheless. Her lips remained closed, though. She couldn't fault a man who wanted to protect her and his fellow soldiers, not over this. Still, despite the fact that the man had attacked her, would have raped her, and that she had held a knife to his throat, she hadn't wanted him dead. Bile tried to rise up her throat but she swallowed it down.

The heat of Sean's fingers on her arm brought her back to the problem at hand. It was all she could do not to flinch away from his gentle fingers. Not because of what he had done so much, but because they burned like brands against her skin. "Are you all right?" he asked in a voice as soft as his touch.

She nodded. "Aye, I am well enough thanks to you. But you should not be up and about."

As if to prove her words right, Sean swayed. She placed an arm carefully around his waist to steady him. "Nor should you. You said you would not leave me."

The wounded, fearful tone in his voice made her heart clench. "I know, and I am sorry but your fever grew worse. I had to. How did you even know I was gone?"

They began to walk back toward their meager camp. Sean's body burned in a line as hot as coals against hers. Only her strong hands and steady steps kept them both upright.

"Cliste woke me when she went runnin' out. It gave me the feelin' somethin' was wrong," he whispered.

Unable to respond past the lump in her throat, Ashlinn just nodded. In the midst of a debilitating fever, he had roused himself out of concern for her. During the course of this war she had become used to being mostly invisible to the soldiers. She had come to accept it was due in part to her quiet manner and inability to comfort them as a mother would. Instincts like those were ones she had never fully developed. But this man saw her, and cared about her well-being. As much as she hated to admit it, she cared for him as well. Anyone who could show kindness and compassion, to the point of endangering their own life for that of a hound, was someone special. She wasn't sure what to do with that.

He made a soft sound low in his throat and patted Cliste on the head. "Even from such a distance, she knew you needed us," he marveled. "This war has made monsters of men and noblemen of beasts."

The words chilled her to her bones, for more than one reason. Glancing back at the still corpse of the man who would have violated her and murdered her, she had to disagree. Some men had come into this war monsters.

Chapter 5

The soft patter of rain on leaves woke Sean. A bitter aftertaste from the tea lingered upon his tongue, making him work it against the roof of his mouth. Pale sunlight caressed the golden locks of Ashlinn's hair that lay strewn across his chest. She felt so wonderful and warm curled up against his side that he didn't want to move. Wicked of him, he knew, but he would allow himself this one little indiscretion, just this once. He had danced intimately with death, after all. Surely it wasn't so wrong to allow himself this one moment of happiness.

Besides, he didn't want to let her go after what she'd been through. Seeing that man attacking her had struck a chord deep inside him, awakening a protectiveness that still resonated throughout him. It was utterly unexpected and a bit frightening. Surrounded by so much death all the time, he tried to keep his emotions locked away. But this woman had found a key, however small.

Outside, the haze of rain made it difficult to see more than ten feet or so. Thankfully, his little nurse had done an excellent job of putting up their tent and very little moisture save for that which seeped up from the ground found its way in. Despite the rain, the day was so warm it crested over from pleasant to slightly uncomfortable. Soft panting and the rhythmic thump of a tail told Cliste, who lay near his head, found the summer day anything but comfortable.

Careful so as not to disturb Ashlinn, he started to prop himself up on the elbow of his good arm. Dull pain throbbed in his side, not enough to take his breath away, just enough to make him move slower. Regardless of his care, Ashlinn stirred.

"What's the matter?" she whispered.

Shaking his head, he smiled down at her. With her blond hair spread out around her shoulders, teasing her delicate collarbones, she truly did resemble an angel. One that looked beautiful and quite alluring in a man's shirt and breeches.

"Nothin'. Just wantin' to see how high the sun is. How long have I been out?"

The back of her hand rose to stifle a yawn. "Not long. Six or seven hours maybe."

She sat up, crossed her legs before her, and reached for his forehead. All the willpower in the world couldn't keep the blood from flowing to his cheeks. He had never seen a woman strike such a casual, unladylike pose, let alone touch a man so readily with her bare hands. A very wicked part of him liked it, a lot. He had to forcibly remind himself that she was being a nurse and he was not being dishonorable by allowing her to do her job.

Oblivious to his embarrassment, she nodded. "Good, your fever broke. How do you feel?"

The crotch of her breeches drew his gaze like a moth to a flame. He had never seen a woman in men's breeches and he decided in that moment that he rather liked it. Then again, it was a very distracting sight.

"Um...uh..."

What had she said?

Cliste leapt to his rescue, literally. She sat up on her haunches and licked his left cheek, leaving it slimy and damp. Laughing, he scratched behind one of the hound's ears, continuing to stroke her head as she laid it upon his leg. Something strange on her collar drew his attention. It felt like a small cylinder, the kind meant to hold medicine or such. For a nurse's dog it made sense he supposed.

"I feel much better."

His gaze shifted to the hazy world outside their small tent. He opened his mouth to speak but she beat him to it, oddly voicing the very words he was thinking.

"We should wait until nightfall to travel."

"Aye, we should."

Half propped up, he relaxed against the pack, mostly to get a better look at her. The cozy tent didn't give them much room, which was both nice and unfortunate, since he wished to be as gentlemanly as possible. Back in proper society he wouldn't even be allowed to be in a room unchaperoned with a lady, let alone in a situation like this. Such things seemed silly after all he had seen and been through, vestiges of normalcy that were forever altered and long gone. Yet they were important to him, vital even.

"How is it you seem to know so much about sneakin' around?" he asked, voice low.

Pink stained her cheeks and her spine straightened. "I am not a spy, if that is what you are getting at."

Palms out in surrender, he shook his head. "No, no, I wasn't suggestin' that. I only meant that you are unlike any other nurse I have ever met, or doctor for that matter."

Her blush deepened to crimson but a smile tugged at her lips. Ice-blue eyes that were ironically warm regarded him with guarded admiration.

"You would liken me to a doctor?"

"O' course. You sewed me up, saved my arm and my life. You are a better doctor than most I've known."

Moisture shown in her eyes before she turned her attention to Cliste. "I became a nurse in this war not only to help save lives, but to try and keep my brothers alive," she said in a soft voice.

"Your brothers are soldiers."

Dry eyes returned to him. The strength and pride in that look gave him chills that felt oh so good. "Aye, they wanted to fight to preserve the Union, said what the Rebels were trying to do was too much like what is going on in our homeland."

"'Tis true," he agreed.

Head cocking to the side, she looked so deep into his eyes that he had to fight the urge to squirm. "Is that why you left Ireland?" she asked.

It took a moment to find the right words to answer her. "No. I am—was—a violinist. When the high society of Ireland had no more room for me, I came to find my way in America." His conscience burned at telling her only a half-truth, but he didn't know this woman well enough to tell her any more. Besides, he had never told anyone any more than that.

Her hands found his, turned them over, fingers caressing his palms. The sensation made his eyes flutter closed and he had to repress a sigh of pleasure. It had been a very long time since a woman had touched him, and never one so enthralling or bold.

"That is what you meant," she murmured.

"What I meant?"

The smile that graced her lips made blood work its way to his groin.

"When I asked you if you wanted me to save your arm and you mentioned your fiddle. I was not sure if you meant that literally."

Silence fell as she set to the task of checking his bandages. After a long moment, her eyes lifted to meet his. The demure way they hid slightly beneath her long lashes made his heart beat so hard it almost hurt.

"What is Ireland like?" she asked.

The wistful tone of her voice tugged at him, bringing to memory the misty fields and rocky coastlines. That's what he wanted to tell her of, but he couldn't deceive her, he wouldn't. He lifted his chin in the direction of the tent opening.

"Not much different than this I am afraid. Death and dyin' all around."

She swallowed hard. "I am so sorry. It must be terrible to have moved from one battle-torn country to another."

One of his shoulders lifted in a half shrug. "'Tis different here. At least half the country is not yet a battlefield, and there is hope."

"Some days it doesn't feel like it," she murmured. Shaking her head and disrupting the waves of hair that cascaded across her shoulders, she drew her hands into her lap. "Why do you fight?"

"'Cause no one deserves to live in chains."

Her delicate eyebrows rose. "Truly, that is why?"

He made himself meet her gaze. There was more to why, but he couldn't tell her, not just yet. "This surprises you?"

Shaking her head, she took one of his hands in hers. Warmth poured into him. Being enveloped in her skin made him a bit dizzy, but in a wonderful way. In proper society a woman wouldn't even touch him without gloves on. He was beginning to enjoy being out of society more and more.

"No, not at all. You seem like a good man. I only meant that many soldiers fight to preserve the Union rather than to end slavery," she was quick to say.

"'Tis a grand reason as well, to be sure, but I believe a country built upon the backs of others cannot stand for long," he admitted.

This made her smile, but oddly, it was one filled with sadness instead of mirth. "What of one birthed out of the blood of the Irish? The 69th, 63rd, and 88th brigades are almost all entirely Irishmen. And I have seen far too many of them die."

The sad tone of her voice told him what her blank expression would not.

"Then it shall be one born of the finest, strongest blood of all."

Eyes brimming with tears met his, and he saw something else shining in their depths—respect. "Two of my brothers have already died and another, my younger brother Michael, has gone missing," she offered up.

His hands gripped hers tighter, thumbs caressing the backs of her fingers. "This country will be better for their sacrifice, but I'm sorry they were taken from you."

Tears glistened on her lashes as she looked away. "Thank you." The words were barely a whisper.

"That is what you were doin' on the battlefield after the doctors and ambulance wagons had already retreated. You were lookin' for Michael."

She nodded. "He needs me."

Cliste's head suddenly lifted from his leg, her ears perking up. Tension pulled her shoulders up, readied her body for movement. Her eyes darted from Ashlinn, to him, and back again. At the same time he moved to grab his stolen musket and pack, Ashlinn put on her satchel, coat, and grabbed the doctor's bag. Part of him admired the fact that he didn't have to prompt her into action; another part of him became saddened that she would know such hardship.

Eyes scanning the rainy forest, catching on each shadow that twilight had lengthened, he moved from the tent in a crouch. Full dark was yet a half hour away, but enough cover existed that they should be able to sneak away unnoticed. That is, if someone else didn't have the same idea. As he scanned their surroundings, Ashlinn reached for the tent. Grabbing her hand, he shook his head and tapped below one ear. She nodded and moved her hand away from the treated fabric.

Nose lifting into the air, Cliste followed them out. The hair along her back rose as her head snapped to the south. Thankfully, she didn't make a sound. She didn't have to. Her mannerisms made it painfully clear. Someone was out there.

Chapter 6

Chills raced through Ashlinn regardless of the warm, damp July night. She knew Cliste's signs all too well. Someone was coming. The rain began to let up, the misty gray created by it slowly dissipating. For once, she actually wanted the constant drizzle of the last few days to come back. Thankfully, their dark blue uniforms would help hide them in the coming night. But it would still be a while yet before full dark fell.

Legs bent to keep low, she crept along beside Sean, one hand buried in Cliste's fur. She had learned that by having direct contact with the hound, it not only calmed them both, but she could feel when Cliste tensed at something. Though he had to be in immense pain, Sean moved with the ease of a seasoned soldier, head scanning, hands ready on his rifle. The gun should have put her at ease, but instead it made her blood pump so fast she became light-headed. If he fired it and there was more than one enemy soldier out there, they'd all know exactly where they were.

The desire to reach for Sean made her muscles ache. Not only did she want to warn him, she wanted the comfort of touching him. But she knew she had to trust him, and that distracting him was a bad idea. Instead she stayed as close to his side as she dared, just out of the reach of the rifle barrel. They moved carefully through the underbrush, sticking to it and using it to hide them. Darkness spread with each moment, helping to cloak them even more.

"I'm telling you I heard something," came a gruff voice from far too close.

Ashlinn exchanged a wide-eyed look with Sean. He grabbed ahold of her, pulled her behind a tree, and pressed her against it. Wrapped in his arms, his warm body against hers, a false sense of safety drifted over her. She'd never been so close to a man she wasn't related to before, and certainly never like this. Sean was all hard planes of muscle against her soft curves. A wonderful rush made her head swim from the contact. His breath warmed her forehead, sending a completely different kind of heat coursing through her.

So distracted was she that she barely noticed the sound of footsteps approaching and passing by the tree they hid behind. Several moments after they had gone, Sean took her hand and started through the forest at a brisk walk. Soon he led them out of the bushes where they could move faster and still remain relatively quiet. They all but jogged through the trees. Even in the fading light, Ashlinn could see the pinched look on Sean's face and knew he had to be in terrible pain.

Again she heard voices, but this time they were too far away to make out any words. Sean kept up their hurried pace until her breath came in gasps that burned her throat. Finally, she reached out and touched his arm. Her other hand hovered over her heaving chest. Sean took one look at her and slowed to a walk. Though full dark had fallen, her eyes had adjusted well enough that she could see the pain etched on his face. Despite what it cost him, he hadn't once made any sound that would indicate the agony he was in. He had slowed for her, not himself.

Almost of its own accord, Ashlinn's hand took hold of his. Inappropriate as it was, she didn't care. Her mother could seethe down at her from heaven all she wanted. Their lives were on the line and if they were going to die, she was bloody well going to do it helping a handsome man stay on his feet. Hard as she listened, she didn't hear another voice. Either they had lost them, or the Reb scouts had decided to pursue them quietly. Still, she wasn't about to let go of his hand, not with the way his fingers tightened possessively around hers. How much she liked it should have bothered her more than it did, but she'd worry about that if they survived the night.

Near her other hand Cliste trotted along, tail wagging. The hound's relaxed demeanor soothed Ashlinn's nerves until finally she was able to stop shaking. Each ragged breath Sean took made her concern for him grow. She moved in close to him so her mouth was next to his ear.

"We should stop and rest," she whispered.

"Do you need to?"

"No, but your wound."

He lifted his chin, pace never slowing. "I will be fine. If we are caught, they will kill me and do worse to you. I will not let that happen."

Though his words were quiet, the emotion behind them made them so powerful chills raced up her arms. From the conviction in his tone, she could tell that arguing would be a waste of time. Besides, how could she when he sounded so gallant? Then there was the scathing memory of the Reb soldier knocking her to the ground, unbuckling his belt…

"All right, but promise to tell me if it gets too much. No need to be overly manly," she whispered.

"I promise." His feather-light breath upon her cheek was just enough to make her wish it were a caress.

Silently chiding herself, she marched on beside him through the dark forest. Every now and then, they came close enough to see the beaten down road the Union army had left in its wake while returning to Harrison's Landing. The hours ticked by and Sean never slowed his brisk walk. Ashlinn's calves and back soon burned from stepping over fallen branches and ducking beneath low-hanging ones. Her breeches and coat had snagged on bushes more times than she could count. That road was so tempting the sight of it made her ache.

Just when she feared she couldn't take the temptation any longer, Sean guided them out onto the road. Moonlight bathed the swath cut through the countryside, making it look like a ghostly river. A glance up revealed clouds retreating. She tugged gently against his hand.

"Do you really think 'tis safe?" She didn't want to doubt him, but she feared the pain might be getting the better of him since he had been denying it for the last few hours.

"Aye, 'tis just around the next bend. Besides, they have seen us, and we do not want to give them any reason to shoot." He indicated the path before them with a lift of his chin.

Her feet were already upon the road by the time the second sentence left his mouth. She halted in midstride, alarm coursing through her. Sean straightened and pulled her close to his side. Next to them, Cliste began to growl low and quiet, not a menacing sound so much as a warning.

"That 'tis far enough. Yer name and rank, soldier," boomed a voice from the trees on the other side of the road.

Sean stepped between her and the voice. "Corporal Sean MacBranain," he announced in an equally loud voice.

"Who's with you?" came the man's voice from the trees again.

"The nurse who saved my life." His hand tightened around hers as he said the words.

Quiet as a ghost, a shadow stepped out of the bushes, making her tense up. Another set of boots sounded behind them. Cliste's growl grew louder, throaty with warning. She had never even known they were there.

Upon seeing the Union blue uniforms Ashlinn let out a breath. "'Tis all right, Cliste," she said, one hand patting the hound's head.

"MacBranain! Bloody hell man, we thought you were dead for sure," came a different voice from behind them.

Ashlinn turned to see a tall, broad soldier approaching, musket lowered, a wide grin lifting his shortly trimmed mustache into cheeks that sported at least a week-long shadow. He paused, eyes going to Cliste. She continued to pet the hound's head in a soothing motion. Slowly, the hair along Cliste's back lay back down. Steering wide of her, the soldier approached Sean.

"Good lord, man. 'Tis that a bear or a dog?" the soldier asked in a deep voice, eyes on Cliste. His accent suggested he was Irish, but his height suggested something else.

Sean laughed. "'Tis an Irish wolfhound. She also helped save me life."

A grunt of pain expelled from him as the man embraced him. The beginnings of a growl rumbled through Cliste again.

"I would have been dead for sure if it were not for this one here," he said when the man let him go.

The tall man looked Ashlinn over, not in the leering way some soldiers did, but as if he was impressed with her. Then again, that could be due in part to her being clad in men's clothing with her hair all done up beneath her cap. "Thank you, lass. You have saved a good man here, you have."

The attention shifted back to Sean as the other two men exchanged greetings with him. Pushed to the side, Ashlinn had to fight back a pang of loss. She didn't want to part ways with Sean. For the first time since this blasted war, she hadn't felt so alone. The thought stirred the beginnings of panic within her. She didn't want to allow herself to get close to anyone ever again, not after what happened to her brothers. As if sensing her thoughts, Cliste pressed against her side, her wet nose finding its way into Ashlinn's palm.

"We best get you back to camp. The lieutenant will be thrilled to know there is another survivor," the tall soldier said.

The man turned him toward the direction of Harrison's Landing, leaving Ashlinn forgotten in the background. Even the second soldier, who began to melt back into the forest, didn't spare her a glance. Such was the treatment of medical folk, especially a woman disguised as a male nurse. Despite being used to it, it stung this time. Part of her ached at watching Sean walk away, a part she very much wanted to deny. The logical part of her knew it was for the best, so she let him walk on ahead. Attachments were more dangerous than bullets in this war.

He stopped, turned, and reached back for her hand. "Ashlinn," he called back to her.

At the sound of that gentle voice, she knew with a sinking certainty. There was no denying it. Already she had become attached to this soldier in a way she'd never allowed herself to become attached before. But she would resist it with everything she had in her. She had to. This man, like so many others, would likely end up just like her brothers. Dead or missing. Yes, she would resist. Tomorrow. Accepting his hand, she realized she would fight the most onerous of doctors to remain at his side and ensure his recovery. But that was all. Once he was better she would keep her distance.

Chapter 7

As they walked through the muddy pathways between soldier tents toward the hospital tent, Sean clung tighter to Ashlinn's hand. Her circulation had to be suffering for it, he knew, yet he couldn't loosen his grip. The care she had taken with him and his wounds was above and beyond what most doctors—and certainly any nurses—could or would have done. Though he was on the road to recovery, his fever last night had proven he wasn't out of the woods yet. He didn't want anyone else treating him. One stolen glance at her and he knew it had more to do with not wanting to be away from her than it did with not wanting someone else to treat him.

The rational part of his mind tried to convince him that forming any type of attachment was a bad idea. People only ended up either disappointed by him, or disappointing him in the end. Those that didn't more often ended up dying during this blasted war. This woman had saved his life as surely as any of the soldiers he trusted at his back and, like them, he felt a bond with her that was unbreakable because of it.

Soldiers began to call out greetings to not only him now, but Ashlinn and Cliste as well, mostly Cliste. Eyes big and round, Cliste looked up at Ashlinn, tail wagging. Laughter bubbled from Ashlinn like water over rocks. The sound sent a warmth spreading through Sean that helped banish some of the pain.

Ashlinn leaned down, almost eye level with the hound. "Go on then, you beggar. But do not beg from those who cannot afford to give."

Tail increasing its velocity until Sean couldn't believe the dog didn't topple over, Cliste bounded off amidst the tents. Eyebrows rising, he turned to Ashlinn.

"The soldiers know her?" he asked.

"Many of them. I almost never have to feed her she is so good at begging." The joy in her voice made him smile.

For a moment, he wondered how he had never seen Cliste before, or heard the soldiers speak of her. Then his gaze drew out to the row after row of tents that dotted the transformed plantation like ants in formation. His tent sat acres away, in the opposite direction from the hospital tent. Never had he cause to go near this place before. The sprawl of tents was like a makeshift city, one big enough that two souls could live within it and never meet.

Several muddy paths later, the horrible reek of carrion filled the air, coating the back of Sean's tongue, making him fight the urge to vomit. They rounded a tent and the sprawling hospital tent—easily ten times the size of even an officer's tent—loomed before them. Dread far chillier than any rainy winter in Ireland seeped into him. The stench came from the hospital tent. He suddenly wanted to be going anywhere but in there. Even the battlefield didn't seem as daunting at the moment.

Slowly, almost reluctantly it seemed, Ashlinn pulled her hand from his. How had he held on that long and not noticed? Shame at his improper manners burned through him. This woman made him forget himself, and that scared him more than a little. As they entered the tent she fell into step behind him, becoming so silent he had to glance back to make sure she was there.

A lone light shone deep within the large tent, casting a sickly yellow glow upon a scene Sean didn't want to get closer to. Cots lined both sides of the tent, easily over a hundred, and all filled with soldiers. Regardless of Sean's reservations, their soldier escort led them inside. With a whine, Cliste sat down at the entrance to the tent and refused to go any farther. Sean wished he could do the same, and for more reasons than the debilitating pain stabbing through him.

Hovering over a table at the opposite end of the tent, wearing a blood-splattered apron, saw in hand, stood a man that appeared more butcher than doctor. On the table before him lay a still body, one leg ending in a gory mess, the other half sawed off. At first, Sean thought the wounded man lay on a dark blanket; then he realized arterial blood covered the table and slowly dripped onto the floor.

The doctor tossed the bloody saw onto a side table strewn with medical instruments. Several of the soldiers lying in cots startled at the sound. One man to Sean's left sat bolt upright, eyes wide and wild. As they passed the man's bed, Ashlinn reached out and patted the soldier's arm. She whispered to him until he lay back down and closed his eyes. Though the light was dim in the tent, Sean could tell by the outline of the man's body beneath the thin blanket covering him that he had only one leg.

"What is this? Another?" came the doctor's voice, heavy with exhaustion and a touch of despair.

He approached them slowly, wiping his crimson hands on his already soiled apron. The wrinkles between the man's brows knitted together so tightly they suggested he hadn't stopped scowling in years. Pain and sadness shone in his eyes, but cold detachment hid it almost completely. Sean stopped walking. He didn't want that man's hands anywhere near his wounds.

"Aye, Doc. A missin' one found his way home," the soldier escorting them said.

Bushy brows narrowed over muddy brown eyes as the doctor perused Sean. "Missing or deserted? I have no time for deserters who are just going to be hanged."

Back straightening, Sean glared down at the shorter man, his good hand curling into a fist. "I am no deserter. I was wounded and left on the field of battle."

The doctor snorted. "And yet here you stand."

A wool coat brushed lightly against his arm as Ashlinn stepped between him and the doctor. One hand went to her hip while her other pointed at the doctor's gory chest. "I will not stand for you disrespecting this honorable soldier. He was indeed badly wounded and I tended to him in the field. We only just arrived because of the severity of his wounds and a fever that laid him low over a day."

The doctor's eyes narrowed to slits. His lips pulled back from his teeth in an expression that resembled a snarl far too much for Sean's liking.

"I should have known that was you." The last word was said like a vile curse. "Been out prowling the battlefield again in that ridiculous disguise, I see. This man is lucky if he survived your convoluted ministrations." Though the doctor's voice was full of contempt, the begrudging desire shining in his eyes contradicted it.

Fingers curling into fists, Sean had to remind himself to breathe before he could push words out through his clenched teeth. "Luck had nothin' to do with it. I would have died if not for her."

Lips pursing, the doctor beckoned to him. "Really? Let us see these wounds then," he said in an unconvinced tone.

Ashlinn helped Sean remove his coat and began to work on his bandages. The doctor stepped closer, ducking a shoulder into Ashlinn, starting to push her out of the way. She pushed him back until she stood before Sean, blocking him from the doctor completely.

"You will not touch my patient with your filthy hands. For the love of cleanliness, man, wash first," she warned, voice filled with cold promise.

The doctor shook his head. "You and your foolish notions. Get out of the way, woman. This is men's work."

He shoved her back so hard she crashed into the foot of a bed. The soldier within it let out a groan and stirred in his sleep. She saved herself from falling, but just barely. The doctor reached for Sean. Quick as a water snake, Sean's good hand lashed out and caught the doctor's hand, twisting and turning it at an angle. Emitting a rather unmanly squeal, the doctor rose up on his toes and turned to try and relieve the pressure on his wrist, but to no avail.

"Release me to her care, and her care alone," Sean demanded in an even tone.

Nose scrunching up, the doctor shook his head. "Unhand me! Her crackpot treatments are likely the reason you developed a fever in the first place."

Sean's gaze flicked to the blood-soaked table and its latest occupant. "Says the man who just left a butchered corpse lyin' on a table."

The wrinkles between the doctor's brows deepened and sadness peeked through his detachment again. Unable to feel anything but contempt for him after the way he had treated Ashlinn, Sean shoved the doctor back into the aisle, releasing his wrist.

The doctor shook his head. "Fine, you daft Irishman. You are released to her care. She alone is responsible for your health now. But, do not come haunting me when she kills you. Now get out of my hospital."

Hiding a wince of pain, Sean tossed his coat over one arm, walked to Ashlinn, and offered her his hand. She accepted it and rose from where she leaned on the foot of a bed. Once on her feet, Sean offered his arm, which she took slowly.

The soldier who had escorted them in cleared his throat and stood taller as their attention shifted back to him. "Right then. I will let the lieutenant know you have returned, Corporal, and the lads and I will bring your things over to a tent beside the nurse's."

Sean gave the man a smile he hoped looked more convincing than it felt. "Thank you, Private, that would be much appreciated."

Turning their backs to the doctor, they started for the exit. Ashlinn trembled against him and he thought he heard her sniffling. The urge to apologize burned the back of his throat but he swallowed it. He could not apologize for defending her. Hard day or not, the doctor had been uncouth and out of line. The very thought of the man touching him with those bloodstained hands sent a shiver of fear through Sean. No, he would far rather his life be in Ashlinn's delicate hands. Looking at Ashlinn's straight back and lifted chin as she all but marched beside him, he couldn't help but wonder if his motives had been more selfish.

Chapter 8

Three hairpins later, most of Ashlinn's blond locks finally had been tamed back into a braid that reached down between her shoulder blades. Still, she fussed with stray bits of it here and there, seeking perfection. With shaking hands, she smoothed the skirt of her simple blue work dress. A pang of self-consciousness twinged within her.

The ladies of New York would scoff at such a drab thing. They, however, didn't have to labor over bleeding men all day. While she didn't either right now, as her day of work was over, she didn't have any other dresses that didn't have bloodstains. The only thing the garment had going for it besides a nicely fitted bodice was a skirt that was scandalously short. Had she been wearing a fancy pair of shoes her ankles should have shown. But all her fancy shoes were a world away back in New York. All she had in this muddy, dreary place was her calf-high working boots.

One last look in the tiny mirror propped upon her trunk made her cringe at the dark circles beneath her eyes. She tried to convince herself that it had to do with the candlelight, but the yawn fighting its way through spoke otherwise. Graveyard rounds were all the doctor would permit her to do, but she wasn't about to let him win by giving up. The soldiers needed her.

Tonight was about one soldier in particular. Three days from their arrival and Sean was finally feeling good enough for a bit of exercise. He had asked her to join him in a walk along the river. The very thought brought heat to her cheeks, turning them a nice color. It was a shame he was bringing along another soldier as chaperone. Often she found herself longing for the time they had spent alone. Such wicked thoughts added a smile along with her blush. Of course, she wouldn't risk her heart by allowing feelings for the man to form, but a little harmless flirting couldn't hurt.

A soft woof came from the opening of her tent. Gathering her skirt so it didn't catch on anything in the cramped area, she went to the flap and opened it. Big tail wagging, a grin exposing her canines, stood Cliste. Beside her, a young soldier stood at attention, his left brow twitching each time Cliste's tail smacked his leg. Ashlinn glanced over at Sean's dark tent, suddenly fearful that he had sent this man along to cancel for him, or worse.

"Hello," she managed through a tightening throat.

"Hello, ma'am. The general has sent me to invite you to a ball to be held tomorrow night to celebrate the visit of President Lincoln."

A hand flew to her chest as if to stop her thundering heart from trying to leap out of its cage. Relief weakened her knees but resolve kept her upright. So many thoughts and concerns raced through her mind that she found it impossible to give voice to even one of them. Perhaps she would be able to speak to a general, or at least a lieutenant, at such an event and try to convince them to send out search parties for missing soldiers. The young soldier extended an envelope and a pencil to her.

"The general asks that you provide your dress and shoe size so that he may send along proper attire."

It felt more like a command than an invitation, one delivered in a polite, respectful tone, but a command nonetheless. It had been two years since she had worn something fine and danced about a ballroom, so she wasn't about to argue. Then, of course, there was the small matter of the President of the United States being present. Surely she'd never get close enough to speak to him, but others perhaps. She accepted the offered objects, opened the envelope, wrote her name and size on the paper inside, and handed it back.

"Thank you, Private," she said with a slight curtsy.

"You are quite welcome, ma'am." He tipped his cap to her and moved on toward another nurse's tent.

All the nurse's tents had been pitched in this small area between the hospital and the grounds of the plantation manor. Not only did the general deem it a safer place for the women, but as the only place on the property left with any grass, it was also the cleanest. He wanted his soldiers' hospital in the best possible location. Ashlinn had gained quite a bit of respect for the man once she had heard that. This invitation, though, she wasn't sure what to think of.

"Has that patient of yours died yet?" An ugly croak of a voice interrupted her musings.

The very sound of the doctor's voice made the hair on the back of her neck stir. Damn, why hadn't she returned inside her tent, or gone to Sean's?

"Of course not. He improves every day."

The temptation to brag about how well his stitches were taking and the lack of any signs of infection grew, but she suppressed it. This man did not deserve to know how Sean was doing and she was not about to tell him simply for the sake of bragging. When it came to treatment of her and the other nurses, this one was far worse than the doctor who had died out on the battlefield.

An almost imperceptible growl rumbled from Cliste as the hound moved between Ashlinn and the approaching doctor. In dark breeches and a beige shirt that bore no visible signs of bloodstains, the man was almost presentable. That was, if you could look past the dark sideburns of hair that clung to cheeks that turned into chops, which Ashlinn could not. It wasn't that she only fell for a handsome face. The deep lines between this man's brows from constantly furrowing them and the wrinkles at the corners of his eyes from sneering too much were hard to look past. Crumbs clung to his bushy mustache and his jaw worked at some type of food or another.

A smile full of anything but joy slid onto the doctor's face. "Well, in that case he will be ready to rejoin his brigade in no time."

His gaze traveled over her body, lashes low like spiders trying to cover their tracks. But she noticed. Oh yes, she noticed. She wished for her coat, a shawl, anything to cover the bit of cleavage her square neck dress revealed.

Ashlinn's throat tightened at the thought but she smiled back to hide her reaction, lifting her chin. "Indeed he will."

For the briefest moment, something like regret flashed in the doctor's eyes. He extended something to her: crackers wrapped in wax treated paper, a rare thing in the midst of war. A slightly sweet scent wafted up from them.

"All the way from New York. Would you like some?" he asked in a voice sweet as syrup.

She turned her nose up. "No, thank you."

His beady eyes shot to Cliste for a brief moment, then back to Ashlinn. "McClellan only wants the women there as pretty play things, you know."

Casting her eyes up and to the side, she shook her head. "The general is much more intelligent than that. He seeks to bring a sense of civility to the president's visit. One can hardly blame him."

"You give the man too much credit; he is still a man." He cleared his throat and stood straighter. "Regardless, a woman should not go unescorted to such a function."

Dread as wet and cold as a New York fall morning seeped into her. Her mind scurried for an excuse to end the conversation but nothing would come to her. Footsteps squished upon wet grass and she turned toward them eagerly.

"Ah, Ashlinn, there you are. I was just comin' to fetch you for our walk," Sean said as he approached.

Tail wagging with such exuberance that her entire backside swayed, Cliste trotted to Sean's side, sticking her nose in his hand. He scratched between her ears, grinning down at her as if she were the grandest thing in all the world. Dark breeches and a blue shirt fit his fine frame quite nicely, revealing just a bit of the swell of his bicep and the curve of his behind. Realizing she was staring, Ashlinn looked down, pretending to smooth her dress. That nicely curved bicep appeared in front of her.

"Shall we?" he asked.

She accepted his arm a bit too readily. "Indeed, before we lose the light."

The doctor puffed his chest out like a red rooster and sputtered several times before getting any words out. "Surely you are not gallivanting about unescorted."

Sean grinned and looked behind the doctor. "O' course not. I may be a soldier, but I am also a gentleman."

The doctor spun around and glared at the uniformed soldier standing at attention behind him. When he looked back at them, Ashlinn had to hide a smile behind her hand.

"Good day then, Doctor," Sean said as he began to lead Ashlinn toward the manor house.

Shooting the doctor a brief growl, Cliste shot out ahead of them.

In her free hand, Ashlinn held her skirts up until they cleared the occasional muddy areas and made it to the dense green grass. Soon they were out of the maze of tents with nothing but the sight of the sprawling southern manor and its surrounding lawn before them. The warmth of Sean's arm looped around hers made her long for him to move closer so she could feel more of his body. To her dismay, he truly did act the gentleman and kept his distance. If only she could cover her ears and block out the constant buzz of the encampment, then she would be able to pretend they weren't in the midst of a war.

"I do apologize if I interrupted your conversation with the doctor," he said after a while.

"Do not apologize for rescuing me. In fact, I hope that you will consider interrupting any time you see the doctor having a conversation with me."

Sean laughed. The deep, carefree sound echoed down into Ashlinn's soul, tingling in the most amazing way. Heat warmed her cheeks and she used the excuse to look back at the soldier following them to hide her blush.

"Very well then. I shall consider it my duty to rescue you any time I see you in his presence."

"Thank you," she managed in a soft voice peppered with pain.

He looked down at her. "You should not let that blaggard get to you."

She swallowed hard, mustering up the courage to speak. "'Tis more than his surly attitude. When my brothers were wounded, it was he who treated them. They died on his table." Why she was being so open and forward with this man, she had no idea. All she knew was that his presence soothed her, put her at ease in a way little did now days.

"I am sorry. I did not think 'twas possible to dislike the man more, but now I do. But he was right about one thing, you know."

Her gaze whipped back up to him. "That, I find hard to believe. What could he possibly be right about?"

His wonderful copper eyes met hers, the sunbursts of darker brown around the pupil drawing her in. "It would be best if you had an escort to the ball, and I would be most honored if you would allow me to be that escort."

Ashlinn's eyes widened before she remembered her manners, swept her long lashes over them, and nodded. "I would be most honored to attend with you."

"It is I who will have the honor. What is your favorite color? I shall send along a request to General McClellan about the dress."

Her blush returned with a vengeance, scalding her cheeks and making her wish the evening were cooler. "No need to go to all that trouble for me. I shall be happy with whatever he sends along."

The devilish grin he gave her made an entirely different kind of heat spread through far more scandalous parts of her body. "Perhaps you would allow me to choose a color."

She inclined her head, mostly to hide her red cheeks. "Certainly. I am curious to see what it will be."

The river soon came into view, undulating along the edge of the plantation property like a lazy snake on a sultry summer day. Cliste bounded right for the water, sending droplets flying everywhere as she plunged in with an abandon that Ashlinn envied. Though clouds still lingered in the sky, it hadn't rained all day, making the combination of heat and humidity stifling. The subdued light cast by the setting sun softened the edges of everything, giving the scene a gentle look that clashed with the chaos behind them. Frogs croaked and bugs buzzed, a reminder that life in nature went on despite their war.

Though he didn't so much as let out a groan, Ashlinn could tell by how he stiffened after a while that Sean's side began to hurt. This was his first real exercise since they had returned. She had insisted he rest for a few days with little activity. Pretending to fuss with her skirts, she slowed her pace.

"Why do you think the president is coming to visit?" she asked as they turned to walk along the grassy riverbank.

Sean let out a long breath and shook his head as he looked down at his boots. "General McClellan wrote him a letter."

"A letter?"

"Aye. He beseeched the president to focus the efforts of the war on preservin' the Union instead of endin' slavery."

The tension lacing his words told her he wasn't exactly happy about that.

"And this bothers you."

His jaw tightened as he cast his gaze out over the slow moving river. "Aye. We cannot be unified when a third of our people are slaves."

They stopped at an old wooden bench beneath a small arbor covered in grape vines. Ashlinn sat down on the bench and motioned for Sean to do the same. Clearly he needed to rest for more reasons than one. After a quick glance around, he sat, but at a respectable distance so their legs didn't touch. Feeling bold, and needing to pull him from his dark thoughts, Ashlinn took hold of his hand. Sean glanced over his shoulder at their chaperone but didn't pull his hand back. The man stood a respectable distance away, staring off into the distance.

"I keep track of every man I have tended, writing down his name, address, and the names of his family members in a book so that if he dies, I can send a letter to his family. There are hundreds of names in that book and I know thousands more have died." She had to take a deep breath to steady her voice. "Focusing on preserving the Union would likely make the Rebels concede at this point. Part of me understands McClellan's desire to end things. It's one thing to tend to a wounded man, another entirely to send him to his death."

Cocking his head, Sean looked at her through narrowed eyes. "You agree with the general?"

"No, not at all. I merely understand where he is coming from. I believe slavery must be ended, and even if it costs an entire generation their lives, it will save the souls of countless more to come."

The wrinkles in Sean's brow smoothed out and his eyes widened. "You are a very interestin' woman, Ashlinn O'Brian."

Laughter spilled from Ashlinn, not the polite giggle expected from ladies but an unrestrained guffaw that she regretted immediately. "I have been called many things, but never that."

For several moments, Sean laughed along with her, putting her completely at ease. His fingers tightened around hers as he gave her a smile of pure joy. "'Tis true. I admire that you think so deeply and speak your mind about it."

She raised one eyebrow at him. "Then that makes you a very interesting man, Mr. MacBranain. Most men prefer their women to be seen and not heard."

"I have noticed that unfortunate fact about men in America. 'Tis not so in our native Ireland, for the most part."

They sat looking out upon the river for a while, enjoying the birdsong and the crickets tuning up for the coming night. In the shade of the grapevine leaves, the heat of the day almost reduced to pleasant. The sweet scent the remaining ripe grapes gave off was a bit cloying in its strength, but well worth it.

Soon Sean leaned close enough that their shoulders touched. Though cloth separated them, the motion felt wonderfully intimate.

"Thank you for this," Sean said.

"For what?"

As their eyes met, he reached up to touch a strand of her hair. "For savin' my life. And for remindin' me there is more to it than killin' and dyin'."

Though she swallowed hard multiple times, she could not get the lump in her throat to go down so she could respond. The warmth and gratitude in his eyes drew her in until she swam in their coppery depths. One of his arms slid around her waist, drawing her closer. Desire filled those lovely eyes, but a tightness remained around them as if he were holding back. Of course he was. He was a true gentleman after all.

"To hell with propriety," she murmured as she leaned closer to him, her lips reaching for his.

Freezing droplets of water struck her all over, followed by the swishing sound of dog's hair moving as it shook.

"Ahhh, Cliste!" Ashlinn exclaimed as she brought her arms up to shield herself.

Sean's carefree laugh filled the evening, more refreshing than a cool summer breeze. Such a laugh was a rare and precious thing in these times, something she hadn't heard much at all in the past two years.

Tongue lolling out the side of her mouth, bent over ears perked as high as they could go, Cliste regarded them both with what could only be humor in her eyes.

"Cliste, I fear you are a better chaperone than my friend over there," Sean told the hound.

The hound's tail wagged, sending more water flying as she came closer. Laughing, Ashlinn waved her hands out before her. "No, no. Do not dare come near me, you wet thing!"

Sean picked up a stick, waved it before the hound, and tossed it toward the riverbank. Emitting a soft woof, Cliste bounded after it, tail flinging a last round of droplets on them as it wagged. The lengthening shadows of twilight soon swallowed her big gray silhouette.

A long sigh filled with regret eased from Sean as he rose. "Well, 'tis gettin' dark; it would be ungentlemanly of me not to get you back to your tent."

Rather than offer her his arm, he offered his bare hand, proving he wasn't completely against being ungentlemanly. Smiling, Ashlinn accepted it and rose to stand closer to him than was ladylike. Another step and they would be pressed together. It was all she could do not to take that step. Whatever had come over her, she decided she liked it. From beneath her lashes, she gazed up at him.

"Being completely gentlemanly is overrated at times," she said.

He draped her arm around his and pressed her hand against his forearm. "Perhaps it is," he said as they began to walk.

With her free hand, she fussed with her skirt, using the excuse to keep their pace slow. Not only was she in no hurry to get back, she didn't want him overexerting himself. All too soon, they were picking their way through the muddy patches that dotted the pathways between tents. Candlelight glowed from within a few of the tents already. Thankfully, the paths were empty of people for the most part. Cliste pushed her nose through the canvas door of their tent and dashed inside, leaving them alone.

Arm withdrawing from hers, Sean took a step back. Before they lost contact altogether, he caught up one of her hands, raised it to his lips, and kissed the back of it. The heady sensation of a man's lips—this man's lips in particular—upon the bare flesh of her hand was entirely new. Men had kissed her hand before, but always with a glove upon it. A thrill vibrated all the way down to her core. Her eyes shot open and she gasped at the pleasure of it. From beneath his dark brown locks, he gazed up at her from where he bent over her hand. Muscles low in her abdomen clenched, widening her eyes even farther.

"Guess I'm not a complete gentleman after all," he whispered.

The husky tone of his voice touched things inside her that she longed for his skin to. Her face was afire with the scandal of her thoughts, and she couldn't care less.

"Like I said, overrated," she said in a breathy voice.

Slowly, and with obvious regret, he let her hand slide from his and took a step back. "Until tomorrow night then." He bowed and shot her a devilish grin before turning toward his own tent less than ten feet away.

Harmless flirting, she reminded herself. Just harmless flirting. Pushing the boundaries like that made it feel like something almost scandalous, which was fine by her. A scandal her heart could survive; a courtship that ended with a dead suitor, it could not. As she undid the remaining ties that held her tent flap closed, she watched him out of her peripheral vision. He gave her a wink before ducking into his tent, flushing her face with heat yet again over having her staring discovered. Definitely scandalous.

Not wanting to risk the doctor "happening" by again while she was alone, she quickly retreated inside her tent and tied the flap closed. The thump of a tail against the ground greeted her. Cliste seemed to smile up at her from where she lay upon an old blanket at the foot of Ashlinn's cot. It amazed her how pleased with itself a hound could look.

Not even bothering to loosen her corset, she flopped onto her back on the cot, letting out a long breath that she felt all the way down to her toes. Never had she been a lady prone to swooning over a man—not even as a young girl. Medical papers, studies, and practice had always been what intrigued her most in life. Men and relationships were a thing she had made little time for. But here this man came out of the blue, capturing much more than just her attention.

This was neither the time nor the place to allow herself to be distracted by matters of the heart. Not to mention, there was the issue of every man in her life having died or disappeared. She wasn't exactly lucky where they were concerned. For both of their sakes, she needed to keep her heart guarded. While she tried to convince herself of that, she couldn't help but long for the hours between now and the ball to pass as quickly as possible.

Chapter 9

Being a corporal, Sean was expected to be present for all the pomp and ceremony of welcoming the president to the camp, but not to participate much beyond saluting and standing at attention. On the outskirts of the triple line of soldiers as he was, he couldn't catch much more than a glimpse of the proceedings. He saw the president's sideburns and his tall, black velvet hat, but not much else. And that only because the man was nearly a half a head taller than anyone else in attendance.

Fascinating as it all was, he was impatient for it to be over so he could pick Ashlinn up for the ball. He had no way to know if the runner he sent along with the request for her dress had been successful or not. The suspense had him fidgeting like a schoolboy. Earlier in the day he had shaved and bathed—not in the river or submerged in a tub, per Ashlinn's medical advice, but with a towel and basin of lukewarm water. He had been careful to avoid his wounds as she had instructed, instead keeping them dry behind the clean bandages she had put on him this morning.

Finally, the general and president entered the manor. The moment the word "dismissed" left his lieutenant's mouth, Sean allowed his body to relax, taking the pressure off the building pain in his side. At least the trimmed, green grass beneath his polished boots had offered a bit of cushion, but even the benefits of that had diminished after almost an hour of standing in the same spot.

The clouds that had held back the sweltering heat began to move across the sky. Beams of sunlight broke through here and there, reflecting off the puddles left by an earlier rain shower. Sean steered clear of them, wanting to keep his boots as clean as possible. The edges of the paths between the tents weren't so bad. Grass even managed to cling in some spots. He stored the best path to memory so he could bring Ashlinn down it and avoid soiling her dress. He wanted this night to be perfect for her. She deserved it, and so much more. In truth, more than he could give.

Tonight was foolish, in more ways than one. Attending a ball while men were fighting and dying seemed horribly wrong. But it was more than that. His heart longed for him to let his guard down and let her in, but his head fought him. He had long ago lost count of the number of friends who had died beside him. While he couldn't help befriending his brothers-in-arms, allowing feelings for a woman to grow at a time like this was something he could stop. Despite the war that raged within, despite the foolishness of it all, he was determined to enjoy the evening. Considering that each moment of this war brought the possibility of death, it would be foolish not to seize a good moment. That was all it would be: a moment.

Having convinced both his head and heart to be on the same page for the evening, he approached Ashlinn's tent. The ball was yet an hour away, but he wanted to take her for a walk along the manor grounds before the festivities began. He drew his hand over his clean-shaven chin as he contemplated the perfect words. A large, gray, furred head poked through the tent flap at stomach height. Ears perked up and canines showing in a dog's grin, Cliste emitted a soft woof of greeting.

Grinning, Sean scratched between the hound's ears. "Hello to you as well." From within the tent came Ashlinn's voice. "Cliste, get out of the way."

Cliste withdrew and a few moments later the tent flap pushed aside. The fine words of formality he had carefully rehearsed fled like birds from a hound. Not even a vestige of them remained for his gaping mouth to grasp upon. Satin folds in emerald green hugged Ashlinn's curves in all the right ways, accentuating her hips, the dip of her waist. The color matched her eyes perfectly. A square neckline edged in Irish lace framed her bosom, showing just a hint of cleavage that would suggest her breasts to be perfect handfuls. Pins that gleamed in the twilight held her golden hair in an elaborate bun atop her head, exposing the long, graceful line of her neck.

Oh how he longed to brush his lips across that pale skin...he would have blushed were there any blood left to make its way to his cheeks. However, it all rushed in the opposite direction. A hand drifted to her chest, not to hide it, he realized by her stunned expression, but as if checking her heart. Her beautiful blue eyes danced across him, drinking in every inch of his finely pressed and fitted uniform—the one he kept tucked away for special occasions. He was suddenly very thankful the general had offered to clean and press the uniforms of any soldiers attending the ball. And even more grateful that he'd had the chance to bathe—with actual soap—and shave for the occasion.

He was the first to find his voice.

"I was right. That dress proves it."

One corner of her mouth quirked up. "Right about what?" The breathless sound of her voice was alluring music to his ears, like a siren's song.

"You bein' an angel." He knew he sounded just as breathless, and he didn't care.

With a flourish, he bowed deeply and offered her his arm. She inclined her head and accepted, wrapping her arm around his. To his dismay, long white gloves reached all the way up to her elbows. He would miss the decadent feel of her bare hand upon his arm tonight, but seeing her in such finery more than made up for it.

"Now, now, Mr. MacBranain, it would not be prudent to make such an assumption before getting to know me better," she said.

They began to walk toward the manor, Cliste trotting along behind them.

A twinge of fear twisted inside him at her words. "Come now, I should think after all we have been through together we are past such formalities." The wise part of him knew this was his opportunity to step back, to stop playing this dangerous game they had started. But the thought of keeping this woman at a distance hurt worse than a bayonet through the side.

Though she smiled, he thought he caught a glimmer of fear in her eyes as well. "Indeed, we are. But it would be nice to pretend for at least one night that we are within proper society instead of the midst of a war."

The knots in his stomach unbound and he rubbed the back of her gloved hand. "Then that's exactly what we shall do, Miss O'Brian."

She leaned a bit closer to him than what was proper, her side touching his in places. Fire spread out from those areas, warming him in a way not even the sultry July evening could. He longed to lean in to that warmth but he didn't dare. If anyone were going to push the boundaries of society, he would let it be her. To a point. To preserve her honor, and his, he would stop the flirtation before it could go too far. But only if it came to that.

"You look quite dashing in your dress uniform. I hope it does not rub too much against your stitches," she said, adding the last part quickly, as if she needed a reason to compliment him.

He smiled down at her. "Why thank you. And no, 'tis all right."

The dirt and mud paths soon gave way to short green grass that was blessedly dry. Much to Sean's surprise, it hadn't rained since this morning, almost as if the weather itself were giving them a reprieve for this event. They rounded the side of the house and entered the landscaped back garden. Many of the bushes and flowers grew untamed since the Union had taken possession of Harrison's Landing, but it was still beautiful. Cobbled paths led here and there, the largest of them going toward an area where dozens of people gathered. Officers in pristine uniforms and ladies in gowns the hues of jewels chatted and mingled as if a war wasn't going on all around them. It made all the killing, dying, and maiming seem a world away. He didn't want it to feel that way, didn't want to disrespect the sacrifices being made.

Could he pretend convincingly enough that they weren't in the midst of such horrors?

One glance at the beauty on his arm and he knew he could. She fussed with her dress, smoothing it where her hand had clung to it, holding it up away from the dirty path they had just left. The full skirt swept out around her like a bell, hiding parts of her that the breeches she had worn when he had first met her revealed. But he didn't need to see the curve of her hips, her buttocks, they were burned into his memory as surely as if they had been branded there. Her face turned up to him, the doubt etched in her eyes surprising him from his wicked thoughts.

"What's wrong?"

She shook her head and put on a smile that didn't reach her eyes. "I was thinking of my patients. I apologize. We deserve to enjoy this night, and we shall."

Knowing she felt the same about this farce of civility in the midst of war made it a little easier to stomach. His already substantial respect for her grew. Lifting her head, Cliste bumped their clasped arms and shot between the two of them and into the crowd. Tail wagging, she approached a pair of uniformed men who greeted her as if they knew her and promptly set to petting her.

"Not shy at all, is she?" Sean said.

Ashlinn smiled after her like a proud parent. "Not at all. But then, she knows just about all the soldiers. She wanders a lot while I work and they all seem to love her."

"What's not to love? She has quite the personality." Heat flushed through him with each word, for he spoke them not just about Cliste, but about Ashlinn.

Among the dozens before them, Sean searched for a familiar face to connect with. Not a man without stripes on his shoulders stood among the crowd, a fact that rankled him more than a little. Finally, he saw a sergeant from the 69th that he recognized. It took a moment because the man now wore a full beard, something Sean had never seen upon him. He leaned heavily on a walking stick, trying to make the pose seem casual while he chatted up a woman in a yellow gown. Of the dozens of men from his regiment that had visited him while he'd been wounded, this man hadn't been among them. Now he knew why. The man had been wounded as well.

Careful to keep the accepted distance between he and Ashlinn, Sean escorted her across the yard to where the sergeant stood. Turned slightly away from them as he was, attention riveted upon the woman in yellow, he didn't notice them approach. Sean waited for the woman in yellow to stop talking and nod in his direction.

"Sergeant Brady, 'tis good to see you."

The sergeant hobbled around to face him, eyes going wide when they set upon him. "Corporal MacBranain! Ha!"

The man grasped his hand and pumped it with vigor. "'Tis good to see you too, man! We thought you were dead for sure."

"I would have been were it not for Miss O'Brian here. She found me in the field, stitched me up, and helped me get back here."

Eyes filling with wonder, Brady nodded to Ashlinn. "Then we owe you a great debt, Miss O'Brian. Sean here is an exceptional soldier."

Removing her arm from Sean's for a moment, Ashlinn curtsied to the man. "I could not agree more, Sergeant. 'Tis a pleasure to make your acquaintance."

After exchanging pleasantries and introductions, they chatted about the weather, the wildlife, the president, anything but the war. The last one was sticky, considering the reason for his visit. It became much like fishing in a lake full of alligators and trying to pretend they weren't there. Thankfully, the band setting up in a nearby gazebo finally began to play a tune and those gathered started breaking up into dancing pairs. There weren't nearly enough women by half, which left a lot of men standing in the garden waiting. Sean felt a bit guilty for being one of the lucky few to have a lovely lady on his arm, but only a bit. The lively sound of a violin made his fingers ache and his feet long to move.

Between the manor house and the band's gazebo lay a cobbled area beneath an awning where the officers sat with the president. Sean could barely see the esteemed man, he was so well protected by the bodies of others standing around. Being only a corporal, he knew this glimpse of the beard and top hat were all he would get, but he was fine with that. The person he truly wanted to see hung on his arm. When Brady paired off with the woman in yellow, Sean turned to Ashlinn.

"Would you care to dance?"

She raised an eyebrow at him, a gesture that made his blood start to pump to areas most ungentlemanly. "Are you sure you are up to it?"

He was up to it and so much more, but he wasn't about to voice that. Instead, he smiled and inclined his head. "No worries, I am in the hands of a fine physician who will no doubt detect when I am in need of rest."

"In that case, I would love to dance, Mr. MacBranain."

He took her left hand in his and placed his right lightly upon her hip. They waltzed out across the green grass as if it were a smooth ballroom floor. She was pliant and responsive in his hands, almost as if she read his intentions before he knew them and responded accordingly. Warmth flowed from her into him despite the bits of satin and lace between them, not the suffocating warmth of a humid summer day, but the simmering of something far more promising. She floated on her feet, moving into each step with the lightest of touches.

The music poured into him, singing through Sean's blood, pulling his body along to the rhythm. A joy he hadn't felt in over two years began to steal over him like mist on an Irish morning. That wasn't quite right, though. This joy was beyond anything he had felt dancing at the society balls back in Ireland and New York. The beautiful golden-haired woman in his arms had much to do with that. Each bell-like laugh and full smile she gave him made his heart swell until he feared his ribs could not contain it. With her bold manners and open practice of medicine, she was unlike any woman he had ever met.

In between dances they visited the table filled with food the likes of which Sean hadn't seen in two years. At the edge of the table, Cliste sat looking ever so patient. Though her head easily reached above the table even while she sat, she didn't reach over to it.

"Such a clever one, you are. How many of these officers have you enticed into givin' you a treat?" Sean asked her.

Her tail thumped against the grass, and if he didn't know better, he would swear she smiled. Ashlinn laughed and scratched the hound's head. "Many of them, I am certain."

Sean scanned the table. "What's her favorite treat?"

Her tail thumped harder as if she understood his words. Ashlinn pointed to a cracker that didn't look much different from hardtack. Sean raised an eyebrow at her, making her laugh again. Oh, how he loved that sound.

"There is no accounting for the taste of a hound. But, 'tisn't as bad as it looks. 'Tis a sweet cracker," she said.

Shrugging, Sean picked up one for himself and a second that he held out to Cliste. Gentle as a babe, she picked the treat from his hand and crunched away at it. He tested a corner of the one he had taken for himself and found it quite tasty. Once Ashlinn finished her punch, he offered her his hand with a slight bow.

"Shall we return to the dance floor, my lady?"

Giggling, she allowed him to sweep her back out onto the open area of grass where the dancers were engaged in a lively waltz. Not wanting any of the men to feel left out, he stepped aside now and again so others could dance with her. She chatted each of them up, often leaving them looking a bit disappointed. Intrigued by her behavior, he listened in as a lieutenant swept her past him in a waltz. They conversed about the impossibilities of sending out a search party for lost soldiers. He spoke to her of how many had likely deserted, and she looked as though she may slap him. That one Sean quickly stepped in on and took over the dance.

Tears glistening in her eyes, she only sniffled and looked away as he swept her around the garden to the tune of the music.

"I'm sorry, he didn't need to be so blunt about that," he whispered.

Blinking rapidly and straightening her back against his hand, she met his gaze. "No, I am sorry for ruining our evening with a doomed plot to find my brother."

He rubbed the back of her hand with his fingers, taking great pleasure in how the touch drained some of the pain from her eyes. "Nonsense. You had to try. There is no harm in that."

By the end of the dance he had her smiling again. Night soon fell, but the blanket of stars above and the swollen half-moon gave more than adequate light to continue the festivities. The general, president, and both their entourages retreated inside the house, but the festivities continued uninterrupted. Sean began to realize that this night was as much for the leaders of the army as it was for the entertainment of the president. Men with renewed spirits could renew the spirits of those they led. Looking around the garden at the corporals, sergeants, and lieutenants dancing with the smiling ladies, he realized it was a brilliant plan. Even Sergeant Brady was managing a few steps with the lady in yellow.

After a few polkas and another slow waltz, his breathing became hitched enough that she noticed. Both the stitches in his arm and side pinched as if driving tiny thorns deep into his skin and muscle. Regardless, he didn't want to stop. Ashlinn's bosom heaved, the hint of her delicious cleavage peeking out from the emerald-green satin threatening to draw his eyes. He resisted, forcing his gaze up across her delicate collarbones that gleamed ever so slightly, not with perspiration, but as if the moonlight pooled there. The ridiculous urge to lap up the moonlight as if it were water, made him drag his gaze up to her face. Pink flushed just beneath her high cheekbones and her mouth was slightly agape as she drew in deep breaths.

The sudden tightening of his breeches forced him to look quickly away.

"I fear I must rest a moment. Would you mind escorting me to that bench over there?" she asked.

The breathy sound of her voice did all kinds of wonderful things to him that made him long for shadows that would hide his condition. Thankfully, the bench she motioned toward was deep within the shadow of a willow tree, so deep in fact that it took him a moment of searching to find where she pointed. It was a bit far from the festivities, barely within sight of them really. To take her there wouldn't exactly be proper, but since she was the one asking...

"I would not mind at all."

Sean looked around for an unoccupied soldier who might be willing to chaperone them, but they all seemed to be having such a grand time that he didn't want to pull them away.

Ashlinn laughed, looped her arm through his, and began to lead him toward the distant bench. "Come, my unfailing gentleman. I promise not to scandalize you, much," she said, whispering the last word. It branded him like an iron straight from a blacksmith's forge.

So caught up were they in their own revelry that no one seemed to notice them leave the festivities. Soon Sean could hear the thundering of his own heart over the music in the distance. He struggled to keep his wits and manners about him as his blood all pumped to one place, making him light-headed in the most delicious way. They passed beneath the drooping moss that hung from the willow. To his surprise, Ashlinn pulled him not to the bench, but around behind the huge tree trunk. Holding tight to his hand, she sighed as she leaned back against the tree, her eyes cast out over the river.

"It is beautiful here," she said.

It took a monumental effort to peel his eyes from her and look out at the tree-lined river only a few yards away. With a star-filled sky hanging above it and fireflies dancing above the grass between them and it, the scene was pristine for sure. As his gaze returned to Ashlinn he couldn't help but think all the splendor in nature didn't even compare. Light from the half-moon played along the blond tresses that had escaped her bun, framing her face with an almost ethereal glow. Something he hadn't seen in her eyes before swam in their blue depths now: happiness. Her gaze shifted from the river to him and filled with something else entirely.

White teeth flashed as she pulled her bottom lip between them, worrying at one side of it like she was trying to hold back words. The sight put him at a loss of words, instead making his body long for action. Compelled by the power of desire in her eyes, he put a hand on the tree to each side of her head and leaned close. Their bodies didn't touch, he wouldn't go that far, but at only inches away, he could feel the heat radiating off her. More than anything he wanted to press into that heat, allow it to consume him, but he didn't dare.

"I will not dishonor you," he whispered in a ragged voice that laid his desires bare.

One of her hands snaked up behind his head, cupping the back of it. "Then allow me."

She pulled him down to her, and despite all his manners and respect for societal boundaries, he was powerless to resist. Their lips touched and the last of his reservations exploded as surely as if they had been hit by cannon fire. His body melted against her soft curves, igniting him from head to toe with a fire that spread from his groin out. As his erection grew, he pulled his hips away from her in a last effort to be at least somewhat gentlemanly. A strangled moan slid from his lips as she raised her hips to press against him.

The moment his lips parted, her tongue slid into his mouth. Reason deserted him. His hands moved over her, one behind her neck, the other around her waist, pressing her tighter to him. When her tongue retreated, his followed. The warm, wet sensation of her mouth made him groan with need. Their tongues danced together, far more intimate partners than they themselves had been not less than an hour ago. Breathless and fighting to keep his hands from wandering to places even less appropriate, he drew back.

"It seems my angel has a bit of devil in her," he gasped.

The laugh that escaped her was deep with desire, the type of sound meant to be heard in only a bedroom, and he loved it. "Does that bother you?" she asked.

He shook his head slowly. "Not in the slightest."

Smart, daring, she was everything he never knew he wanted. If they were back in New York, he'd be asking her father for his permission to court her and calling on her whenever she'd see him. However, her father was dead, and New York felt a world away.

"Then why do you look sad?" she asked.

He allowed a very sated smile to spread across his lips. "Only because I wish I could court you properly. You deserve that."

Fear showed in her widening eyes a moment before desire drowned it. She grasped her hands together behind his neck and looked him straight in the eye. "I have spent much of my life either with my head in a book or covered in blood with sutures or a scalpel in my hand. A proper lady I most certainly am not."

His head cocked to the side. "You have a point there, and I must admit, that's part of what I enjoy most about you."

Her mouth gaped. "Truly?"

Hand splaying out wide across her back to touch as much of her as possible, he drew her back to him. "Aye, truly."

Rising up onto her toes, she pressed her lips to his again. This time they were hard, eager as they forced his lips open, giving her tongue access to dive into his mouth. The moan that slid from her flowed into him like the sweetest, most potent whiskey, burning all the way to his soul.

"Unhand her this instant, you filthy mick!" A harsh, male voice shattered the perfect moment into a million pieces.

Head turning toward that voice, Sean shot away from Ashlinn as if she were on fire. A man of slightly shorter and considerably softer stature than himself stomped toward Sean. He crossed between shadows cast by the tree branches overhead, and Sean caught a glimpse of his face. Square jaw clenched so tight his jowls shook beneath his sideburns; the doctor was the very image of spitting mad. His fist rose and Sean braced himself. Every instinct in him screamed at him to move, but he didn't. He deserved this. The impact stung and turned his head, but that was it. He hit like the Englishman he was.

A blur of green satin and blond hair shot before him. Shoving the doctor back with both hands, Ashlinn moved between them. "Doctor Taylor, how dare you strike a soldier!"

Eyes going wide, the doctor stammered, words catching in his throat. Two deep barks broke the night, followed by the kind of growl that set a man's hair on edge. Hackles raised and teeth bared, Cliste stalked up beside Sean, her gaze fixed upon Taylor.

One dainty hand went to Ashlinn's hip. "And you would do well to watch your tongue. I am Irish as well and do not take kindly to you using such nasty slurs against not only a fine man, but my kind."

Taylor took a step to his left, putting Ashlinn between him and Cliste. Baring his teeth like an animal, he pointed a shaking finger at Sean. "That *man* is not your kind. He seeks to dishonor you, and I have come to see that he does not, at least not any more than he already has." His eyes narrowed at the last part.

Anger under tight control, Sean stepped out from behind Ashlinn. "My intent is not to dishonor the lady."

Taylor's finger shook at him again. "Oh, but you already have. Or have you forgotten that in society a man only kisses a woman who is engaged to be betrothed to him, or who is a whore."

Right hand curling into a fist, Sean took a step forward. "Watch your tongue, man, or so help me, I will defend her honor, even if you are a doctor."

"Puff up all you want, mick, but you cannot deny that what I say is true. You cannot honestly tell me that your intentions for this woman are honorable, not in a time of war." The words stung far worse than the punch had, their truth cutting deep as a knife.

Ashlinn moved back between them, her head thrust high and her teeth bared. "His intentions, and mine, are not your business, Taylor." She reached back, looped her arm around Sean's and gave him a tight smile. "I am feeling rather tired. Would you please escort me safely back to my tent, Mr. MacBranain?"

Nodding his head deep in a show of respect to her, Sean began walking. "O' course, Miss O'Brian."

On the way past Taylor, he allowed his shoulder to collide with the man, shoving him back a step. Pain lanced through his arm at the impact, but the seething look on the doctor's face was worth it. Snarling and teeth gnashing sounded behind them but Sean didn't turn to look. If Cliste wished to bite the man, he wasn't going to stop her. A quiet, high-pitched whimper sounded from the doctor. He pleaded with the hound in a soft voice that slowly drew away.

Not wanting to be seen by the others, Sean skirted around the edge of the garden where they were quickly hidden from the revelers by a row of tall, flowering bushes. Feet stomping into the grass as if it had affronted her, Ashlinn muttered to herself. For a woman not born in Ireland, she had a firm grasp on the curse words of the language and used them with great abandon. It was almost enough to make him smile.

Not even the lovely way anger flushed her cheeks red could bring a smile to him, though. As much as he loathed the doctor right now, he had to admit—at least to himself—that the man was right. Nothing good could come from the two of them getting involved right now. It was anything but honorable. If tonight were any indication, she would very likely let him spoil her. Wonderful though it would be, no matter how good his intentions were of making an honest women out of her once the war was over, he knew the chances of him seeing the end of the war were slim at best. The 69th infantry was the first to the fore and it showed in their constantly depleting numbers. It was becoming the norm for scores of them to die in each battle. He had already cheated death once; it wasn't likely that it would happen again. He couldn't put her honor at risk.

At Ashlinn's hurried pace they left the grounds of the manor in no time at all. The music faded until it was nothing but a memory, one that saddened him beyond words to leave behind. His fingers ached to hold his violin, his arms ached to hold Ashlinn, and his wounds simply ached. The night couldn't have gone more wrong. Neither of them spoke until they reached their tents, then both started at once.

"Go ahead," Sean said.

"No, you."

Steeling himself for words he did not want to say, Sean straightened. "I must apologize for my behavior tonight, 'twas anthin' but gentlemanly."

Concern wilted the edges of Ashlinn's smile. "We agreed being gentlemanly all the time is overrated."

He took her hands in his, wishing the gloves weren't keeping their skin from touching—and chastising himself inwardly for wishing it. The words got caught in his throat and she spoke before he could.

"Please do not allow anything that hateful man said get to you. He only wishes to cause me misery because he believes women have no place in the field of medicine. That, and I think deep down he fears I know more about it than he does."

Sean lifted her chin with one hand until she met his gaze. The way the starlight lay softly upon her skin threatened to take his breath away, but he sucked it back in. He had to get this out.

"But he is right about one thing."

Loose locks of her hair bobbed as she shook her head. "No."

"Aye, I am afraid so. The honorable thing to do is to wait for this war to end, then court you properly when we return to New York, if you are interested. And I must do the honorable thing by you. You deserve no less."

Her breath hitched. Starlight glistened off moisture in her eyes. "You have not acted at all dishonorably today. It was I that enticed you. Please do not feel as though you are to blame."

Lips pulling up into a smile, he shook his head. "I am a grown man and I shoulder my fair share of the blame. I will act the proper gentleman from now on, I promise."

"But you could die tomorrow." The pain in her voice threatened to crumble his resolve but he held fast to it.

His finger traced up the line of her jaw. "Not possible. I have a guardian angel."

She leaned into his hand, her skin wonderfully soft against his callused palm. The patter of a heavy four-legged creature trotting closer told Sean they were no longer alone. He glanced down at Cliste. "Two, in fact."

A short laugh thick with unshed tears came from her. "Until then, we will be friends at least, I hope."

Lifting her hand, he hovered over it for a long moment drawing in the scent of lavender soap and underlying iodine. He kissed her hand slow enough that the warmth of her skin radiated through the satin and lace to heat his lips. Even as he wondered how in the world he would be able to keep his distance from her, he released her hand and stepped back.

"The very best of friends," he promised.

Hand crossing over his abdomen, he bowed deeply to her as he took another step back in the direction of his tent. "I bid you a good evenin'."

She swallowed hard and gave him a joyless smile. "You as well." The words were but a choked whisper.

False smile firmly in place, she turned and ducked inside her tent. It killed a part of him to know she was in so much pain, and that he had caused it. If only he had been a gentleman all evening as he had intended, none of this would have happened.

A huge, wet tongue rubbed along the side of his hand. Cliste looked up at him with forlorn eyes before dashing in. Sean watched until the light of a candle from within revealed the silhouette of Ashlinn sitting upon her cot with her head in her hands. It took every ounce of willpower he had left not to go in there and comfort her. But he didn't dare, not when he knew where such a thing might lead. If she pushed the issue, he would be helpless to resist. How he was going to remain only friends with a woman that had such power over him, he had no idea.

Chapter 10

Over and over Ashlinn flipped the end of her braid through her fingers as she walked from the hospital to Sean's tent. The repetitive motion helped her relax, focus. For almost an entire week, she had been able to avoid the man. With him now attending drills, it hadn't been hard. He was not participating in them—he had assured her the first day he attended—just going to reconnect with the men he would soon be fighting alongside. The words had sealed her resolution that day to keep her distance.

Hate it though she may, she had no choice but to see him now. His stitches had to come out.

Each night that he walked by her tent on his way to his own Cliste perked her head up and whined. That he chose to take the route leading alongside her tent had her worried perhaps she was in his thoughts as much as he was in hers. If so, the fact that they were keeping their distance was for the best. Harmless flirting was one thing, but attachments were something neither of them could afford right now. If that was the case, she had misread him terribly and was more than a bit embarrassed to admit it even to herself. Embarrassed and secretly thrilled. But considering how the men in her life died or disappeared, distance was the best answer.

Besides, she needed to remain focused on finding Michael. He was out there somewhere; she could feel it in her gut. If he were dead, she or Cliste would have found their family's other hound, the one that had attached itself to Michael. Since neither he nor his corpse had shown up, she held onto hope that he was out there somewhere with her brother.

Today Cliste pranced alongside Ashlinn, happy as could be, as if she knew where they were going. She wished she could share the hound's enthusiasm. Stopping at Sean's tent, she cleared her throat. The flap opened before she could get any words out.

For the briefest moment joy flashed in Sean's eyes, brightening the lighter brown in them. But the emotion was gone as quickly as it had appeared, replaced by a guarded expression. His hair hung down nearly into his eyes, making her want to brush it back, plunge her hands into it, and pull him to her. So much for her control. Yet wanting a thing and acting on it were two very different things. She could do this.

"Miss O'Brian, what brings you to me tent?"

Had she been standing there long without saying a word? She didn't know. Time seemed to have stopped. She cleared her throat.

"Ashlinn?" he said more softly, the word almost a caress.

Determined not to act like a lovestruck lass with no sense, she linked her hands before her to look more official while keeping them occupied at the same time.

"It is time for your stitches to come out," she said, proud that her voice didn't sound even a little breathless.

His brows rose and he nodded as he stepped aside, sweeping a hand out to invite her in. She hesitated at the threshold. Could she trust herself if she went in there? To get to the stitches she'd have to have him remove his shirt. Heat scorched her cheeks and she looked down. Damn, why had she worn her hair back? A canine head bumped into her back hard enough to push her forward a step. If she didn't know better, she would think her own hound was working against her. Sean let the tent flap close behind her.

Candlelight illuminated the small area well enough that she'd be able to see all she needed—and all she didn't need to see. Then again, it helped reaffirm her hope that all she felt for him was desire. As his fingers worked at the buttons on his shirt she struggled to keep her focus on why she had come here.

"Have the wounds been causing you any pain or discomfort?" She kept her voice professional, detached, everything she didn't feel right now.

When he opened his shirt and began to peel it off, she cast her gaze to the ground. Hard planes of muscle flashed in her peripheral vision. Despite the cool, rainy day, the temperature inside the tent became stifling. She would have to look at him eventually; she just couldn't bring herself to do it yet. This was ridiculous. She had seen him half naked when she had stitched him up for goodness' sake. Then he had just been another soldier, one of the masses of men she treated and sent back into the fray to die in some other horrendous manner.

"Less and less every day," he said.

The sound of his voice made her look up. Her eyes raked across solid pectorals, down hard abdominals, to a dark line of hair that led from his belly button and into the low waist of his breeches. Had she asked him a question? She couldn't remember. Oh how she wanted to touch all that bare skin... The strength of the pull helped her label the feeling for what it was—desire, not something deeper. A sigh of relief slid between her lips. Realizing that helped, a little. Telling herself he would just die on her like every other man in her life helped a lot more. Her eyes caught on the red scar dotted with black knots of thread on his left side.

"Have the stitches loosened?"

He touched one of the black knots, moving it slightly. "A bit."

The nurse in her began to awaken, carrying her across the small space that divided them. She pulled a small pair of scissors from her pocket. "Hold as still as you can."

His soap, oil, and gunpowder scent wrapped around her as she closed the distance between them. In many ways it was similar to any other soldier's scent, but there was an underlying pleasant musk that was all him. That singular smell poured down her throat, wrapped around her self-control, and began to dissolve it.

Focus. She had to focus.

She snipped each of the stitches and put the scissors away lest she stab him due to her shaking hands. The thread resisted, forcing her to place a hand upon his skin to manipulate it into letting go of the stitch. Heat from his body seeped into her. An eternity later, she had all the stitches from his side wound out. He didn't flinch once.

"Let me know if I hurt you," she said.

He made a noncommittal grunt that she suspected held a double meaning. But then, maybe that was just her imagination. To hurt him in any other manner, he would have to have feelings for her, which he could not. Not thinking, she ran her finger over the clean, pink scar. Sean shivered and made a sound low in his throat that sent heat rushing through her. The desire to run her fingers over more of his bare skin was so strong that she had to pull away, reminding herself that desire and feelings were not the same thing.

"It has healed quite well," she said in an attempt to distract him from her own reaction.

"I had an excellent surgeon." There was no teasing or sarcasm in his voice, just honesty.

Unable to resist any longer, she lifted her eyes to his. A maelstrom of emotions swirled within the coppery depths: pain, longing, desire. All were reflections of her own inner turmoil, the first two ones which she wanted to deny more than anything. She had expected cold detachment, or raw desire alone—not this.

"Thank you." The two words were so thick with emotion that they laid her soul bare, but it was too late to take them back. Besides, appreciating the fact that someone recognized her medical ability was not the same as having feelings for them. She hated how much that the thought made it feel as though she were trying to convince herself.

His shaking hand reached out to tuck a stray lock of hair behind her ear. Seeing him shake almost undid her. Surely, desire alone couldn't cause such a reaction.

"You are welcome. 'Tis true. Had anyone else found me out there I would have likely died of infection."

"Aye, you would have."

Warm fingers traced down from her sensitive ear to her jaw. Pride swelled in her that she didn't shiver, but her eyes did flutter closed. She forced them back open and looked at the arm so close to her, at the scar marring it. Scissors rising, she set to the task with an air of detachment that she hoped did not appear as false as it felt. The swell of his bicep distracted her in the most delicious way, causing muscles low in her abdomen to tighten. Ignoring her raging heart, she finished removing the stitches from his arm.

"This is not what I meant, you know." Sean's voice startled her.

"What is not what you meant?"

Her gaze remained fixed on his arm. She couldn't meet his eyes again or she would crack and beg him to tell her how he truly felt. For both her heart's sake and her pride, that was the last thing she wanted to do—the last thing, and the only thing.

"Avoidin' each other is not bein' friends. 'Tis the opposite. We are adults, we can control ourselves enough to be friends, surely," he said, desperation hidden beneath his careful tone.

That, she feared, was precisely the problem. If they controlled their passion, their friendship would grow. And if that grew, the sensation warming the frozen edges of her heart may grow as well. Better to allow desire to take them over.

The daring brush of his fingers against her cheek encouraged her. Keeping as much emotion from her eyes as she could, she met his gaze again.

"Aye, of course we can," she said.

A deep sigh eased from Sean and a smile crept onto his lips. "Good."

Eyes sweeping low, head tilting as she stepped to the side, she purposefully turned herself so that he would have an excellent view down into her cleavage. The opportunity to tease him a bit in retaliation for being shirtless was just too good to pass up. She did not want to leave, not with him standing there looking like a work of art. Her gaze strayed to the cot, along with her thoughts. What she really wanted to do was…

Something different on his carefully folded uniform that sat on the edge of the cot caught her eye, grinding her lascivious thoughts to a halt. Three stripes adorned his shoulder, not two. Feet moving of their own accord, she crossed the narrow space and picked the uniform up. Her fingers traced the sergeant stripes. Her spirit soared on a wave of hope. Sergeants came across her table far less often than soldiers of lower rank.

"You have been promoted."

He walked to her side, hovering close enough that she felt the heat of his body. "Aye, sergeant of a fine company of men. I start runnin' drills with them tomorrow."

She turned to him, forcing her eyes to meet his, to stay away from the planes of his chest, the swell of his biceps, for now. "I do hope you will be careful for at least another two weeks. You are still healing."

One side of his mouth quirked up into a partial grin. "Doctor's orders?"

Brows pulling together, she gave him as stern a look as she could. "Indeed." The look melted away and she could feel hope creeping into her eyes. "Does this mean you will be in less danger?"

Sean looked away. "Not exactly. But as I said, these are good men. They will watch my back."

The words worked like a bucket of cold water on her hope, washing it away with an unpleasant shock. Small though it had been, that hope had managed to melt a bit more of heart.

"As my doctor, you would o' course be welcome to watch the drills, to ensure that I am not overdoin' it."

A different kind of hope thrilled through her. Watching him work out could be quite enjoyable, and could keep her focused on her desire. "That would be prudent."

Her thoughts took a turn that threatened to lead her down a path she could not go if she wished to maintain her dignity. Should he spurn her advances now in the name of honor, she may lose the chance at using desire as a shield. Best to keep him wanting. She started for the tent opening, hands again clasped before her to ensure she kept them to herself.

"Our first drill is at sunrise tomorrow at the northeast side of the property, if you would like to observe it," he called after her.

Hand on the tent flap, she allowed herself a glance back. All that bare flesh and hard muscle burned into her memory. "I will be there."

Before she could lose her resolve, she ducked quickly out of the tent and let the flap close behind her. Cliste sat waiting, tail sending up small clouds of dust as it wagged back and forth across the ground. Mouth open in a huge grin, tongue lolling out one side, the hound looked quite pleased with herself.

"Do not look at me that way," she whispered.

Rising to her feet, Cliste led the way back toward the hospital. She got no more than half a dozen yards before a man stepped out from behind a tent directly into her path. Dark brow furrowed so deep it nearly swallowed his beady eyes, the doctor shook a finger at her. Against all physician-like instincts, she wanted desperately to break that damn finger.

"Watch it, woman, or you will end up ruined, and no man will want you for a wife."

Ashlinn waved the scissors at him. "Not that it is any of your business, but I was removing his stitches." Scissors tightly in hand, she shoved past him.

"Humph. Well it would have been prudent to do so in the hospital instead of the man's own tent."

Teeth grinding, Ashlinn turned halfway back toward him. "And did it ever occur to you that I may want to be more than just someone's wife?"

The man's face turned such a bright shade of red that she suspected he might be holding his breath. Good, let the fool pass out. She had rounds to do. Growling in frustration, she stormed off toward the hospital tent. The last of her tolerance with men telling her what she should want to be and how she should act had been exhausted. It was time she started taking matters into her own hands. And when that came to Sean, she intended to make it quite literal. If she kept their relationship physical, it may help her keep him out of her heart.

Chapter 11

A second line of men moved forward to seamlessly cover the first line that went through the motions of reloading their weapons. Not a single shot was actually fired, but they went through each step as if it had been. After two weeks of running drills with his men, they had become a finely tuned company that moved and thought as one. He couldn't be more proud of this fine group of one hundred Irishmen from New York. And he would do everything in his power to do right by them.

More than once, he had stolen a glimpse into the shade of the willow tree near the riverbank. In a simple dark blue dress that hugged her curves and transformed her into something stunning, Ashlinn lounged upon a bench there. Her golden hair spilled about her shoulders like sunlight. Locks blew about in the breeze created by the small fan she waved before her.

Longing so powerful it made his chest ache forced him to look away. She came to watch at least once a week, to monitor his improvement and make sure he didn't overdo it, supposedly. Why she really came was clear by the longing in her eyes and the ease of her smile. Every day he awoke with the hope that it would be the day she came to watch. The times he got to see her were fewer and farther between now that his tent had been relocated amidst his company. Sometimes entire days would go by without so much as a glimpse of her. Those were the hardest. Remaining honorable and proper had never been so difficult.

A soldier cursed as his rifle slipped from his sweat-slickened hands. The man quickly picked the weapon back up with one hand while wiping the other across his dripping brow.

"Sorry, Sarge," the man said as he continued the drill.

Sean walked along the front line, correcting positions of some, complimenting others. When he reached the man who had dropped his weapon, he stopped. "'Tis all right, Corporal Ferguson." He stepped back to look at the line of twenty-five kneeling men and the subsequent three lines standing behind them.

"Good job, men. Let's call it a day and take a dip in the river before chow. Dismissed!" he announced.

Whoops and hollers filled the sultry air as men rose to their feet and started toward the river. Each one took care with his weapon, taking it with him and storing it along the bank. Pride swelled within Sean at the sight. They were learning. Clothes began to fly off but some men splashed right into the water, uniform and all. He longed to join them but didn't dare do so with Ashlinn waiting and watching. That would certainly cross the lines of propriety. He wasn't sure of her family's standing, but from the pristine way she talked and her careful manners, she was a lady of high society for certain. And high society would never tolerate such lewdness as skinny-dipping. Worse than all that, though, he would miss the chance to talk to her.

Hoping he didn't stink half as bad as some of his men did, Sean walked to the shade of the willow tree where Ashlinn sat. The smile she gave him made his heart thud harder as it pumped blood to some wonderfully inappropriate places. His breath caught as he watched a bead of sweat trickle down her neck and into her cleavage. She reached down and caught the drop just before it could slide to the point where her breasts met and suddenly Sean's knees went weak.

Air swirled around him as Ashlinn rose to her feet and stepped to his side. She placed a gloved hand upon his arm, the touch sending sparks dancing down deep into him.

"Are you all right, Sergeant? You did not overdo it now, did you?" she asked in a chastising voice that had just enough of a teasing tone to it that Sean suspected she knew exactly what was wrong with him. Perhaps skinny-dipping wouldn't bother her after all. This woman would be the death of him.

With a deep breath, he regained his composure and offered her his arm. "Quite all right, thank you. I fear the heat may be gettin' to me a bit is all."

"Hmm, well, we should get you out of it then." With that, she led him along the edge of the river, beneath the shade of the elm trees that grew in abundance there.

Cliste leapt to her feet and trotted alongside, ears pricked up, eyes watching them closely as if it were her solemn duty to chaperone them. Grinning, Sean scratched between the big hound's ears.

This was the long, secluded way back to his section of camp, around the back of the manor house through the landscaped garden. His heart pounded harder at the thought of being alone with her—or as near to it as one could get here. He knew he should stop, ask one of the soldiers to chaperone them. But they were all occupied and he didn't want to pull them away from their much-deserved relaxation. No, he would simply have to keep his distance and his control. She was his nurse, after all, just measuring his improvement.

Every time he had seen Ashlinn over the past two weeks, their encounters had been short and very sweet, with more than a little flirting. Any time he asked anything personal, though, she remained aloof. Nor had she been bold with him again, no skin-to-skin contact, and certainly no kissing. The secret smiles she sometimes hid made him wonder if she was doing it on purpose. It was starting to drive him mad with desire, making him seriously regret not asking for the right to court her then and there. But he couldn't, he wouldn't. They were in the midst of a war and he had his company to focus on; honor demanded it. A daring part of him wished to allow nature to take its course. To do so would be to compromise his honor, and worse, hers. That was something he would never do.

Her gloved fingers brushed slowly along his arm. His eyes closed and he had to remember how to breathe. "How is the arm doing?" she asked.

If she insisted on torturing and testing him, he could at least return the favor. "Much better. I shall show you once we reach my tent."

Her right eyebrow rose and she cocked her head. Was that a glimmer of hope in her eyes? It left too quickly for him to tell, but it was long enough to send blood burning in a rush to his groin. Had her pace sped up or was he imagining it? Just the possibility made his head swim.

"How are the wounded?" he asked.

With great fervor, she delved into the description of her day, going over each man she had treated and his improvements or lack thereof. It had become a routine of theirs. He loved listening to her talk about her work. The passion that filled her voice when she did so thrilled him like nothing else ever had. While technical bits of surgeries and wound care exceeded his understanding, they also fed his growing respect for her intelligence. And her stories of recovery and tales of things the wounded soldiers told her only served to solidify his belief that she was an angel.

In no time at all they reached the edge of the field of tents. Leaving the gardens of the manor house behind, they wove through the maze of the encampment. Soldiers milling about called greetings to both of them, some casting Sean a knowing, envious look. They would never be so crass as to comment in the lady's presence, but they had begun to tease him good-naturedly in her absence. Once they reached the area where his company's tents lay, they found themselves alone. It would be at least a short time until his men returned from the river, leaving them with only Cliste. Temptation reared within him, but he tamed it easily enough.

They reached his tent and she asked him to wait a moment for her. Disappointment flashed in her eyes as he ducked inside, leaving her standing alone on the dusty path. His libido raged at him as his mind played out the possibilities of inviting her inside, but he ignored it like any good gentleman would. His regiment put honor and loyalty above all other virtues. Since he led a company now, they looked to him, and it was more important now than ever that he remain honorable. Scooping up his violin and bow, he dashed back out of the tent.

The light that filled Ashlinn's widening eyes when they set upon his violin made his heart pump faster. Hoping to walk off the jitters, he led her over to an open area filled with logs and rocks that the men had gathered for seating. With a nod, he invited her to sit. Gathering her skirts, she did so, bright eyes fixed upon him. Cliste sat beside her, the huge hound nearly eye level with her.

His fingers shook a bit as he placed the violin on his shoulder and fussed with the pegs. Each night for the last two weeks, he had played for the men along with the company's drummer and bugler. They loved it, but he suspected their exposure to such music was limited at best, and that they would have enjoyed it even if he were terrible. Being a lady of society, Ashlinn would likely know if he made a mistake. He drew the bow across the strings, filling the air with the sound of perfect notes. He grinned at Cliste as her head cocked to the side.

The feel of the instrument upon his shoulder and the bow in his hand soothed him, taking away some of the anxiety. As he began to play a sweet, slow song, his fingers stopped shaking. A few chords in and he became so caught up in the music that it carried him along, flowing through him as though it were a living, breathing thing. Pure rapture transformed Ashlinn's lovely face into a thing of such beauty that it made Sean's heart swell until it felt as though it barely fit within his chest. Moisture glistened in the corners of her light blue eyes.

When the song came to an end, she stood and applauded. Beside her, Cliste rose to all fours, tail wagging.

"Bravo, Sean! 'Twas amazin'!" The slip of her perfect English into an Irish brogue spoke volumes of how much the music affected her, leaving him speechless.

A grin so wide he felt his cheeks dimple spread across his face. Lowering the violin, he dropped his head. Over the years he had been playing at society functions both in Ireland and New York; many had paid him compliments. This one meant more than all of them combined.

"Thank you."

"Do play another! Please!"

Cliste barked as if in agreement.

In a flurry of blue cotton skirts, Ashlinn sat back down and leaned forward. Elbow upon her knee, she rested her chin in her hand like an eager child. Cliste let out another bark, her gray rear end swaying from the vigorous wagging of her tail.

Sean lifted the violin back to his shoulder. "How can I deny such faces?"

Slowly, he drew the bow against the strings, pulling out a long, beautiful note that resonated all the way to his core. The music swept him along as it always did, guiding his hands and fingers as if he were no more than the tool through which it flowed. His eyes fluttered but he did not allow them to close like he usually did. How could he with the sight of Ashlinn before him, her own eyes closed, a euphoric smile upon her lips, not a crease of worry on her face? For the first time, he had found something as breathtaking as the music itself. So caught up was he in watching her that he didn't notice soldiers from his company had started to gather until halfway through the song.

Men soon filled the makeshift seats, many of whom watched him almost as raptly as Ashlinn did. The fair-haired drummer, a man of barely twenty from Five Points, New York, soon joined in. Another soldier brought out a flute and did a fine job of playing along. Not a word was said, or needed. They all knew the old Irish song from their homeland. Once the song ended, the applause of over a dozen men filled the air, punctuated by Cliste's occasional bark.

The drummer started in with the catchy beat of "The Battle Hymn of the Republic" and Sean and the flute player were quick to join in. To the cheers, whoops, and hollers of the men—and surprisingly Ashlinn as well—they played song after song. They took turns singing lyrics to some of the songs, even goading Ashlinn into singing a few parts. Unlike most women, she had a lower voice that hit the notes of their battle songs just right, giving them a sexy sound that made the men cheer and made Sean light-headed from the racing of his heart.

More and more gathered until his entire company seemed to be present, many sitting upon the ground when seating ran out. Feet tapped along in time to the rhythm, hands clapped with the beat, and cheering rose at the end of each tune. The bugler soon joined in, as did Fergusson on harmonica, adding a decidedly American sound to the Irish tunes. Darkness began to fall and still they played.

Toward the end of the latest song, Sean noticed a runner making his way into the camp, darting around those gathered, coming straight for him. The young man's flushed cheeks and wide eyes drained all the mirth right out of Sean. He lowered his violin and bow. The other instruments slowly stopped. It became so quiet he could hear the runner's ragged breathing as the man came to a stop before him.

Bent over, hands on his knees, chest heaving, the man struggled to speak.

"Easy, lad. Just breathe a moment," Sean told him.

Left with no other choice, the man did as he was bid. Finally, he straightened and saluted Sean. "Sergeant MacBranain, your presence is requested by Lieutenant Briggs."

Men started to rise, many voicing questions. The runner grinned, but it was a look filled with more fear than joy. "Rebs have been spotted on the hill."

Chills coursed through Sean, stripping away the heat of the day. "The hill" had to be Malvern Hill. Images of corpses littering the countryside flashed behind his eyes. Sucking in a sharp breath, Ashlinn stood and came to him. The fear clouding her blue eyes cracked his heart. It seemed he was bound to return to hell despite the angel at his side.

Chapter 12

Each step was like a reoccurring nightmare, only worse because she was awake. Grass squished beneath her boots, ripe with moisture from the day's rain. Most of the bodies strewn broken upon the field wore gray coats, but not all. The one mercy lay in that there were not that many, not compared to the other battlefields she had scoured. This had been more of a skirmish than a battle, ending with the Rebels scattering, so she had been told. Of Sean and his company, the others had no word.

No, she decided. *This is worse than the reoccurring nightmare.*

In her nightmare, she had only ever searched for her baby brother. Now she searched for two men. The pain threatening to crush her heart, the unshed tears burning her eyes, the storm of hopelessness waiting behind the windows of her soul—they were exactly the things she had been hoping to avoid. It had become glaringly clear now that keeping things flirtatious and physical had not worked. Desire alone didn't cause this empty pit of fear and nausea in her at the very thought of him being harmed.

Since the ambulance wagons came in after the troops were already withdrawing, she had missed seeing many of the soldiers who left of their own accord. Sean and his company were not among those she had seen. For all she knew, they could still be out there fighting, chasing the Rebels down. A new and horrible fear rose in her. What if he disappeared like her baby brother had? Could she be doomed to search endlessly for them both?

A huge gray shape loped toward her from the edge of the trees. Had she not known better, it may have looked like a pony from this distance. But the loping gait of a canine with its head hung low, nose sniffing the air, was unmistakable. Cliste's slow gait and relaxed manner allowed Ashlinn to let out the breath she had been holding. Out of habit, her hands went to the small cylinder attached to Cliste's collar. A push of a button popped it open and released the tiny scroll inside. Her shaking fingers struggled with the slightly damp paper. As it had been every day since her brother's disappearance, the writing upon the scroll was only her own. The old familiar disappointment stung more this time than it had the last. Perhaps because a part of her had been hoping for a message from Sean, which was ridiculous considering he didn't even know about the hidden scroll.

Eyes going to the last withdrawing ambulance wagon, Ashlinn patted the hound. "Come on, Cliste. Time to go back," she said through a sigh.

Nose flaring as she tested the air, head dropping low, Cliste bounded ahead. A pang of sadness for the hound's own heart pinched at Ashlinn. She wasn't the only one searching for someone on the battlefield. Their family had a second hound, a male that had attached itself to Michael. The male was Cliste's mate. If they found one, they would inevitably find the other. To their combined heartache, neither turned up no matter where they looked.

Steeling herself for a long walk, Ashlinn followed the swinging gray tail before her. She did not want to be left alone in this place again after dark. Too many ghosts flitted along this hill, some of them manifested by her own horrible memories. It no longer felt like a place for the living. The last of the soldiers fell into line around her and the ambulance wagon to escort them back. Their presence was both a comfort and a disappointment. Why couldn't it have been Sean's company tasked with such a duty?

Gazing upon the trees that lined the worn road around them, she tried to banish such thoughts. To wish one man's safety over another's was wrong, she knew, but she couldn't help it. She was tired of this damned war taking men she cared about from her. That thought stung in more ways than one. Playing with the fire of feelings had been beyond foolish. More than ever, she wished for the South to see reason and surrender.

Following an easy path with such an escort made for a much shorter trip than the last time she had walked from that hill. In no time at all it seemed Harrison's Landing came into sight. Every fiber of her being screamed for her to go straight to Sean's tent, but she resisted, instead following the wagon to the hospital. The wounded had to take precedence over her own pained heart. She could never hope to call herself a physician, even if only in her own mind, if she did not put others' health first. And heavens knew if she left these men to this butcher of a doctor, it would be leaving them in mortal danger.

With only a handful of wounded she was able to see to them in no time at all. Their wounds were thankfully minor for the most part, and nearly all would recover so long as she kept a close eye on them over the next few days. As it was every time she entered a hospital tent, memories of her own brothers bleeding out on tables haunted her each time she closed her eyelids. Yet she soldiered on, because she had to. On her way out the door, she forced herself to take the time to stop by each cot and check on the other soldiers as well. Hours later—though it seemed days—she made it to the last cot. A figure moved into the doorway as she started for it. Her heart caught—with hope, fear, she wasn't sure—but it was not who she hoped for.

The awful, caterpillar-looking mustache of Doctor Taylor rose in a sneer. "What, not out tending to your corporal?"

"He is a sergeant now, and he is not *mine*." For the sake of the soldiers laying abed in the room she kept her voice low, doing her best to keep her hatred from leaking into it.

Taylor gave her a sort of sideways nod, his muddy eyes filled with contempt. "That is right; he was only playing at courting you to get what a man wants from a woman he does not intend to marry. Which I fear by your attitude he has already obtained and moved on."

Overcome by a tidal wave of fury, Ashlinn reared back her arm and slapped Taylor so hard his head whipped sideways. An angry red welt in the shape of her hand stained his face. Raised with three brothers, she knew how to hold her own, and then some.

"How dare you!" she hissed through clenched teeth.

Hands closing into fists, he started toward her but jerked to a halt. Glancing down, Ashlinn saw that the soldier in the bed close by had a hold of the doctor's arm.

"You are not goin' to be wantin' to do that, Doc," the man said.

Glaring at him from beneath a deeply furrowed brow, Taylor tried to yank his arm free and failed. Heavy wool blankets rustled and several sets of feet slapped against the packed dirt. Soldiers began to stir in their beds all around, some even beginning to get up. The doctor's beady eyes flicked about the room. He opened his fists and held his hands up, palms out.

"You are right, of course, soldier. I almost allowed my passion for propriety to get ahead of my reason."

With a forced genteel air, Taylor turned to her, shaking his head. "It saddens me that you would turn your back on an upstanding gentleman such as myself for the attentions of a man who clearly means to dishonor you."

Her own hands now clenching into fists, Ashlinn took a step toward him. "You are out of your mind to think I would ever welcome advances from you. Two of my brothers died by your hand!"

Brows pulling up toward his receding hairline, Taylor shook his head and looked down. "No, Miss O'Brian. It was the war that killed your brothers, not I."

Out of her mind with rage, she slapped both hands against Taylor's chest and shoved him back a step. "Bullshit! My eldest brother bled out from a botched amputation that you did, and my second brother died of infection from your filthy instruments and hands!"

Taylor's face took on an expression of tolerance, as if he were dealing with a petulant child, but mirth danced in his eyes. "Such a temper. Careful, that detestable brogue is slipping back into your voice."

The words threatened to catapult her over the edge. She reached for his neck, only to find a tall, broad soldier with a bandage wrapped around his arm standing in her way.

"Easy now, Miss O'Brian," he said.

The man gently took hold of her hands and lowered them. Hooking an arm through hers, he led her out into the hazy light. Fresh air flowed into her lungs, clearing her head and melting away some of her fury. He looked familiar. Then it fell into place. It was Fergusson, the harmonica player from the mini-concert Sean had put on for her the other day. A day that seemed a world away now. The soldier patted her arm, careful to do so only where her dress covered her skin.

"Don't let him get to you. He's a filthy blaggard not fit to breathe the same air as you. And he knows nothin' of the good sergeant's intentions toward you," he said.

"Thank you. Private Fergusson, is it?" she asked in a voice that only slightly shook with residual anger.

He nodded.

"You are from Sean's regiment, are you not?"

Again he nodded, but showed no other response.

"Is he all right? I searched for him…" Her throat closed up, not allowing her to finish the sentence.

Brow rising, Fergusson shrugged. "I am sorry, Mrs. O'Brian, but I was knocked out by shrapnel and only just awoke recently. Last I saw him he was alive and fightin'."

Some of the concern keeping her muscles rigid drained away, leaving her feeling as though she may collapse. But she couldn't, she wouldn't dare. She was no swooning lass; she was a nurse who was a damn score better than most doctors she had met. Straightening, she smoothed her skirt and gave Fergusson a humorless smile.

"Thank you, good sir. I appreciate you stepping in between the doctor and me."

"You're most welcome," he said from the hospital entrance as she began to walk away toward her tent.

Almost as an afterthought, she called back to him in a soft voice. "And thank you for your kind words about the sergeant's intentions as well."

She turned away so quickly it was hard to tell, but she thought she saw the beginning of a smile pulling up the man's mustache. Glad for the way the fading light of dusk hid her expression, she strode out onto the muddy path and walked briskly to her tent. The doctor's words had brought back the staggering loss of her older brothers like twin blows from a cannon. It was all she could do to make it to her tent, throw the flap back, and step inside before the tears started to flow.

Through the watery haze covering her vision she saw something impossible. Sean sat upon her cot, button-up shirt undone down to his pectoral muscles and coat discarded beside him. Damp brown hair curled back from copper eyes that drank her in as if she were the finest wine. He rose as she flew at him, catching her in his strong arms, holding her when her legs no longer would. For a few precious moments, she allowed herself to cling to him so tightly that there was no way he'd be able to draw breath until she let go. The sob climbing up her throat never made it out, but a few errant tears slid down her cheeks.

Only when she could speak, did she finally let loose of him and pull back. To her delight—and torment—he didn't let go of her. "I could not find you" was all she dared say lest her voice crack.

One arm wrapped firmly around her waist while the other brushed her hair back from her brow. "I'm sorry. I wanted to come to you straightaway, but my company did the final sweep of the hill to ensure the Rebs were good and gone."

She wanted so badly to lean into the fingers that brushed her brow, but she refused to allow herself to. The very fact that he was here, in her tent, touching her so tenderly, stirred far more than just desire in her, and that scared her. In the copper striations of his eyes, the depths of his intentions lay bare. The power of emotions therein made her close her eyes against the honesty of it. Emotions, not just desire. It came as no consolation to know she wasn't the only one who had lost control of her emotions.

He drew in a shuddering breath. "About what I said—"

"No, Sean." She shook her head, dropping it down so he wouldn't be able to see the emotion in her own eyes.

"About waiting…" he continued.

She leaned her head against her chest, still shaking it. "Today I walked the field looking for not one body, but two. Dreading not only finding my baby brother whom I failed to protect, but you as well." She wanted to say more, had to say more, but her voice caught.

Ignoring the entire first half of what she had said, he asked, "How old is your little brother?"

"Twenty."

Sean's hand rubbed her back in what felt like an automatic need to comfort. "He's been a man for a few years now. 'Tis not up to you to protect him anymore."

She lifted her head and met his gaze. "But 'tis. You don't understand. My brother lacks common sense and often makes the wrong choices. I promised his wife, and our other brothers, that I'd look after him. He can be a bit...sketchy." While the words were meant to be joking, the truth in them made them ring a bit harsher.

She bit her bottom lip as she realized the weight of that confession had allowed her accent to slip through all those careful language lessons. While the hint of a smile tugging at Sean's lips showed he liked it, the slip served to remind her of how much her mum had invested in those lessons. She had wanted to give Ashlinn every advantage in a world that hated her simply because she was Irish. Letting the accent slip felt like a betrayal to her.

Again Sean stroked her hair, threatening to shatter her defenses. "War has a way of sharpenin' a man's common sense, of makin' him a survivor," he said.

"You think he is alive?" she asked so softly he may not have heard had he not been inches away.

Taking her hand, he sat down on her cot and pulled her down beside him. "Aye, 'tis quite possible. Someone could have found him just like you found me."

By the tightness around his eyes, she could tell there was more he wasn't saying. Like how the Rebels could have found him and he could be in a prison right now. A powerful shudder coursed through her. That possibility had haunted her, tormenting her in her dreams, since the day her brother had disappeared.

"If the right people found him he would be back here, among his regiment," she whispered.

Turning sideways on the cot, Sean drew a knee under himself so he could scoot closer to her. His hands enfolded one of hers. The wonderful warmth that encompassed her hand also made her heart ache. All she could think about was that warmth leaving and that she might never feel it again.

To deny herself now seemed like a mercy that would save her heart later. She tried to pull her hand free but he held fast.

"Not necessarily. He could be with another regiment. You have to think positive, for both his sake and yours," Sean said.

She nodded slowly. "I know, and most days I do. But today…"

Her eyes closed tight against the sting of tears. Crying was not an option. If she dropped her guard, she would collapse into Sean's arms and she could not let herself do that. Already she had lost too much. Opening up her heart had been a mistake she had not intended to make, and now intended to remedy.

"Was it just my late return, or did somethin' else happen today?" Sean asked, suspicion putting a protective edge on his tone.

Protecting her heart was one thing, but she couldn't allow him to feel as though her distance was all his fault. "I confronted Taylor today about killing my brothers."

Sean sat up straighter, his body going rigid with tension. "He killed them?"

Though she met his gaze, she saw right through him, to the sight of her brothers lying on a bloody table. "Aye, he did not pull the trigger, but he may as well have. He amputated my oldest brother's leg and he bled out from the botched job. My other brother died of infection caused from Taylor's treatment with filthy instruments."

His thumbs caressed the backs of her hands while his eyes tried to swallow her whole. It would be so easy to lose herself in them. She wanted to… But she couldn't, because if she did, she may never make it back if something happened to him.

"I am so sorry," he whispered.

Drawing in a breath to steel herself, she drew her hands from his and rose. "Thank you, Sean. Your friendship means everything to me, but right now that is all it can be. I am not sure I could survive losing you if I allow myself to get any closer." As she spoke, she took a step back, putting a bit more distance between them.

Nodding, Sean stood. Though the small space forced him to pass by only inches from her, he did not touch her as he made his way to the door. Before leaving, he turned back. So much lay in the depths of his copper eyes that she wasn't sure what to make of it.

"I understand. Only yesterday I myself was committed to keepin' our distance for that very same reason."

"What changed your mind?" she had to ask.

The hint of a smile dug a dimple into his right cheek. "You, and the skirmish. Life 'tis too short not to seize what happiness we can, when we can. But I respect you and your decision. I only hope you will still welcome me courtin' after this is all over."

The joy such words caused brought a smile to her face that felt like a ray of sunshine coming from within. "O' course. I would love nothing more."

His smile spread as he opened the tent flap.

"I would like it if you visited me, though. To ensure me that you are all right, as friends would do," she called after him.

Those copper eyes stared back at her out of the dark outside her tent. "O' course."

The words wrapped around her like his arms, strong, warm, and full of promise. Was it a mistake to invite him to visit her? Perhaps. The alternative was an unendurable torture, for if she didn't know he was all right, she would find little peace. She tried to tell herself that concern over a friend would be easier to handle than concern over a potential lover. But, as she collapsed onto her cot and snuggled into the warmth his body had left behind, she feared her heart may already have begun to hold him as more.

Chapter 13

The orders to march came with dawn, and not just for Sean's company, but the entire 69th brigade. All through the organized chaos of breaking camp, he didn't catch sight of Ashlinn once. Nor did he during the grueling march to Charles City, then on to the Chikahominy River and across. The heat of the day mingled with the malignantly pregnant rainclouds to leave him a sweaty, stinking mess by the time they stopped for camp. Thankfully, they ended up close enough to a creek that he was able to take a dip, clothes and all.

After spreading all but the essential articles of clothing necessary to remain decent out in his tent to dry, he took up his violin and went walking. The dark made it difficult, but he managed to find each of his men and ensure they were fed and resting. Many had collapsed beneath their hastily raised tents. These he shook awake and reminded to eat, drink, and check their weapons before he moved on. He gave them words of encouragement, joked, and laughed with them.

His aching feet begged for him to join them in their respite, but he couldn't, not just yet. One tent remained that he had to visit before he could succumb to the exhaustion that tugged at him. It had taken him too much time to see to his men. The thickening darkness worked against him now, making each tent look the same. A powerful desire to sink down somewhere—anywhere—and sleep began to make his vision fuzzy. Still he walked on, refusing to give in.

The panting of a dog sounded off to his left. He turned toward the sound, not daring to hope just yet. Eyes at about the level of his stomach shown in the dark.

"Ha! Cliste! How are you, girl?" he called.

The hound trotted to him, thrusting her head into his hand. He scratched beneath her ears while telling her what a good dog she was. As if in agreement, she woofed and began walking. Hoping she wouldn't just lead him out on a merry chase, he followed along as closely as his long legs would allow. They wound through a maze of tents. On and on they walked until Sean began to wonder where it was the hound usually wandered off to at night, fearing she may be taking him there. Just when he was about to give up, she stepped into an open tent.

Inside, a candle sitting upon the ground burned low. The dim light revealed a figure lying on a cot clad in breeches and a tunic, unbound blond hair pooled around her. Soft, rhythmic breathing told Sean she was sound asleep. The curve of a hip led his eyes along a most appealing silhouette. Relief eased the tension from his body, taking the last of his energy with it. While there had been no skirmishing in the center of the march where she had likely been, he had still worried.

That feeling was the very one he had wanted to avoid in the beginning—the one he had hoped waiting to court her would put off. But during the skirmish on Malvern Hill he had realized it was already too late. His feelings for her had grown into a wildfire he couldn't control. Seeing her here so peaceful and beautiful, he wanted to protect her from all the pain and bad things in the world. If keeping his distance could save her from heartache, then he would do it, he had to. Within reason, of course.

Just barely inside the tent opening, he sank onto the dry ground and opened the pack that held his violin. Setting the bow to the strings, he started to play a slow, sweet song. Eyes closing, he let the melody carry him away until he saw the rolling green hills of his homeland dotted with flowers as they had been in his youth. Among them he imagined Ashlinn walking, her long hair unbound as it was now, her hands trailing along the tops of the yellow and red poppies.

The patter of soft, padded steps pulled him from his imaginings but not his music. He opened his eyes to see Cliste approaching. Big eyes fixed on him; she lay down beside him, placing her head upon his leg. Though her eyes drifted closed, her ears perked up as if she were listening intently to his playing. Halfway through the song, movement came from within the tent. Hiding a yawn behind her hand, Ashlinn rose and walked over to them. She sank down in the opening across from him, leaning her back against a bracing pole.

The smile she gave him warmed him in ways he hadn't even realized he was chilled. Folding her legs before her like a man might, she watched him as he played, eyes going from his face to his hands. Once the song was over, she raised her eyebrows and gave him a bit of a nod. Smiling back at her, he started into another soothing song. By the third song, her head had rolled back against the poll and her eyes slid closed. By the fourth, her steady breathing indicated sleep had stolen over her once again. Just for good measure, Sean played one more before setting his violin aside.

At the movement, Cliste rose, walked deeper into the tent, and lay down on an old blanket folded in the corner. Sean went to Ashlinn and scooped her up into his arms. A groan of protest came from her, but the effects of deep sleep slurred it. Holding her closer to his chest than was necessary, he carried her to the back of the tent and laid her down upon her cot. Her eyes never opened. Seeing that she still had her boots on, he unlaced and removed them, along with her stockings. Though the smooth, bare skin of her perfect little feet begged for his touch, he resisted and instead covered her with her blanket.

Every bit of him wanted to sink down onto the cot beside her, wrap her in his arms, and sleep along with her. Watching her chest rise and fall, her long lashes brush against her cheeks as her eyes moved in the world of dreams, it was all he could do to take a step back. But he did it. Then he took another, and another. Soon he was out the doorway and back in the arms of the night.

* * * *

All through August they marched from one point in Virginia to the next, barely stopping to rest. When they finally did, Sean wished they hadn't. Not only were they joining fourteen thousand-plus other soldiers, but they moved swiftly into action near Antietam.

On a sunken road between a hill and a cornfield, death rained all around Sean and his men that September day. Bullets seemed to fly at them from all directions, dropping man after man. The humid air became so thick with the scent of blood and perforated guts that Sean could taste the horrid, sickly sweetness on the back of his tongue. Gun smoke choked the air so thickly that he had to squint and pray as he checked the color of the man's uniform he shot at. As they had practiced, a second line of his men covered the first as they reloaded their muskets. Even as disciplined as they were, they kept falling, one after another after another.

During a lull in the battle, Sean crouched among the bodies of his fallen men and reloaded his musket yet again. Moisture stung his bleary eyes, but whether it was from the smoke in the air or the sight of all the bodies littering the road, he couldn't tell. A quick glance around told him that of his one hundred men, less than half still stood. The realization was enough to shake his resolve to go on. Yet he had to. He couldn't let Ashlinn down.

The thought of what finding his body would do to her kept his mind sharp, his senses alert.

Finally, the Rebels stopped flowing out of the cornfield and down the road. Bright red blood splashed all across the trampled cornstalks before them, standing out in stark contrast against the pale yellow. In that moment Sean decided he never wanted to eat corn again. Once his ears stopped ringing he realized the rifle fire he could still hear was far off and getting less and less by the moment. From looking around him, he had to guess that was because the majority of soldiers were dead—on both sides of the battle. Just as many blue coats dotted the road and field as gray.

Movement among the bodies down the sunken road drew his eye. At first, it looked like a man bent over. He almost dismissed it as medical staff seeing to the dying and dead, until he realized the figure moved on all fours. The huge thing trotted out of the settling smoke straight toward him, carefully hopping over and skirting around bodies. Its varying hues of gray made it appear as though it were a thing born of the smoke. Relief and concern warred within Sean as he realized the huge beast was Cliste.

The soldiers left alive between him and the hound reached out to pet her as she trotted by. She licked hands, faces, and arms, but didn't slow her progress. Despite how they had first met, seeing her amidst all this death didn't seem real. He hoped to Heaven it didn't mean Ashlinn was out here. Upon reaching him, the hound licked the tip of his nose and sat at his feet. Ears drooping, she pushed her huge head into his hand that didn't clutch his rifle.

"Ah, Cliste. What are you doin' here, girl?" he asked softly.

Instead of wagging her tail as he had half-expected, she whined so quietly he almost didn't hear her.

"Is Ashlinn all right?" he asked.

He felt a bit ridiculous for doing so, but those of his men left standing all focused on loading their weapons or catching their breath, not on what he was doing. Though she looked up at him with profoundly sad eyes, Cliste thumped her tail once. He decided to take that as a yes, because to do otherwise would mean losing his mind. Setting his rifle to the side, he scratched both sides of her neck.

"Good girl," he murmured.

Again, her tail thumped once. As he scratched her, he felt something upon her collar. The little cylinder attached to it. He had forgotten about it. Inspiration sent a thrill through him. If Ashlinn truly was all right, wherever she was, she knew about the amount of dead coming in and was likely out of her mind with worry over him. Perhaps he could put her concerns to rest a bit. Digging around in his coat, he found the pocket that held his sheet music and pencil. On one side of the paper, a partially written song was scrawled across the page, but the other was blank. He instantly set to writing her a letter.

Once finished, he rolled the letter into a small scroll, released the mechanism on the tiny cylinder on Cliste's collar, and hid the letter within. Ensuring the box had latched tight, he patted Cliste on the head.

"You get that back to Ashlinn for me now, you hear?" he whispered.

Cliste perked up but didn't move.

"I'll be along soon enough. Go on now, go back to Ashlinn," he commanded a bit louder.

Ears perking up, Cliste stood, turned, and took off like a shot up the hill behind him. Sean watched until the hound was out of sight before turning his attention back to the body-filled road he stood within. It was time to round up what remained of his company and get out of this hell.

Chapter 14

Hands bloody up to her elbows, Ashlinn stepped back and tried to wipe a strand of hair from her brow with her bicep. When that didn't work, she cursed softly in Gaelic and turned for the washbasin. The sight of the pink water within the bowl made her cringe.

"Fresh water, please," she called over her shoulder.

An ebony-skinned nurse hurried over with a new basin, thick gloves protecting her hands from the hot iron.

"Careful, Miss Ashlinn, still hot from de stove dat is," the nurse said.

Despite the despair weighing her down, Ashlinn gave the dear woman a kind smile. "Thank you, Abigail."

Not only was she a very capable nurse, unlike most, Abigail listened to her and seemed to agree with her ways regarding clean hands and instruments. The moment the toll of dead and injured had risen too high for the hospital to handle, Ashlinn had volunteered to work in another tent and had asked to take Abigail with her. Too busy hacking apart wounded men to argue, Doctor Taylor had no choice but to agree. For the past two days, she had been able to work in relative peace with no one questioning her practices. Relative in that her heart clenched at each new soldier they brought in until she saw his face and confirmed it wasn't her brother or Sean.

At this point she knew it was silly to expect to see her brother, yet she couldn't fight the desperate hope that he might still show up, wounded but alive. Silly, yes, but her little brother was fickle and lost his way often. The fact that neither of them had shown up dead was all that kept her going back in the hospital tent most days. She was angry at herself for allowing Sean to worm his way beneath her skin and expose her to more heartache. But she couldn't dig him out from beneath it, no matter how many men she treated, bodies she carried out, or nightmares of her brothers' deaths she had to endure.

Looking out across the dimly lit tent packed with cots so close one could scarcely walk between them, she began to question the wisdom of her request to work in a tent of her own. At first it had been only five wounded they had brought in. That five quickly became ten, then on the third day that ten became twenty-three. Thankfully—and sadly—no more had come.

Rather than wash her hands in the still steaming water, Ashlinn retrieved her surgical tools from the table beside her latest patient and dropped them in.

"Another for ya hands, ma'am?" Abigail asked.

Unable to voice anything that wouldn't either be a cuss word or turn into a scream, Ashlinn nodded. Without a word, Abigail ducked out the back of the tent. A moment later, she returned with another pot, this one steaming less than the first. Raising a ladle from it, she gave Ashlinn a questioning look. Ashlinn held her hands out and nodded. The freed slave slowly dumped the ladle of hot water over her hands. It burned a bit but she ignored it and scrubbed away as much blood as she could. They repeated the process until her hands shone clean in the candlelight.

After a nod from her, Abigail took the remaining water and went to the cot of the soldier they had just finished sewing up. She hummed softly as she began to clean the blood from the unconscious man's dark-skinned leg—a leg Ashlinn had managed to save by digging the bullet out. Over half the soldiers in the room were Negros. Doctor Taylor turned them away to treat the white soldiers first, something Ashlinn refused to do. It saddened her that the irony of allowing the very people you were fighting for to die was lost on him. But then, she supposed, people like Taylor weren't fighting to end slavery; they were fighting to preserve the Union.

A noise at the tent's back entrance drew her attention. Cliste pushed her nose through the closed tent flap and trotted inside, tail slowly wagging. The movement of her tail caused a spike of hope to plant within Ashlinn. The hound hadn't showed even the slightest sign of happiness since the troops had marched off. Eyes glued to the tent flap, she waited and prayed for Sean to walk in. But he didn't. She jumped a bit when Cliste pushed her head under her hand. On instinct, she began to scratch between her ears, but Cliste pushed past her hand until Ashlinn's fingers rested on her collar.

"There you are. Done searching for Scáth, are you?" she whispered, partly because she was too exhausted to speak louder, partly because she knew the Gaelic name of her family's second hound would be frowned upon by any English who overheard.

Out of habit, Ashlinn opened the cylinder and withdrew the paper from within. She nearly dropped it when she realized it wasn't the note she had left in there, but a sheet of music instead. Not from her brother, for certain, but no less remarkable for that fact. Her fingers shook as she carefully unrolled the tiny scroll. On the other side of the song-in-progress was a note written in beautiful script.

My Dearest Ashlinn,
Bold and quite improper to call you mine, I know. But when facing death a man must have his dreams. I am alive and unharmed for the time. Far too many are not and I know the amount of those already returning to you no doubt has you fretting. The sun is near to setting and due to the cease in enemy engagement, I believe we may be returning to camp soon. I could not bear the thought of you searching the battlefield for me and putting yourself in danger. When Cliste showed up, I embraced the chance to send you this letter. I pray that she makes it back safely to you, for I hold both her and you close to my heart. When we return I shall find you tonight.
Yours Truly,
Sean MacBranain

The letter began to fall from her trembling fingers but Abigail's dark hands were suddenly there, catching it before it could land on the muddy ground. With a tentative smile, she handed it back, holding on to it until Ashlinn was able to grasp it.

"A letter from ya sergeant, ma'am?"

Ashlinn nodded.

"He is a'right den?"

Clutching the letter carefully against her chest, she nodded again.

Hands rising up, Abigail's eyes looked to the roof of the tent. "Praise de Lord!"

While she shared the woman's joy, her heart was also heavy from the amount of dead and dying that had already returned. The amount of wounded in the hospital, as well as in this overflow tent, combined with the bodies stacking up like cordwood outside, made it clear over half the soldiers sent out today weren't coming back. And when they did, they would be exhausted and dispirited.

Ashlinn folded the letter and tucked it into a pocket in her dress. After a quick scan of the room to ensure the wounded were resting as comfortably as they could, she started for the back door.

"Ya've de look of a woman on a mission, ma'am. Anythin' I can do to help?" Abigail called after her.

Hand on the tent flap, she looked back. "Aye. Gather all the nurses you can, leave one you trust here to watch over the wounded, and bring the others to help."

"What we goin' to do, ma'am?"

"Set up the tents for the 69th. They will be in no shape to do so when they return and I will not have those men sleeping under the stars after what they have been through."

Brilliant white teeth shown from within the gloom of the tent as the nurse grinned. "Yes, ma'am!" she said with so much enthusiasm it energized even Ashlinn's tired soul.

Trusting the nurse to do as she asked, she removed her bloodied apron and marched off through the dreary encampment to the place she had seen the regiment drop their knapsacks. If she hadn't taken careful note of the location upon their arrival, she never would have found it among the thousands of tents that spread across acre upon acre of land. The gently sloping fields of Bolivar Heights would have been lovely if not for that.

Dressed as she was in men's clothing with her hair bound up and tucked beneath her cap, she felt secure enough that none of these strangers would recognize her for a woman. Most soldiers wouldn't harass a nurse anyway, but she liked to take extra precautions whenever they joined a new group, especially one this large. Then, of course, there was the deterrent of Cliste trotting along her side like a small horse.

The moment she reached the pile of knapsacks she had seen the 69th drop, she began searching for Sean's. It wasn't until she heard the approaching footsteps of the other nurses that she finally found it. His violin was still safely within. Letting out a sigh of relief, she removed the tent from the top of the knapsack and began opening it, pausing when she didn't see Abigail with the other three nurses.

"Where is Abigail?"

An older woman with her hair done up in a bun so tight it pulled at the corners of her eyes, straightened and let out a huff. "Said she would stay behind, see that things were done the way you liked them to be."

Ashlinn smiled as she turned her attention back to the tent. "Good. Thank you all for coming; I know how busy things are back at the hospital."

Another of the younger nurses picked up a second knapsack. "Yes, well, as you always say, we must tend to the living, too," she said with false cheer.

The haunted look in the woman's eyes told Ashlinn her cheer wasn't faked because she didn't agree with the words, but more because she was clinging to them like a life raft. With all the death they'd seen that day, she more than understood.

"How many do you think we should set up?" the third woman asked.

The answer stuck in Ashlinn's throat. Clearing it, she was able to force one word out. "Half."

Her estimation was based off the amount of dead she had seen return, along with the wounded that filled both the huge hospital tent and the secondary tent she had been working. While all weren't from the 69th regiment, enough were that she had a staggering idea of how many they had lost.

The youngest of the nurses sniffled but none spoke as they set to the task of erecting the tents. Orange and red streaked across a horizon that began swallowing the sun by the time they finished setting up one hundred and fifty tents in perfect rows that mimicked those nearby. Knowing each soldier had his own blankets and such that he liked, they left the knapsacks in a pile near the beginning of the rows of tents. As much as Ashlinn wanted to make up their beds and put their things within the tents, she didn't want them losing their precious belongings. Seeing as they had been sleeping on the battlefield for days, a dry tent alone would likely be enough to offer them relief.

Hands raw and sore from pounding in so many poles and tying off lines, she rubbed her fingers together as she turned back for the hospital tents. Something more than a lack of shared companionship held her back from following the other nurses right away. She called her thanks out to them and they responded kindly enough, but she couldn't yet make herself move. Bending back down to the pile of knapsacks, she picked up Sean's. His violin would be safer with her, and she knew he'd come find her and she could give it to him.

The sound of dozens of feet plodding rhythmically in a semblance of a march pulled at her. Though her mind told it was just another routine patrol around the edge of the camp, her heart insisted otherwise. Her eyes went to the distant horizon. Surrounded by the soft light of sunset, what remained of the 69th marched slow and steady into camp. The different companies began to break off at sound offs from their superiors, presumably heading toward their sections of camp. She counted scarcely more than a hundred: the size of a single company. Men shuffled past her as if she were invisible, some ducking into tents to collapse, others moving on to another section of camp. One came straight for her.

Though the light behind him only allowed her to see his silhouette, from his build and gait alone she knew it was Sean. The armor around her heart fell away piece by piece with each purposeful step he took toward her. Even splattered with mud and blood, hair sticking up in complete disarray, he looked amazing to her. His haunted copper eyes remained locked on her despite the flow of people that passed between them. The only thing that slowed him was Cliste trotting up to him to lick his hand. He scratched her head in a seemingly unconscious gesture and kept walking. Slinging his rifle back over his shoulder, he stopped before her, close enough that she had to crane her neck back to hold his gaze.

The pain of loss etched within the lines of his face brought moisture stinging to her eyes just as much as the sight of him alive did. With all the blood on him, she couldn't tell if he was wounded, but he stood straight enough and had walked well enough that she didn't think he was. She wanted to ask him, but she found she had no voice. If she opened her mouth, she feared a sob may come out, so she clamped it shut tight. Everyone else had either slipped into tents, or floated away like ghosts.

Slowly and with such gentleness that it made her ache, he took her face in his hands, bent down, and placed his lips upon hers. It didn't matter that blood and gunpowder covered his hands, or that he smelled of death. She wasn't in much better shape herself. The kiss set her on fire in a way she had never realized something so chaste could do. He pulled back, his hands sliding down and around her back to clutch her tightly to him. Pressed so close, she couldn't draw breath, but she didn't care. So long as he was holding her, she didn't need to breathe.

For the longest time they stood locked in an embrace, oblivious to the world around them that was swiftly falling into darkness. Wonderful though his embrace was, she couldn't help but keep her eyes on the other soldiers, not out of fear of compromised propriety, but to search their faces for her brother. She was beyond grateful for the miracle of Sean's safe return, but hoped one miracle might lead to a second. Ridiculous, she knew, considering how long Michael had been missing, but one she hoped for nonetheless. Soon she felt the rumble of Sean's stomach and drew back.

"You must be starvin'. Come along, I will make you somethin' warm to eat," she said.

"So long as 'tisn't corn," he said. The same haunted quality she had seen in his eyes earlier darkened his words, warning her not to ask.

"No corn, I promise."

She took his hand and began to lead him back to her tent. Keeping him at a distance wasn't an option right now. Maybe it never had been. The man needed her help as much as any physically wounded soldier, and she would not deny it for her own sake. He was a friend—a very dear friend—who needed her. Tail unusually still and head low, Cliste trotted ahead of them.

Sean resisted, eyes scanning the mound of knapsacks. "I have to get me…"

She handed his knapsack to him. The barest hint of a smile touched his lips like a mirage as he accepted it.

Motioning with his head, he indicated the rows of tents as they left. "You did this, didn't you?"

In an almost unconscious attempt at propriety, she let go of his hand and looped an arm around one of his as they walked. "Aye, myself and the other nurses."

"You're amazin'. Thank you."

A smile almost made it to her lips, but exhaustion of both her body and soul made it impossible. They walked the remainder of the way in silence through the quiet, dark encampment without encountering anyone. Ashlinn wouldn't have cared if they had. At this point, she didn't care if people talked. All she cared about right now was doing what she could to ease that haunted look in Sean's eyes.

Sean stood motionless in the darkness of her tent while she lit a candle and filled a washbasin. In the candlelight, his eyes looked so distant it seemed his soul was in another world entirely. She wished she couldn't imagine what it was like, but she could. She had walked the battlefields collecting the dead and wounded enough times to get a strong feel for the horror the soldiers faced. Taking his knapsack, she set it aside and started to unbutton his shirt, but his rifle strap got in the way.

"I will need you to remove that so we can get your uniform washed," she said gently.

He reached for it, but hesitated. Slowly, his eyes came to focus on her; he removed the rifle, and set it carefully aside. The only movement he made as she removed his shirt was to lift his arms and help the process. Some of the blood had soaked through, forcing her to peel the shirt away from his skin. Thankfully, she found no wounds to indicate that any of it might be his. The sight of his muscled chest would have sent a thrill through her at any other time, but right now, it simply made her relieved that he wasn't injured.

She had to fight back the impulse to bury her face against that chest and cling to him as tight as she could. This time she didn't resist because she was afraid for her heart; she resisted because it would be for her, not for him. And right now he needed her to be strong for him. She took a step back.

"If you will remove your socks and breeches, I will wash those as well." Though she tried to sound like the professional nurse she was, the woman in her made her voice shake a bit.

Some of the nurses talked about how a few of the soldiers didn't wear drawers beneath their breeches. Whether or not Sean did, she had no idea. She stepped around him and faced the tent entrance to give him as much privacy as she could. Bootlaces slapped against leather, a belt buckle jingled, then wool fabric brushed against skin. Calling up every lesson in etiquette she had ever undergone, she did her best not to picture him standing naked behind her, and failed. She extended a hand that shook slightly out behind her. Clothing draped over it a moment later.

"Feel free to clean up. There is a towel on the table beside the basin. I will be right back," she called as she stepped out into the night.

Due to the amount of blood she typically had on her at any given time, she kept a washtub next to her tent. Rounding the edge of the tent, she stopped in her tracks when a figure cloaked in shadow intercepted her. The tension blew from her in a rush when she saw Abigail's kind brown eyes regarding her with concern.

"Lemme wash dose for ya, Miss O'Brian."

She took the clothes from her with one hand and extended something to her with the other. On instinct, Ashlinn held her hand out. Abigail placed a wooden serving tray upon her outstretched hand, waiting until she grasped it with both hands before letting go. The spicy scent of stew wafted to her from the heavy, warm tray.

"Abigail, I…" Her first instinct was to refuse the kind gesture, but the words died on her tongue. She didn't want to insult her, and besides, Sean desperately needed to eat.

Abigail patted her shoulder and moved toward the washtub. "Ya just take care of your sergeant."

The urge to correct her, tell her he was not "her" sergeant, burned on her tongue, but she swallowed the words in fear of what Abigail would say. She did not have the energy for an argument right now, and she did not want to offend the woman. She started back for the tent. Just before turning the corner, she looked back at Abigail, who had already submerged the first item of clothing. "Thank you, Abigail. You are a true friend."

Straightening abruptly, Abigail turned her head in Ashlinn's direction. Though she couldn't see her expression in the dark, Ashlinn could feel the emotion in her words. "Thank ya, Miss O'Brian."

"Please, call me Ashlinn."

"Ashlinn." She sort of rolled the name around as if it were a delicacy to savor.

It was unheard of for a white woman—even a Northern one—to call a Negro "friend," Ashlinn knew, but she didn't care. Buried in her medical studies as she had always been, friends weren't something she had really taken the time to foster. That, and most women could not stomach the conversations she found stimulating. But Abigail was nothing like those women. Coming as close to a smile as she had in three days, Ashlinn stepped back into the soft glow of her tent.

Beads of moisture all across Sean's bare chest glistened in the candlelight. Her eyes followed a few of those beads as they zigzagged their way between his abdominal muscles, past his belly button, and sped along the line of hair leading into his knee-length drawers. The white linen drawers did very little to disguise the contours of his groin. Slowly, he drew a towel along his arms. She knew she should look away—had too—but her head refused to turn. Warmth spread from her center in a rush, concentrating between her legs.

Despite her desire to protect her heart, her resolve began to melt away like the final snow clinging to hills in spring. Seeing him standing there with such a forlorn look on his face made her realize it wasn't just herself she had been hurting by denying her feelings for him. She wanted nothing more than to go to him, embrace him, lose herself in him. Mustering all of her willpower, she turned her back to him and took several bracing breaths. "I apologize. I should have announced myself," she said in such a breathless voice, were it not for the still night he likely wouldn't have heard her.

"'Tis all right. 'Tis not like you haven't seen me half-naked before." A touch of humor lightened his troubled tone.

Were it not for that tone in his voice she would have been mortified at the impropriety of the situation. But that tone, that defeated hopelessness shrouding him made all the rules of society seem pointless.

"You are a bit more than half-naked this time," she said, trying to make her voice sound teasing. Instead it turned out dark, husky, and very unladylike.

"My apologies. I would take my leave, but I am without my clothes."

Was that a teasing note in his voice as well? It was hard to tell through the darkness that still haunted it. She could find him another set of clothes, but she couldn't let him go. After all he had been through today, she didn't want him to be alone.

"There is no need to apologize, Sean. Please, stay awhile. Rest and have somethin' to eat while your clothes dry."

The cot creaked and wool brushed against wool. "There, I have covered the bits you have not seen." While his words were light, his tone was anything but.

Hearing him like this made her heart ache but she did her best to hide it with a smile as she turned and walked to him. He sat on one end of her cot, a wool blanket draped over his lower body. Breaking at least a dozen rules of etiquette, she sat beside him on the cot and handed him a bowl of stew. Without a word, they set to eating. Despite the hunger that had to be gnawing at him, Sean ate slowly and with all the manners of a gentleman. Only when every bit was gone did he set it aside. The moment he did Cliste leapt to her feet, trotted over, and began to lick it clean.

"Where did you get that? I think there was rabbit in it. I haven't had meat that wasn't dried in months."

Ashlinn grinned as she set her own bowl aside and handed him a waterskin and cup. "There was indeed. It was from the nurse that I have been working closely with, Abigail. That woman is nothing short of a marvel."

After gulping down a cup and refilling it, Sean nodded. "I have to agree."

Ashlinn gathered the bowls and cups, placed them on the tray, and rose from the cot. Before she could take a step away, Sean grabbed her free hand.

"Please stay with me. I will be a perfect gentleman, I promise. 'Tis just that... I do not want to be alone."

The vulnerability in his tone struck a chord deep inside her. Not waiting for an answer, he lay down on the cot, turned his back to her, and pulled the blanket up over his shoulder. In only moments, his breathing deepened into that of sleep. Sighing, she set the tray down and began the arduous task of removing her gown, corset, and all their accoutrements. Several minutes later, standing in her pantaloons and chemise, she hesitated at the edge of the cot. In all her life, she had never imagined climbing into a bed with a man that wasn't her husband. It simply was not done.

Sean made a sound in his sleep that was close to a whimper, and her decision was made. Leaving the blanket tucked tight around him, she lay down beside him, spooning her body against his as they had done in the woods for warmth what seemed like a lifetime ago. Behind her closed eyelids the faces of all the bodies she had seen return from the battle, and of all the men in the hospital, reminded her of how lucky she was to have the one lying before her. She snaked an arm around his waist, buried her face against his neck, and finally succumbed to exhaustion.

Chapter 15

Darkness still clung to the encampment when Sean gently disentangled himself from Ashlinn's arms and eased off the cot. She was so exhausted that she barely stirred. A few soothing words soon had her snuggling beneath the blanket, breathing deeply again. Leaving her was the last thing he wanted to do, but he had to. If anyone saw him leave her tent they would begin to talk, and he did not want her reputation tarnished. It was bad enough that he knew he had spent the night with her, innocent though it had been.

The night air cooled his skin as he stepped outside in his drawers and unlaced boots, carrying his knapsack and rifle. Only snores greeted him, allowing him to breathe a bit easier. Around the corner of the tent he found the washtub and his clothes hanging on a line above it. He quickly dressed, not bothering to lace up his boots. Paws padded upon the packed dirt as he slung his rifle over his shoulder and picked up his knapsack. Moonlight shone in Cliste's big eyes as she looked over the washtub table at him.

He scratched behind one of her ears. "I'll be fine, don't you worry about me. Watch over Ashlinn now," he whispered.

Her tongue dashed out to wet the back of his hand before she turned and lumbered back into the tent. It still amazed him that such a huge, fierce-looking dog could be so gentle and affectionate. She was a marvel to be sure. Much like her owner. Sean couldn't allow his mind to drift there, or else he may find his feet carrying him back inside the tent. Even if she agreed to let him court her, he could never been seen compromising her honor in any way. If something did happen to him during this war, he wanted her reputation intact so she could find another suitable husband. It suddenly struck him. *He* wanted to be that suitable husband, more than anything.

As he walked, he contemplated why. Having grown up in a family that showed one another little to no affection, among other issues, he knew he had insecurity issues that made him need someone the way he needed her. But knowing that, he had always been good at fighting the instinct and seeing a relationship for what it really was. No woman had ever captured his attention the way Ashlinn had.

The respect he felt for her intelligence, the warmth he experienced from her kindness—they weren't just because she would be a good wife. Possibly the contrary. She would be a woman who insisted on having her own life, healing others despite the fact that it was something women simply didn't do. She would be stubborn, set in her ways, and she would be…amazing.

Holding a hand to his nose as he walked by the rows of bodies awaiting shipment back home or burial, he made his way to the smallest hospital tent. He knew immediately that this was the one Ashlinn had been working in because there were far fewer corpses lined up outside of it than the larger hospital tent. Pride in her abilities swelled through his chest, for he knew it was no coincidence. A glint of muted starlight shown off glass near his right eye, cluing him in to duck a moment before he would have collided with the hanging lantern.

Sean found a box of lucifers on a small table near the tent's entrance, struck one, and lit the lamp. Not wanting to disturb the patients, he turned the wick down as low as it would go without extinguishing the flame that danced on its end. The soft glow revealed a room packed with at least twenty cots from which a wide variety of snores issued. He couldn't help but wonder how many of these men would walk again, or hold the hand of the woman they loved again, all because they had the good fortune of being brought to Ashlinn's tent instead of the doctor's. At the opposite end of the room, he saw a figure slumped in a chair, sound asleep. By the voluminous skirt that surrounded the person's legs, he was guessing it was the nurse on duty. Holding the lantern aloft, he began searching the sleeping faces for his men. Some of them did indeed belong to his company.

Several stirred awake at his approach and he offered them words of encouragement and praise for a job well done. For those that asked, he danced around the topic of how many had died and whether or not they had won. Truly, he didn't know if they had. If he had to guess—which he told a few of them—he would have called the battle a draw. To his surprise, more than a few of the men in the room were Negros. Once he had spoken to each man that roused, he bid them all good night and good health and moved on to the largest hospital tent.

Upon entering, the rotting stench of putrid flesh forced him to cover his nose with one hand. The beds within this tent outnumbered the other by at least five and half times, which could have contributed to the smell, but Sean knew better. It had a lot more to do with the differences in Taylor's and Ashlinn's medical practices than it did with the sheer volume of patients. He would have bet his rifle on that. Forcing himself to breathe through his mouth, he made the rounds, stopping by each cot and chatting with each man that awoke at his approach. Though some were in dire shape and likely wouldn't make it long, he maintained his smile and positive attitude for each of them.

Canvas brushed against canvas—loud to Sean's soldier's ears—drawing his gaze to the tent opening at the back. A paunchy figure a good half a head shorter than him strode up with enough aggression that Sean instinctively reached back for his rifle. Seeing that it was only Doctor Taylor, he didn't draw the weapon around, but he didn't let go of the stock, either. The man brushed crumbs from his mustache in a hurried motion.

"Who is this disturbing my patients?" Taylor barked, his harsh tone far more disturbing than Sean could ever be to the men.

In a much quieter voice that managed to sound far more menacing, Sean answered, "'Tis Sergeant MacBranain, and I'm checkin' on my men."

Taylor took a step back, and straightened to stand as tall as he could. "Well then, Sergeant MacBranain, you have no doubt seen that they need their rest. Shall we leave them to it?"

Sean had to grind his teeth against a reply to the question that wasn't a question at all. He did his best to keep his response even and quiet. "I shall indeed, after I've seen to each of them, and not a moment before."

Emitting a huff, Taylor's somewhat bulging eyes skitted to Sean's hand that remained on the stock of his rifle. He gave him a curt nod and retreated to the back of the tent to plop down in a chair. Grabbing a cracker from a plate, he resumed eating, but Sean could see him watching him out of the corner of his eye. Not sparing the man another thought, Sean completed his rounds with deliberate slowness. When finished, he made his way to the other end of the tent, doused the lamp, and walked out. Hurried steps pounded on the packed dirt floor behind him but he let the tent flap go anyway.

Canvas slapped against flesh, making the corners of Sean's lips curl up into a grin. Not wanting any further interaction with the despicable man, he kept walking. His spirits, and his tolerance, sank as he heard steps slapping the ground behind him. Sean didn't slow his pace and soon the overfed man was huffing.

"I desire a word with you, Mr. MacBranain," Taylor snapped.

The lack of his title meant Taylor no doubt wished to speak to him man-to-man instead of doctor-to-sergeant. As it was not a conversation Sean wanted any part of, he kept walking.

"That was several, so good evenin', Taylor."

The man's sweaty stench preceded him as he sped into a jog, passed Sean, and stood to block his path. Tempting as it was to simply plow right over him, Sean stopped, fearing he wouldn't leave him alone until he had his say.

"What's it you wish to discuss with me?" Like his patience, his words were clipped short.

If this fool persisted, he wasn't sure he could hold his anger in check, not after what he had been through over the past several days. Everything was still too raw.

The man's chin thrust up in an attempt to peer down his hawkish nose at Sean, which only resulted in him glaring at his chest. "It is regarding your intentions toward Miss O'Brian."

Was that a hint of sweet cracker he smelled on his breath? The bastard had to be spending a small fortune to get a hold of such a thing, a fortune that would be better spent on medical supplies. Sean didn't think his opinion of the man could drop any further. He had been wrong. Then something far worse occurred to him. Had the man seen him leave Ashlinn's tent? Surely not; he had been too careful for a fool like him to notice.

"That is none of your business, Mr. Taylor."

He deliberately dropped the man's title to remind him that they were speaking man-to-man and in doing so, he was not bound to the etiquette of a soldier. Would such a formality fly with his lieutenant if this led somewhere bad? Probably not, but Taylor didn't know that.

Though he pulled back a bit, Taylor puffed his chest out. "It most certainly is, as I intend to officially court her."

Sean's fingers tightened around both the strap of his knapsack and his rifle. "Without the man of her family available you would have to gain her consent, which you have not."

He started to shove past him but Taylor stepped back and to the side to block his path again. The man's bushy brows pulled together over his muddy eyes like two caterpillars preparing to mate. "But I will, for certainly she will not spurn a man of means who can both provide for her and ensure she maintains the high social standing a woman of her wealth is used to. From the look on your face, I am going to venture a guess that you did not know her family was wealthy."

The straps bit into Sean's palms, his hands convulsed so tightly. Not bothering to let go, he dropped his shoulder down, shoved it into Taylor's own to knock him aside, and marched past him. If he stayed to listen to any more of the man's dribble, he would end up pummeling him.

"Until she accepts your proposal, she and I are none of your business," he threw back as he kept walking.

"Oh, she will. You can bet on it, because I can give her everything you cannot, MacBranain," he called after him, twisting his name as if it were something dirty.

It took the last shred of his control not to turn back around and pound the man into the ground. But that would no doubt accomplish exactly what he wanted, and Sean wasn't about to let that happen. He marched on, breathing deep of the cool night air, letting it and the darkness drain his anger away. In the absence of anger, though, doubt set in. Ashlinn had never mentioned that her family was wealthy. Had she hidden that deliberately from him? Surely not. She wasn't shallow. Or was she? He had suspected her family was wealthy, but he hadn't been sure until now. What else about her didn't he know?

Chapter 16

Head ducked low to keep the rain from dripping down the back of her collar, Ashlinn pulled her cap tighter down onto her bound hair. Mud splashed up onto her boots as she walked the soggy path from one hospital tent to another. At least in breeches she didn't have to worry about gathering up her skirts to keep them clean. Why more of the nurses didn't don men's clothing, she could not fathom.

Just before she reached the second tent, a figure stepped out of it. The pelting rain misted around the person, obscuring their features from view. Were it not raining hard enough to make a devout man want to build a boat, she would have taken a detour to avoid the person. Every day for the past week, Doctor Taylor had been seeking a private audience with her. Fearing she knew what he wanted, she had begged off and avoided him so far.

To make matters worse, she had not seen Sean the whole week, either. That night after Antietam, her resolve to keep him at a distance had begun to melt away a bit. When she had inquired after him to his men, they informed her that he had been placed on picket duty at the far edge of the encampment. Never had he been assigned to such a duty before. When she asked the men from his company about it, they voiced suspicions that someone had complained about him to their lieutenant. She knew of only one person that would do that, and it wasn't a soldier. Had she not been so busy tending to the wounded (and searching for her brother among them), she would have gone out to visit him.

As she turned to go around the figure, she saw too late that it was Doctor Taylor, as if her suspicion alone had conjured him. The man stepped into her path and shot an arm out to surround one of hers in a semblance of an escort.

"Miss O'Brian, I am so glad I encountered you. May I have a moment of your time?" he asked so sweetly it made her teeth ache.

She tried to pull away but he held fast to her arm. "Now really is not a good time. I am hardly presentable."

"I do insist. I have been eager to speak with you for over a week now." An edge worked away at the sweet tone.

Again, she tried to tug her arm free. He held on so tight that to get away she would be forced to make a scene. Despite the wet conditions, the midday hustle of the encampment meant there would be a lot of witnesses to her unladylike behavior. Had she not undergone so many lessons in etiquette as a young woman, she would have done it anyway.

Muscles going stiff, she stood as straight as she could with him latched onto her arm. "Fine then. What is it you wish to speak to me about, Doctor Taylor?"

"Since you have no living male relative or benefactor, it is to you personally that I must state my intentions to." His tone was all business, but she feared she knew what he was about to say next was as personal as it could get.

"Doctor Taylor, this is highly unorthodox—"

"I wish to court you, officially. And let's be frank: you really can't do much better than someone of my wealth and standing. You have no need to offer a dowry of any kind. I am a man of adequate wealth and means and I understand that no male relative is living that can arrange a dowry for you." He interrupted as if she hadn't even spoke.

Anger fed her strength. How the man could continue to be so arrogant and clueless was beyond her. With a violent twist, she pulled free of his grasp. "If I have no living male relative, it is thanks to you, and I yet might. My younger brother is still missing, which makes your proposal not only terribly untimely, but highly inappropriate."

Shaking his head, Taylor gave her a tolerant look that she wanted to claw right off his face. "The war took them, not me, as I have explained. And if your younger brother is still alive, it is because he is a deserter, which is only one more reason you should find my proposal quite attractive. There are not many men that would take in the sister of a deserter, especially with no dowry on top of that."

With a speed and power that surprised even her, she lashed out and slapped the man across the face. Teeth clenched, his head whipped back to her, eyes no more than dark beads between angry slits.

"Certainly you do not wish to court me because I am from a wealthy family with no male heir and my husband-to-be stands to inherit all of my family's fortune. Not with you being a man of wealth and means," she said with more than a little sarcastic bite to her tone.

Blood stained Taylor's slightly crooked teeth as he grinned at her. The sight sent chills racing up her arms. She took a step back.

Droplets of blood flew as he hissed through his teeth. "When no one else will have you, it will not really matter, will it? If you are waiting on your soldier to court you, you will be sadly disappointed."

One hand doubled into a fist. She stood her ground as he loomed closer. "I will not allow you to speak ill of Sergeant MacBranain."

He let out a bit of a crazed sounding laugh. "I do not need to. Look around." His arms swept wide to indicate the encampment. "How many of these soldiers were here when we first arrived two years ago? None. They all die, as will he."

Her mind worked desperately to try to recall a single soldier from two years ago. She couldn't. Tears stung her eyes but thankfully, the rain masked them. Words jumbled around in her head, eluding her attempts to formulate an intelligent argument.

"Miss O'Brian, there you are! I've been lookin' for you," came a familiar voice that she associated with the sound of a harmonica.

She turned in his direction. "Private Fergusson. What is it I can do for you?" Relief allowed her to force a false sense of cheer into her voice.

The tall, ruggedly handsome man stood with his hand on the strap of his rifle. His green eyes narrowed at the doctor with warning. The three-day shadow of a beard darkening his face only served to make him look more menacing. "One of your patient's wounds needs to be looked at. If you'll come with me, I shall escort you there."

So great was her relief that she nearly gasped from the power of it. She moved quickly to his side and took his offered arm. "O' course."

"We are not finished here, Miss O'Brian," Taylor called to her.

She shot a glare back at him. "Oh, we most certainly are. The answer to your question is no, and it will always be no."

With a disciplined clip, Fergusson turned them in the opposite direction and began walking, water splashing beneath his boots.

"You will change your mind, and you will beg me to ask you again before this war is over," Taylor called after them.

Ashlinn paused long enough to smile back at him. "Please, *do* hold your breath until then."

As they walked through row after row of tents, Ashlinn concentrated on slowing her pounding heart and swallowing her tears. She didn't realize she was muttering under her breath until Fergusson laughed and complimented her on her Gaelic curse words.

Embarrassment scorched her face. "I apologize, Private. That was most unladylike of me."

Fergusson's trimmed mustache arched up on one side. "No worries, Miss O'Brian. Nothin' could color my view of you as a lady, rest assured."

The words made her smile. "You are very sweet, thank you."

"'Tis true. And you handled yourself quite well back there. I particularly enjoyed the part where you slapped him."

Though humor lightened Fergusson's tone, an underlying hardness suggested he didn't like the doctor very much. Ashlinn knew exactly how he felt. As they left the tents behind and started across a well-trod meadow of yellowing grass, it occurred to her that he was leading her somewhere. The rain had reduced to a drizzle, making her wonder how long they had been walking. While she trusted the young, strapping soldier, she hardly knew him, and strolling off into the wild with him was far from appropriate.

"Private Fergusson, where are we going?"

With a thrust of his head, Fergusson indicated the tree line not more than ten yards away. "Your presence is requested by the gentleman there."

She realized someone was walking toward them out of the trees. The confident gait of the lean figure made her heart pound faster. She would know that walk and silhouette anywhere. Warmth spread through her, banishing the chill brought on by her damp coat. Realizing she was a soaking wet mess, she had to fight the impulse to fuss with her hair and tuck it up beneath her cap better. Her breeches clung to her legs and rear, making her suddenly very self-conscious. After a week of not seeing Sean, she was glad no matter the circumstances, but she would have preferred to look more presentable. She knew she needn't fuss over such things since they were only friends. Yet the surge of emotions at seeing him well felt like anything but friendship, and certainly, so much more than desire. Trotting alongside him, tail held high, was Cliste.

Fergusson let go of her arm and suddenly snapped to attention, right hand rising to his forehead in a sharp salute that Sean returned. Ignoring them both as if she had seen their exchange dozens of times, Cliste bounded up to Ashlinn and licked her hand.

"Sergeant MacBranain, the lady was in a bit of distress when I found her in the presence of the doc. I thought a walk in the fresh air may do her a bit o' good."

"Thank you for lookin' out for Miss O'Brian's well-bein', Private. 'Tis much appreciated," Sean said.

"You're most welcome, sir. As is the lady." He turned and gave her a slight bow before returning his attention to Sean. "If you'll excuse me, sir. 'Tis my time to report for picket duty."

"O' course. Carry on, Private."

Again they exchanged salutes; then Fergusson marched off toward the tree line.

Rain poured from Sean's cap as he grabbed the brim and tipped it slightly to her. "Good day, miss. May I have the pleasure of escortin' you back to your tent?" he asked in a formal tone that still managed to be quite warm—due in no small part to the handsome smile that graced his lips.

It took a great deal of effort to pull her gaze from those lips up to his eyes. She longed to taste them again, but she didn't dare. That hadn't worked to guard her heart before. It certainly wouldn't work now. Still, she was in need of an escort back to camp. Even inside her own head that sounded like an excuse to touch the strong arm he offered her. But it was a good enough one, for accept it she did. Even through both of their coats, the warmth of his arm seeped into her, taking some of the chill away. She shivered involuntarily and he drew her a bit closer. His side touched hers, sending more heat rushing through her. He led her not directly back to the camp but toward the trees that ran along the edge of it.

"You're chilled. I apologize for havin' him bring you all the way out here in such weather," he said.

She shrugged. "'Tis all right. I would have gone anywhere so long as it was away from Taylor." *And toward you* almost slipped out, but she held the words back at the last moment. What on earth was wrong with her?

They reached the trees and the leaves caught the misty rain before it could fall upon them. The occasional drop from the yellow or green water-laden leaves reached them, but it was considerably less than in the meadow. Ears perked up, Cliste ran on ahead, no doubt after some poor forest creature by the enthusiasm her wagging tail exuded.

"I apologize for bein' absent for the last week. Someone told my lieutenant that I was bein' improper with one of the nurses, so he put me on picket duty until I sorted things out."

She glanced at Sean out of her peripheral vision. Was that a blush darkening his cheeks? Had his words not inflamed her, she would have smiled. But thoughts of Taylor going to Sean's commanding officer and speaking ill of him made her want to do anything but smile.

"That son of a—"

"Now, now. Best not to waste your energy on him. Besides, 'twas a good thing. It gave me time to think things over," he said.

"Things?" Ashlinn didn't trust herself to say more. She did not want him to hear the mixture of hope and fear in her voice.

With his free hand, Sean swept aside the drooping branches of a willow tree and led her beneath it. The ground around the base of the tree was so dry it didn't squish beneath her boots in the slightest. Letting go of her arm, he took her hand in his and leaned back against the trunk of the tree. His copper eyes captured her gaze and held it. The raw emotion in his eyes made her swallow hard.

"Us." The way his voice dropped low and became husky made her want to look away to hide her own reaction, but she was held fast.

"I have little more to me than me name, and even that's not much where I come from. The doctor tells me you are from a wealthy family in good standin'. You deserve much better than the likes o' me."

She shook her head, trying to ignore how the direction of this conversation was splintering away bits of her heart. Her hand tightened around his. Though he had made no move to let go, she feared he would, and heaven help her, she didn't want him to. "You are a good man. That's a rare thing worth more than all the wealth in the world," she whispered.

The smile he allowed to shine through his mask was genuine. "You may feel differently when we aren't in the trenches of hell. And I wouldn't fault you for it."

Jaw clenching, she turned her head away. He took hold of her chin and turned it back to him ever so gently. "But I would like the chance to get to know you better, and for you to get to know me better. So that when that time comes, you can make your decision with all the cards showin', so to speak."

Still, fear kept her from allowing hope into her heart. "What are you saying, Sean?"

"You've captured me, Ashlinn. You're wicked smart, independent, and you stand up for what you believe in. I can't imagine a more intriguin' woman." Through all that, he remained confident, holding her gaze, but then his eyes dropped as if he were suddenly self-conscious. "Before I ask you what I want to ask you, though, there's somethin' you need to know about me."

He wouldn't look up at her. Concern for him, as well as for herself over whatever it was he had to say, churned within. But there were things she had to say as well. The battle of Antietam had shaken her resolve to its core, making her realize friend or otherwise, she cared for this man and did not want to waste what time she had with him. Seeing him so devastated after Antietam had changed something in her, broken it open.

"If you are destitute, I do not care. A widower, I do not care. Estranged from your family, I do not care." She lifted his chin with a finger and stared straight into his frightened eyes. "There is very little in this world that could make me see you in a bad light," she told him. And she truly didn't, heaven and all the powers that be help her.

Palm against a birch for support, Sean turned away. His head dropped and his breathing hitched. The last of her resolve to keep him at a distance melted like lingering snow in June. She reached out to him, hand hesitating inches away. Breath held, she waited, giving him time to find the strength on his own.

* * * *

Swallowing hard, Sean straightened. Come what may, he had to get this out before he went any further. Honor demanded he do so.

"My parents betrayed our people to the crown. But I didn't, I swear by all I hold dear, I didn't. I knew nothing about what they were up to." A few shuddering breaths and he went on. "We were run out of our home in Kilkenny by the IRA. My parents stayed in the North, where those loyal to the crown remain. But I couldn't. I had no love for the crown. So I came to America."

Not a single soul outside of Ireland had ever heard that story. Telling it lifted a weight from his shoulders that he had become so accustomed to bearing, he shuddered. Were his hand not against the tree already, he might have staggered. Still, he couldn't look at Ashlinn, couldn't bare her rejection over this. Yet bare it he would, if he had to.

Slowly, she pulled his hand from the tree and took both of his in hers, squeezing them hard. "You do not need to bear the sins of your father. There is no shame in leaving a situation like that. You are a good man, and the good you have already done in this country has redeemed the MacBranain name. Now, Sean." When his eyes dropped again she ducked low to keep in their sight. "Ask me what you want to."

Disbelief lingered with a blossoming hope in his chest. "I would like to court you properly, startin' now if you'll have me. There is no sense trying to guard my heart from you. You have already found your way in." He paused and swallowed hard. "If afterward you decide you find me suitable I'll not ask for, nor accept, a dowry, for 'tis you I want, not your family's wealth. But if you desire a man of higher standin', I'll understand." He swallowed so hard he had no doubt she heard it. "I have no intention of dishonorin' you. I merely want the chance to get to know one another, official-like, in a manner that no one would look down upon."

An inner turmoil broiled within her eyes and she was silent so long the birds in the tree above them began to tweet once again. Despair drove him to speak.

"Unless you have already accepted someone else's courtship. Then o' course I would respect that, but—"

She rose up on her toes and stopped his words by covering his lips with hers. That slight contact broke the dam of control he had built into a million pieces that he'd surely never be able to recover. Ever since that evening after Antietam, he had wanted nothing more than to kiss her again. Well, that wasn't entirely true, he wanted much more, but it all started with a kiss. His arms wrapped tight around her, pressing her against him. Clinging to a shred of honor, he kept it chaste and sweet, his lips parting only enough to tease her with his warm breath.

The smile on her beautiful face nearly made his knees weak. "May I take that as a yes?"

She laughed, the sound sending a shiver through him and making his eyes flutter closed for a moment. "Aye, you certainly had better."

He pushed away from the tree, stepped back, and offered her his arm. "Well in that case, I fear we have broken all etiquette and leapt ahead of the process. If we're to keep company now, then we shall have to do it proper so none may claim I have spoilt you," he said in his most official sounding voice.

Sighing deeply, she dropped her gaze until her lashes brushed her cheeks, and accepted his offered hand. They began to walk through the forest once again, Cliste trotting ahead of them.

"I hope this does not mean the end of our stolen kisses and embraces," she said softly, watching him out of the corner of her eye.

The come-hither look along with the words sent blood pumping to places that would make it quite difficult to hide. Right now he could scarcely bring himself to care. One corner of his mouth quirked up into a half smile. "I did not say that."

Up ahead Cliste bounded to a soldier in blue that leaned against a tree. He greeted her and patted her head. He glanced at Ashlinn out of the corner of his eye, secretly pleased at the disappointment that shone in her eyes. He was quite serious about doing this proper, all the way down to the escort. As much as he wanted this lady, he wanted to do it right. Telling her his story only strengthened that resolve. Now, if he could only hold on to that resolve in the midst of war.

Chapter 17

Arms and lips still burning with the wonderful feel of Ashlinn, Sean marched straight for his lieutenant's tent. He wanted to head this off at the pass before word had a chance to get out. Or more specifically, before Taylor came crying to his commanding officer yet again. This time he would not allow that blaggard to make it seem as though he were out to dishonor Ashlinn.

The flap to the lieutenant's tent was tied open and the sound of a wire brush moving against steel came from within. Behind a table, the man sat cleaning his rifle. For a moment Sean considered backing away and returning later, perhaps when the man didn't have a weapon in his hands.

Without shifting his focus from the weapon, he addressed Sean. "What is it you need, Sergeant?"

Upper lip twitching as he fought the impulse to cringe, Sean snapped to attention and saluted. Only just now looking up at him, the lieutenant put his bore brush down and returned the salute. Gun oil and soot smeared across his forehead as he did so. Picking up a rag, his attention returned immediately to his work.

"I wish to have a word with you, sir. But I can come back when you aren't busy."

"That 'tis a mythical time that doesn't exist. Please, have a seat." He motioned toward the empty chair on the other side of his makeshift desk.

Sean marched in and sat in the chair, his back rigid, eyes forward.

"At ease, soldier. Just tell me what 'tis on your mind."

The man's casual tone should have relaxed him, but it didn't. He wasn't a hard man, his lieutenant, just a fair and honorable one that expected no less from the men he commanded.

"Well, sir, I thought a lot about what you said, about not dishonorin' the good ladies who are workin' as nurses for the 69th, or even allowin' it to appear as though we are."

When he paused to carefully consider his next words, the man waved the rag at him. "Go on."

"And what I feel for Miss O'Brian is not a passin' fancy. I intend to officially court her, and I wanted to head off any rumors before they start."

At that, the man stopped what he was doing, put the rag and weapon down, and looked at Sean. He figured it was best to leave out the part about how he had already asked her, and she had accepted. The look of warning in his lieutenant's brown eyes hurried Sean's next words.

"We are at war, I understand that. My men and the war come first and that will not change, I assure you. Courtin' Miss O'Brian will give me incentive to work harder and fight harder. It will not distract me. In fact, I will work so hard you'll want to promote me."

It wasn't hard to sound convincing; he meant it. No lives would be put at risk due to him courting Ashlinn, of that he was utterly determined. And the last part, about a promotion, he definitely intended to work hard toward. Not only to serve his country and his men better, but because he knew to truly have a chance with Ashlinn he needed to earn and save as much coin as he could. Once this war was over, a beautiful woman such as herself would have no shortage of suitors, likely all of them far better off than him. If he wanted to be able to compete with them, he had to start now.

The lieutenant's eyes narrowed to slits and he pursed his lips for a moment, as if thinking hard. Sean couldn't help but hold his breath. He didn't know what he'd do if the man refused him. Something that would no doubt land him in a heap of trouble if he were caught. But one thing was for certain, no matter the consequences, he couldn't walk away from Ashlinn now.

"On those very conditions." Before Sean could thank him, the man held up a hand. "But, if I see even one sign of it distractin' you, or movin' your focus away from your men or this war, I will bust you back down to private, and that is if I'm feelin' generous."

Propelled to his feet by his excitement, Sean saluted the man again. "You won't, sir, I assure you. You'll be hard pressed to find a more dedicated soldier."

The man set his rifle and rag down and leaned back in his chair, arms crossing over his chest. "We shall see about that. Since you're so eager to prove yourself, ready your men for reconnaissance to Halltown. You leave at first light."

Sean covered his disappointment with what he hoped was an eager smile, hand remaining at his forehead in the salute. "Aye, sir. We shall make you and the Union proud."

Sighing, the lieutenant sat up and returned the salute. "See that you do, Sergeant. Dismissed."

Body rigid, Sean shot the man a smile that he didn't feel, snapped the salute down to his side, turned on his heal, and marched from the tent. He tried to tell himself that he hadn't just unknowingly led his men into danger. That the lieutenant would have chosen his company for the mission anyway. And it was likely, but that didn't remove the weight in his stomach. The man could have chosen any of the companies of the 69th for such a detail. Deep down, Sean knew he had unwittingly given the man a reason to choose his.

Knowing the possibility of others seeing him leave the lieutenant's tent was high; he maintained his false smile and confident march until he was well into the darkness of the outer edge of the encampment. The doctor wasn't the only one who talked. He had to be careful. Only once darkness encased him did he allow his shoulders to sag and his smile to melt away. Once he headed in the direction of his company's tents, he started to whistle a tune in hopes of some very sensitive ears picking up on it.

His heart sank as he turned down the soggy path that led between the first row. The patter of huge paws splashing through the mud pulled his attention back behind him. For a long moment, he feared it was merely hope playing tricks on him; then he saw a huge gray shadow moving past the glow of the tents. The hound bounded up to him, nudging his thigh with her big nose.

"Good girl," he whispered as he scratched behind her ears.

If he didn't know better, he would almost think she had followed him and been waiting for his call. But it was far more likely that she had just been out in the area making her rounds and mooching off the other soldiers. He took a piece of paper from within his coat and wrote a quick letter to Ashlinn on it letting her know he would be gone for a few days. Cliste dropped her head as if waiting for him to open the small cylinder on her collar. Shaking his head, he rolled the letter into a tiny scroll and placed it within. At the click of the cylinder closing, Cliste perked up, let out a quiet bark, and bounded off into the dark.

Wonder filled him as he watched the hound fade into the night. Unfortunately, the moment he turned back to his camp, pain wrenched at him as if his guts had twisted. Just when he had built up the courage to ask Ashlinn to allow him to court her, he had to leave her. While he had gotten what he wanted, he had also ended up with more than he had bargained for.

Chapter 18

Crouched in the yellowing grass of the field, Ashlinn could almost pretend a large portion of the Union army wasn't camped behind her. The warm, unusually dry October day had enticed her and Abigail out to gather the white flowering yarrow before it withered away and disappeared for the year. Glimpses of the robin's egg-blue sky that stretched above the orange, red, and yellow draped trees lifted her spirits and reminded her of home. Fingering the soft, fernlike leaves of a flower she had just plucked, she paused before dropping it into the half-full basket beside her. Serenaded by a few birds and Abigail's soulful humming, she almost didn't hear the sound until it was nearly upon them.

Something large moved through the waist-high grass to their right. A mixture of hope and fear swirled within her. Instantly, her thoughts turned to Michael.

"Cliste?" Ashlinn whispered as one hand reached to her waist where she kept a bowie knife.

A soft woof came from the swaying stalks. Letting out the breath, Ashlinn sat back on her heels as Cliste trotted up to her. After pushing against her hand for a quick scratch, the hound lay down on her belly and dropped her head. Knowing what she wanted, Ashlinn reached for the cylinder on her collar.

She and Sean had been exchanging letters like this ever since he had returned from reconnaissance at the end of last month. Thankfully, he hadn't been gone long and hadn't had been sent back out since. However, his commanding officer worked him nearly from sunup to sundown, leaving little to no time for them to see one another. The approval of the courtship ended up making things more difficult, keeping them apart more effectively than when she had decided to keep him at a distance. So they had to be creative, and thankfully, Cliste seemed to enjoy it as if it were a game.

Unfolding the letter, she fought to control the girlish smile that turned up her lips. Once upon a time opening the cylinder on Cliste's collar had brought her a great deal of stress as she had hoped—and feared—it would be a letter from her missing brother. An echo of that old pain remained, and she still thought of him each time. But now it had become the highlight of her day, often many times a week. She unrolled the tiny scroll and began to read, aware that Abigail had gone quiet beside her.

My Dearest Ashlinn,

It is my fervent hope that you will do me the honor of walking with me this evening to take in a bit of fresh air and the sight of tonight's full moon. Should you be so inclined, and unobligated, I shall be by your tent to pick you up at sunset.

Yours,

Sean MacBranain

The formal manner of his words didn't detract from the excitement that rose within her. A moonlit walk with him sounded like heaven, and not only because they had scarcely seen one another in three days' time. Of late, she had come to understand her mother's old saying, "'tis better to have loved and lost than never to have loved at all." Each moment, each word with Sean was a treasure she held dear. Denying herself those treasures had been a mistake. But then, that was easy to say with him still alive and well, she knew. Yet it was a risk she was glad she had accepted. If only she could see him more.

"Too tender to share, ma'am?" Abigail prompted from beside her.

More than the usual eagerness lay in her tone. Sharing the letters with Abigail had become a habit and pleasure the two women indulged in together. Abigail's slightly too-wide eyes and pursed lips made Ashlinn wonder.

"Not at all. He says he wishes to take me walkin' tonight," she told her through a grin.

In Abigail's presence, she found herself allowing her carefully disciplined English to slip and the Irish in her to shine through. Something about Abigail put her at ease and made her feel more herself than the company of any other woman—even her own mum—ever had. It didn't hurt that Abigail never judged or corrected her, unlike the women back in her circles at home.

"Um hum, be a fine night for it, de moon out and all," Abigail said through a sigh as she cast her gaze skyward. "In that case, ma'am, we'd best get ya back and cleaned up. Sunset ain't more dan two hours away at most."

Rising, she brushed back the dense curls of black hair that had come free of her thick braid. Again, Ashlinn got the sense that there was something else in her friend's smile. Was it hesitance, a touch of nerves?

"Are you worried about me walkin' with Sean at night?"

The hesitance melted away in the wake of a big smile. "Oh no, ya sergeant is a real gentleman."

Ashlinn fished out the pencil she kept in her breeches pocket, flipped the note over, and wrote a quick but sweet reply back accepting his offer. She rolled the paper back up, tucked it into Cliste's collar, and scratched beneath the hound's chin.

"Take that to Sean now," she told her.

Ears and tail perking up, Cliste seemed to grin at her before turning and bounding off into the tall grass. Basket in hand, Ashlinn rose and brushed the dirt from the knees of her breeches. Her smile grew as she watched the grass sway after Cliste's passing. If they could get a moment alone perhaps tonight she could coax more than a kiss out of the oh-so-proper sergeant.

* * * *

Smoothing an imaginary wrinkle from her dark blue working dress, Ashlinn wished for the thousandth time that she had something less plain to wear. No wonder the man wasn't trying to ravish her at every turn; all he had ever seen her in was this drab thing and men's clothing. There had been the one fine dress she wore to the ball, but that had been months ago, and she feared the image had faded from his mind. It could also be his deep sense of honor and propriety that made him evade her every attempt at intimacy. No matter how she tried to convince him that desire didn't detract from his honor, he refused to budge on the matter. The stain of his parents' transgressions darkened him no matter how much she tried to convince him he was clean of it.

The rhythmic sound of bristles brushing the tangles out of her hair calmed her, as did the quiet humming Abigail made as she brushed. Soon, her long hair draped around her shoulders like a wavy shawl of gold. She usually wore it bound up in a bun but tonight she wanted to try something new. While she didn't expect to take Sean's breath away clothed in her working dress, she hoped leaving her hair unbound might at least stir him. Not that she didn't think he was attracted to her, he clearly was. But she had to do something to shake his restraint or else she was going to explode from desire.

Abigail's humming stopped, as did the brush. "No need to fret now, Ashlinn. Ya look beautiful." Even after a few weeks of being on a first name basis, Abigail still whispered Ashlinn's name each time she said it, as if it were something forbidden to her. It made her both proud of the woman and sad for her.

Fur brushed against canvas as Cliste pushed her way through the tent flap. She stood beside Ashlinn's stool, eye-to-eye with her, tail wagging.

"I do believe dat means ya sergeant is here."

Despite the fact that Abigail had brushed it into perfect waves, Ashlinn smoothed her hair as she stood. Before Sean could announce himself, she strode across the small space with three eager steps, and swept the tent flap open.

In a pair of dark breeches and his woolen coat, she could almost imagine he were just a suitor come calling and not a soldier in the middle of a war. Waves of his dark brown hair fell to his clean-shaven cheekbones, which were accented by delicious dimples. Candlelight erupted across the copper striations in his eyes as they widened to take in the sight of her. His tongue darted out to wet lips that turned up into an impressed smile. The sight of that pointed pink tongue sent warmth flooding toward the apex of her legs. Scandalous plans of ditching their escort began to form. But she couldn't do that to poor Abigail. Another glance at how nicely he filled out those breeches and she thought just maybe she could.

Sean bowed slightly to her, eyes remaining locked on hers. "Miss O'Brian, you look lovely this evenin'." The conviction in his voice made her feel as though she stood there in a fine gown rather than a worn working dress.

He turned sideways and offered her his arm. "Shall we?" Was she imagining a hint of suggestion in his tone?

Inclining her head, she gazed at him through a curtain of her golden hair. His breath drew in sharply and his eyelids fluttered. She accepted his arm and stepped from the tent.

"We shall indeed."

Behind them, the candlelight extinguished, plunging them into the soft glow of twilight. A tail thumped against Ashlinn's leg as Cliste jogged past to take up the lead. Abigail's soft footsteps followed behind far enough back to give them a bit of privacy, but close enough to be a proper escort. As they walked, they exchanged pleasantries about the weather, news they had heard from New York from various people about anything that didn't have to do with the war. Such conversation had become a bit of a routine of theirs, a way to feel normal amidst so much abnormality. Occasionally a soldier called out a greeting to them, but for the most part, they passed through the camp unnoticed.

Shortly after they left the encampment behind, Abigail dropped back a bit farther. Ashlinn turned her head away from Sean to hide a smile. She would have to thank the woman for that later. To her delight, Sean pulled her in closer until their sides touched. Both the heat of his body and the heat its nearness arose in her chased away the chill of the October evening. Ahead of them and to the right stretched an orange and red sky that glowed with the false promise of warmth. Still only a pale ghost in the slowly darkening blue sky, the full moon hovered near the opposite horizon as if awaiting its turn for dominion.

Ashlinn's gaze went from the sunset to the encampment and back out to the moon. "I do not believe I have been this direction before."

"Aye, you have not." The mysterious tone of his voice made Ashlinn wish she could see his face better in the lengthening shadows.

The edge of the forest approached and each step closer it seemed to grow darker and darker. "Is it safe so far from camp?" she whispered.

His free hand came to rest atop hers, the rough feel of his palm against the back of her hand sending shivers up her arm. She had purposefully not worn gloves in hopes that he would touch her like this. The feel of his calluses, most of which were formed from years of holding a violin and a bow, stirred her in a way she couldn't explain.

"No worries, I shall always keep you safe," he said, voice low enough to feel like a caress all on its own.

She leaned her head against his shoulder as they walked, partly because she wanted to touch him more and partly because his words made the world sway. "Are you takin' me somewhere special?"

A soft "hmm" of pleasure vibrated through him. She smiled, knowing her lack of careful etiquette in allowing her accent to come through had caused it. The fact that he loved it when she showed her heritage touched her as deeply as his kisses did. Deeper, even.

"I am. But I have a confession to make. We won't be alone."

The smile melted from her face and she lifted her head from his shoulder to fix him with a hard look. "Why, Sean MacBranain, are you leadin' me on?" she teased.

Eyes widening, he shook his head. "Oh no. I would love nothin' more than to spend this evenin' with you, alone." He leaned close to whisper the last word in her ear.

Shivers raced from the sensitive skin of her lobe all the way to her core. Continuing to walk, he straightened and returned his focus to the forest they were about to step into. "But, I have a feelin' you may enjoy this nearly as much."

She glanced back to make sure Abigail was far enough back to be out of hearing range before she whispered to him, "I doubt that."

His deep laugh sent shivers dancing across her skin. "I will take that as a compliment."

Curiosity piqued, she paid special attention to their surroundings. The darkness of the forest wrapped around them like a cloak seeking to hide them from the rising moon. Air crisp enough to be refreshing but cool enough to portend the changing season filled her lungs with the taste of pine and alder. They walked through the trees for some time, fallen leaves crunching beneath their feet. Well, hers at least. Somehow, Sean seemed to avoid making any sound at all as he moved. It was a soldier's skill that she could mimic when she had to but couldn't do it unconsciously like he did.

Up ahead she began to notice a soft glow that was definitely not moonlight. For one, its yellow hue suggested a low fire or candlelight. The most convincing reason was that it emanated from about waist high. Cliste bound straight for it and shadows soon swallowed her. For a moment, she had hoped he had been referring to only Abigail when he said they wouldn't be alone, but then she heard voices. They were soft as if the people were whispering, and from the din, she guessed at maybe fifteen people, possibly more.

"Sean, what..." Her voice trailed off as the trees parted.

Gathered in a small clearing, seated on stumps and logs, were eighteen people, both men and women, white and Negro. Several of the men wore bandages. In the center of the group was a small fire over which sat a cauldron. An ebony-skinned man rose and hobbled over to them, leaning heavily upon a walking stick. The bandage around his leg was dark with blood.

"Thank ya for comin', Sergeant MacBranain and Miss O'Brian," he said in a deep voice filled with pain.

"You're most welcome, Jedidiah." Sean motioned to those gathered, then looked at Ashlinn. "After hearin' the stories of all you've done for the soldiers, these fine folk would like to learn your methods."

Ashlinn could hardly believe his words, even as she looked at the eager faces gazing at her from around the fire. "You... You want me to teach you?"

Surely that couldn't be what he meant. Her methods were frowned upon by nearly all the medical people she knew, and definitely by all of the doctors serving in the war.

White flashed as Jedidiah grinned. "Very much so, ma'am. If ya will have us as students."

Abigail stepped around from behind them to join the group, one shoulder ducking under Jedidiah's to help hold him up. The way her big brown eyes looked anywhere but at Ashlinn made her think the woman had more than a little to do with this.

"You all know what the doctors say about my methods, do you not?" Ashlinn asked.

The group exchanged glances, each falling at last on Jedidiah and Abigail. Jedidiah nodded to Abigail and it was she who spoke, finally meeting Ashlinn's gaze.

"They do, ma'am. But they also know dat ya patients survive, and many of dem do not lose der limbs. Ya way is better. We all know dat."

An amazing feeling began to spread out from her chest. These people wanted to learn from her. Never had she imagined anyone would acknowledge her medical skills, let alone ask her to teach them. Her ways—her father's ways—were patterned after forward-thinking doctors in Europe, men ahead of their time. People in the medical profession in America had yet to embrace practices so foreign to them. Yet here these people were asking her to teach them. Sure, they were nurses and soldiers, most of them freed slaves, but the situation was no less miraculous to her because of that small fact.

Eyes brimming with the power of her emotions, she looked up at Sean. Respect for her was etched all over his face. The last bit of the icy wall she kept around her heart melted upon seeing it. Suddenly he was no longer just a handsome man that she cared about; he was someone special and precious. A heavy breath rattled through her as she turned her attention back to the gathered crowd and nodded toward Jedidiah.

"You have wounded, I assume?"

Abigail smiled, eyes full of pride, pride in Ashlinn. Damn if these people weren't bound to make her cry tonight.

"We do, ma'am." Abigail helped Jedidiah ease down onto a blanket that spread out near the fire.

Casting Sean a smile that she hoped held all the promise of things she would say to him later, she started toward the group. "I see that you have begun to boil water, good. Clean hands and instruments are the first key to avoiding infection."

She gathered her skirts up in one hand and knelt beside Jedidiah on the blanket, wishing Sean had at least given her a clue about the nature of the night's outing so she could have worn breeches. Then again, if he had, she wasn't sure she would have come for fear of not living up to these people's expectations. But, since she was here...

"When were you wounded, Jedidiah?"

The big man grimaced as she moved aside the tattered edges of his pant leg. "Earlier this mornin', ma'am. Stepped on somethin' durin' picket duty that exploded."

Chills raced through Ashlinn. Had the Rebels come up with some new barbaric weapon that didn't even require them to be in the area? This war was truly was turning men into monsters. Shaking the thought off, she returned her focus to the task at hand.

"Bring a few of those candles closer and fetch me some of that water."

People rushed to do as she asked and soon candlelight poured over her and Jedidiah. After peeling away what remained of the man's pant leg, she drew in a deep breath and set to washing her hands. Multiple lacerations tore upward through his calf and shin, many deep enough to see muscle, one deep enough to see bone. She was going to need a lot of stitching material.

"Can ya save it, Doc?" Jedidiah whispered.

Realizing she had been quiet for some time as she planned her approach, she looked at Jedidiah and smiled. "Quite possibly. Many of these scars won't be pretty, but we can likely save your leg so long as we clean it out proper now and you keep it clean while 'tis healin'."

Moisture glistened in Jedidiah's eyes before he bowed his head. "Thank ya, missus doc, thank ya so much." The emotions in his thick voice choked Ashlinn up.

She had to swallow hard and look at his wound again to force her mind back to a medical state. Holding her hands out for Abigail to pour water that was just short of scalding over them, she began to lecture those gathered on the importance of cleaning wounds, hands, and instruments. Many knelt around her and Jedidiah in a circle, their eyes following her every move. As she talked she glanced at Sean who had seated himself upon a log in the shadows beside the fire. The pride shining in his eyes humbled her and lifted her up at the same time. That combined with what Jedidiah had said put her in an almost euphoric state that she had never even imagined possible. Doctor. The man had called her "doctor."

Chapter 19

The late-night lessons continued once a week, sometimes more often when the nurses brought a special case for Ashlinn to treat. Watching her teach brought him a measure of peace and joy he hadn't even realized had been missing in his life. She was so good at it, attentive to her pupils and instructive in the most positive way.

It was becoming difficult to find the supplies she needed. Taylor horded laudanum and opium for use on officers and those he deemed worthy, and he suspected the man was hiding iodine simply because he knew Ashlinn wanted it. At least he seemed to be backing off and avoiding her for the most part. But then, Sean's frequent visits likely had a lot to do with that.

Throughout October and into November their subtle courtship continued with long walks, visits by a communal fire, and the occasional concert he and his men put on. While she still pushed the limits of his sense of honor with her delicious kisses and suggestive caresses, that was different now. She was often content to sit and talk long into the night, or just listen to him play his violin.

Then, on November 5th, the order to march came once again. The 69th brigade and their medical personnel packed up and left Bolivar Heights behind. With all the good memories he and Ashlinn had made, he was sad to leave but glad to be on the move again. At least then it felt like they were doing something. He wanted this war won and over with so the two of them could get back to New York and begin a real courtship. The days ticked by into weeks as they marched through the cold rain to Warrenton, then to Rectortown, and on through Manassas Gap. Only the outer edges of the regiment encountered resistance, and even then the skirmishes were few and far between. Sean did his best to visit Ashlinn every night after he had checked to ensure his men were settled, but more than once he collapsed into his tent from exhaustion without seeing her. Most of those nights Cliste had come to him so he at least had been able to send Ashlinn a letter.

Finally, twelve days later, they stopped and prepared to set up a more permanent camp in Falmouth, Virginia. Though his feet ached and his muscles struggled to hold him upright, Sean saw to his men. Many shivered in their wet, woolen coats, cold fingers fumbling with tent strings and poles. After gaining his lieutenant's approval, Sean picked out five of the men who looked as though they could remain upright the longest and sent them to gather wood from a nearby area. As they turned to leave, he took the canvas tent from a soldier's hands that shook so badly he was about to drop it anyway.

"Why don't you have a seat while I get this for you, Johnny?" he said with a smile.

Nodding, Johnny sank down onto his knapsack and laid his rifle across his knees. Elbows resting just behind the weapon, his head drooped and soft snores sounded from him before Sean had even laid out the tent. By the time Corporal Fergusson—recently promoted thanks to Sean's recommendation—returned with the group gathering the firewood, he had helped erect over twenty tents. Before darkness could fall, they had two fires blazing. Warming his hands by the flames for a brief moment, Sean watched the rest of the brigade begin to cover the countryside like ants.

"Feels like we've walked the whole of Virginia durin' this blasted war. Not exactly how I wanted to see America," Fergusson said from across the fire, where he sat with his feet propped toward the flames.

"For certain. Is that what you'll be doin' after the war? Seein' the country?" Sean asked.

Fergusson nodded. "Figured I might as well. How 'bout you? Plannin' to settle down after?"

Sean fought the smile that tried to form. As he opened his mouth to respond a figure approaching behind Fergusson drew his eye and held his tongue. Followed by a retinue of nurses that paused to check each soldier they came across, Ashlinn strode with an ease that suggested she hadn't been marching all day. But Sean knew she had; she just hid her exhaustion well so no one would suggest she see to her own needs first. Giving him a smile that was genuine but not quite as big as normal, she stopped at Fergusson.

She walked around the corporal's side, ensuring he saw her before she placed a hand on his shoulder. Sean loved how sensitive she was to a soldier's quirks like that.

"How are your feet?" she asked.

"Right as rain," he said through a smile so big it could be seen through his bushy mustache.

The man was in worse need of a shave than Sean was. But then, Fergusson always wore at least a few days' shadow. The thought made him run a hand over his own bristly face and grimace.

Ashlinn dropped her bag and put a hand on one shapely hip. "I am not a lass with some weak constitution that you need to protect. The truth, out with it."

Smile falling into a look of shame, Fergusson let out a long sigh. "They hurt, but I'll live, Doc."

For a moment, the weariness dragging down Ashlinn's eyelids banished and Sean caught a glimpse of her blue eyes widening, filling with tenderness. Since she had begun teaching the other nurses back at Bolivar Heights, many of the soldiers had taken to calling her doc, and it never ceased to elicit a reaction from her. She hid it well, but Sean always saw it.

"Let's have a look then," Ashlinn said, just a trace of the tenderness from her eyes entering her voice.

She pulled over a log and sat near his feet.

As he erected a cooking pot over the fire, Sean watched them, fighting the urge to laugh at the defeated look on Fergusson's face. It wasn't so much that the man was trying to be tough and impress Ashlinn. Like himself, Fergusson wished for their men to be seen to first. The rare trait was part of why Sean was so fond of the corporal.

Grumbling about how fine he felt, Fergusson slowly unlaced and removed his boots. His socks came off much slower, sticking to his skin and making a horrible peeling sound that suggested blood might be involved. Bright red blood and the broken skin of raised blisters confirmed it. Not even cringing, Ashlinn opened her bag, removed a bottle, and took one of his feet in her hands.

"This is going to hurt," she warned a moment before she began pouring it over his wounds, catching the excess with a clean cloth.

Crying out, Fergusson flinched. "Bloody hell!"

"I warned you."

Was that humor in her tone? Sean grinned.

"You didn't say it would be like pourin' fire over my feet." Fergusson sounded like a young boy again.

"Aye, well, I thought you might be a bit tougher," Ashlinn said in all seriousness, but Sean could see the smile tugging at one corner of her mouth.

She continued to clean his blisters as she talked, effectively distracting him from the pain. When she finished, she handed him a small jar of ointment.

"Put this on the wounds and stay off your feet for as long as you can. When you must walk, wrap the wounds in this." She handed him a clean cloth. "'Tis clean, and it needs to stay that way. Let nothing that has not been boiled and dried touch your feet for at least a day. Anything else could introduce things into the wound that could cause infection."

She rose and placed his heels upon the log she vacated.

"Yes, ma'am."

The look he gave her must not have been very convincing because she turned to Sean with a hand on her hip. "You see that he does as instructed."

Sean hid his grin behind a stern look. "Yes, ma'am. I'll see that he follows your instructions to the letter." He walked around the growing fire and offered Ashlinn his arm. "I shall show you to the worst off of the men if you'd like."

Both hands going to his arm in an intimate touch of skin on skin, she smiled while he tried to swallow his rising desire. True, it was only her palms on his arm, but even that touch made him light-headed. "Thank you, Sergeant MacBranain, but you have work here to do. The other nurses and I can manage."

She turned away, leaving him chilled, but the warmth of her gaze flooded over him again as she cast him a heavy-lidded look over her shoulder. "But I shall be back to ensure that you are properly watchin' over Corporal Fergusson there."

The slip of her accent made that warmth spread down to his groin, stirring much more than her touch alone had. With a slight inclination of her head to both him and Fergusson, she strode off toward the tents.

A pinecone smacked into Sean's side, forcing his attention from the curves of Ashlinn's backside as she walked away. "Right then, quit blockin' the fire, 'cause clearly you don't need the heat anymore," Fergusson demanded.

Grinning, Sean picked up the pinecone and pitched it back, hitting Fergusson in the shoulder.

"Hey! Wounded man here. Have some respect!"

Laughter erupted from both men, easing the tension of the long march from Sean's chest. "Wounded me arse! You just wanted me lass's hands on your feet."

"You're just sore you didn't think o' it first."

While his feet were sore, he didn't feel the telltale damp that meant blisters, but still…"Aye, perhaps I am a bit at that."

He clapped Fergusson on the shoulder as he walked past. "You do as she instructed. I expect to find you right there when I return."

"Is that an order, sir?"

Though Fergusson's voice was half-teasing, Sean ensured his own answer was quite serious, otherwise he knew the man wouldn't listen. "Aye, 'tis."

With a few of the men who were in better condition at his side, they worked together to erect the remaining eighty tents. Those who couldn't move another step he helped to unroll their bedrolls and get tucked safely within. As he worked, he came across Ashlinn and her nurses from time to time, treating blisters, minor wounds, or simply bringing the men water. Their tenacity and care impressed him deeply, considering the women had marched as long and as far as the men had. It only strengthened his belief that while men may be physically stronger, women were the more enduring sex by far. Each time he encountered her they shared an affectionate look and a tender touch when they could get away with not being seen. She gave him the strength to keep going.

Quite some time after full dark had fallen, Sean and the last of his men standing erected the final tent. A chill that reached deep into his bones turned the air crisp, making it almost painful to breathe. Rubbing his hands together to get the feeling back, Sean bid his men good night and started back for the heart of the camp. The glow of the fire guided him back to where not only Fergusson sat, but a slew of others had gathered as well. Not a single woman sat among them—but then, the nurses did not linger once their work was complete. Still, he had hoped to find Ashlinn here checking on Fergusson and waiting for him. Hours had passed; surely she had finished making her rounds.

He checked Fergusson's feet, ensuring the man hadn't moved as he'd been instructed. They were still bare of bandages and warm from the fire that blazed only a few feet away. "Have you seen the doc?" he asked quietly.

Heavy-lidded eyes barely open, Fergusson shook his head. The daft fool still sat upon the bare ground leaning back against his knapsack. Sean wrapped the clean linen Ashlinn had left around both of the corporal's feet, ducked under one of his arms, and helped him rise.

"Into your tent with you, you fool. The cold ground is no place for the livin' to sleep."

He bore the majority of the bigger man's weight to keep him off his feet as much as possible as they hobbled over to his tent.

"But the fire..." Fergusson protested in a sleepy voice, reaching a hand back toward it.

"'Twill not keep the frost from coming up through the ground to freeze your arse," Sean said as he helped the man into his tent, laid him down atop his bedroll, and threw his blanket across him.

"Thanks, Sarge," he mumbled as he burrowed into the blanket.

Sean laid the man's rifle next to his bedroll, within reach but far enough away the he wasn't likely to roll over it in the night. One hand on the tent flap, a foot out into the darkness, he paused.

"Are you sure you haven't seen her?" he tried once more.

"*Brónach*, Sarge, *nil.*"

Sorry, Sarge, no.

It was no less comfort in his native language. That the man had slipped into Gaelic spoke volumes about how tired he was. Even here in America their kind were careful about when and where they spoke their language. For too long it had been forbidden to them in their own country, punishable by all manner of cruelty by any English soldiers who may overhear it. Here they were merely frowned upon for it, as if it made them less human than others.

"'Tis all right, Corporal. You get some rest," Sean told him.

Chilly fingers fumbling in the dark, Sean tied the tent flap closed to help keep the cold out. Soft chatter from the rest of the men gathered around the glow of the fire told Sean they would be aware enough to get tucked into their tents before their arses froze to the ground. Nevertheless, he stopped by to throw a few more branches into the flames, pat shoulders, and offer words of encouragement. Those illuminated by the orange glow either sat upon logs roasting squirrels or rabbits over the fire, or lounged upon blankets, their breath puffing white upon the air. None of them had seen the doc, as they called Ashlinn, since darkness had set in.

The moment he stepped away from the fire the bite in the air made him button up his coat and put his hands in his pockets. For good measure, he made another pass through the tent rows of the 69th, just to make sure Ashlinn wasn't lingering to take care of someone. Four fires blazed throughout the regiment's area, one near each set of twenty-five tents. Around each, Sean found men gathered, warming either themselves or their food, but no nurses remained. No one had seen Ashlinn for hours. Though logic told him she had likely returned to her own tent, or gone to see to the setup of the hospital tent, a nagging sensation wouldn't allow him to listen to it. Regardless, he decided to start there. The clear, star-filled sky bathed the encampment in a considerable amount of light, but it also made it much colder. He found the large hospital tent with little trouble, but Ashlinn wasn't wandering its quiet rows of cots.

Dousing the lamp, he hung it up where he had found it and stepped back out into the dark. Eyes scanning the nearby tents, he whistled low and soft. She usually erected her tent right around the vicinity of the hospital tent, but he couldn't exactly go checking in each tent for her. The general would not respond well to complaints from the nurses that he had peered into their tents. His whistle wasn't answered, and worse, Cliste didn't come bounding to him.

Unease crept up and wrapped around him, raising bumps along his skin. If the hound was anywhere in the area, she would have come to him. Slowly, he made his way through the rows of tents surrounding the hospital, whistling as he went. On occasion he stopped and listened. For good measure he made two passes through the rows of nurses' tents. Not a soul stirred in this area that he could ask about Ashlinn. Even after what felt like at least an hour of wandering, only the hoot of an owl in a nearby tree answered him.

Stomach feeling like he had swallowed a handful of lead, he stopped at the edge of the encampment where the last of the nurses' tents met the edge of a nearby forest. Cold seeped up from the ground, making him pace in place to keep his feet from going numb. On one hand the numbness would take away the pain, but on the other, he wouldn't realize it if frostbite began to set in. The air began to stiffen his nose hairs with each inhale. His concern grew into something that edged on the border of panic. It was too cold for Ashlinn to still be outside. Exhausted as he knew she had to be, her tired muscles could only keep her warm for so long.

He tipped over that edge into panic and started for the tents once again, intent on checking each one if he had to. Rustling in the bushes to his left stopped him in his tracks. A soft whine preceded the emergence of a huge gray shape that was the size of a thin bear. Breath blowing from his lips in a puff of white, Sean reached out to scratch both sides of Cliste's huge head as she reached him.

"You're a sight for sore eyes, girl," he whispered.

Again Cliste whined. That combined with how her head drooped and her tail was tucked, sent a shock of concern through him. His hands quickly checked the big hound for any wounds but didn't find any. She gave a short woof, turned, and bounded back into the trees. Dread turning to guilt, it hit him that he should have realized Ashlinn had gone searching for her brother. Any time they came to a new camp she searched the area. One hand on his rifle to keep it from bouncing, he took off after Cliste. The hound ran so quick through the underbrush and around tree trunks that he had a hard time keeping up. More than once her ghostly gray shape slid out of sight, pushing him faster. Just short of a mile or so, she finally stopped.

A body lay at the hound's paws.

Sean plunged into an all out run the last few yards, collapsing to his knees beside Cliste. Blond hair spread about her like spilt gold, Ashlinn lay upon a bed of leaves. While she wore a coat and gloves, the garments would scarcely do any good after long out in this cold. Her face was pale—even for her milky complexion—and her eyes were closed. For a moment, he couldn't breathe, couldn't speak. A panic the likes of which he hadn't felt since the IRA came for his parents clenched tight around him.

At last, he forced words past the lump in his throat. "Ashlinn, can you hear me?"

She didn't so much as stir.

"Please, angel, say somethin'," he begged through a sob as he gently shook her shoulder.

When she didn't respond, he leaned close to her face. After an agonizingly long moment, he finally felt her breath upon his cheek. Tears of relief sprung to his eyes and a breath left him in a rush. He scooped her up, cradled her against his chest, and rose to his feet. Bumps rose along his skin from her chilled body touching his. She was light as a feather—a bony feather. It made him wonder when she had eaten last. He tried to recall seeing her eat and couldn't. Food had been scarce during their long march, but he had thought she was getting enough. Head tucked down so his breath could warm her pale face, he strode toward the encampment.

Light as she was, exhaustion pulled him down with every step he took. But he refused to give in. She might die if he did, and he wouldn't let that happen. His tired muscles began to cramp but he ignored the pain. At least it made them burn, and that allowed him to forget for a while how bloody cold it was. The starlight upon Cliste's bobbing tail kept him moving forward like a beacon that promised refuge. He only hoped the hound was leading them back to camp, because as blurry as his vision was becoming, he surely couldn't do it.

A fallen limb caught his foot and sent him to a knee. The frozen ground jarred his kneecap and made him bite back a curse. Ashlinn stirred in his arms. Starlight glinted off her blue eyes as they slowly opened.

"Sean... We have to find Cliste," she said slowly, as if her tongue wouldn't work quite right.

He knew how she felt. The cold tightened his jaw muscles and made it hard for him to respond. The sound of her voice, no matter how faint, eased the weight of worry crushing his chest. "We found her, angel. Nothin' to worry about."

The wrinkles between her brows smoothed out and her eyes slid closed. Fueled by desperation, he cradled her against him again and rose to his feet. One breast moved against his chest as it rose and fell with her breaths. The feeling nearly would have made him weep with relief if he'd had the energy. Once he was up and took the first step, the forward momentum kept him moving despite the ache in his legs and arms. Scar tissue in his side popped and shifted, breaking free of the muscles it had adhered to and sending white-hot shards of pain into him. He ground his teeth against a cry and kept marching. Cliste paused to look back at him.

"Go on, I'm fine," he assured her.

The hound made a soft sound that Sean would have sworn was disagreement, but she kept going. A few heartbeats later, they emerged from the woods at the edge of the encampment. The sight of all the tents was almost enough to make Sean's knees give out. But he didn't dare give in to relief yet. Not a soul stirred within the dark camp as they made their way through the rows of tents. Being within the camp made him even more desperate to get her warm. No fires burned in this area, and he knew he'd never make it carrying her back to his section of camp. Left with no other choice, he followed Cliste, knowing the hound would take them to Ashlinn's tent.

At last, when the large hospital tent came into view, Cliste entered one of the smaller tents near it. Sean ducked inside and carried Ashlinn to the cot at the back of the tent. She stirred when he laid her down, but just barely. He returned to the tent opening, closed the flap, and tied it closed. Fumbling around in the dark, he found her trunk and more importantly, the candle that sat atop it. His searching fingers found a small wooden box, removed a lucifer from within, struck it against the iron hinge of the trunk, and set the flame to the candlewick. Meager though it was, the small flame would help heat the room. All the while Cliste sat near the cot, her head resting near Ashlinn's.

Ashlinn stirred when he began to remove her boots. Taking her freezing hand in his, he knelt by her side. "Hey, angel, I'm sorry but I'm goin' to have to remove your clothes. They're frozen solid in places and will only make you colder as they thaw." He wanted to go get Abigail or another nurse to do it for her. But she didn't have time for him to search them out. He had to get her warmed up immediately else frostbite—or worse, hypothermia—could set in. If that happened... No, he couldn't let himself slip into despair.

Her right cheek twitched twice and a moment later that corner of her mouth rose in what he thought might be an attempt at a smile. "Sean?" she asked in a voice that sounded thin as a summer fog.

Eyes squeezing shut tight against the hot tears that threatened them, Sean bent to kiss the back of her hand. "Yes, 'tis me." The chill from her skin seeped through her gloves and into him, turning his lips icy in moments. He peeled her gloves off, cringing at the white bits of frost that broke free from them and fell to the floor.

"Are you able to sit up?"

For a moment her eyes fluttered, then slowly opened back up. She only hummed a reply and her head dropped in what may have been a nod, but may also have been from exhaustion. Her body was fighting too hard to warm itself up, no doubt leaving her with very little energy.

He lifted her to her feet and held her close against him, hovering over the candle. After a few long moments, she reached out and braced herself against the nearest tent post. Drawing reluctantly away, Sean set to removing her clothing. While he was no saint, he had never removed a woman's clothing to such a degree, and it quickly confounded him. The dress was easy enough to get off but then came the underslip, her corset cover, and the corset itself. By then thankfully his fingers had warmed up enough that he could feel them and manipulate the strings of the corset.

Soon she stood in only her cream-colored silk chemise and ladies' drawers. She began to shiver and sag as if her legs would give out at any moment. Sean scooped her up and carried her once again to the cot. This time he tucked her beneath the blankets. She grabbed his hand, her grip stronger than he thought possible in her state.

"Please, do not leave."

Sitting down on the cot beside her, he began to remove his boots. "I won't. You'll never get warm enough on your own." He wanted to say more, to explain how sorry he was to break propriety and have to do this, but he couldn't lie to her. Sorry was the last possible thing he could feel about lying beside her. He also wanted to say how he would be a proper gentleman, but there was nothing proper about lying mostly naked beside a woman one wasn't married to. Yet he had to, for her sake, society views be damned. He would not let her die because others thought this improper. For her life he would compromise his honor. Hell, he would compromise anything.

Oblivious to his inner turmoil, Ashlinn had turned over. Whether she was simply nestling deeper into the blankets, or trying to give him a sense of privacy, he wasn't sure. Soon he could hear her breathing in long, steady breaths and he had his answer.

Like a bad whiskey, he forced his gentlemanly senses down and stripped to only his knee-length drawers. Skin to skin was the fastest way to warm her. As he returned to the cot, Cliste retreated to lie on a blanket in the corner of the room, seemingly satisfied that he had saved her master. The hound's absence removed the last lingering feeling of propriety. Now not even she would oversee them. Hand on the blanket, he hesitated as he fought against everything he had ever been taught. He had to do this. Her body might not warm up enough on its own.

He crawled beneath the blanket and squeezed onto the small cot beside her. Wrapping an arm around her, he pulled her up against him. Every inch of her was cold as ice. Ever so slowly, the cold receded like the withdrawing tide. For several minutes she shivered from head to toe, but it eventually passed as his body heat brought her own temperature back up.

Chapter 20

Wrapped in Sean's arms as she was, it took a while for Ashlinn to realize she was truly awake and not just dreaming. His warm, mostly naked body convinced her as surely as anything else could. She was not experienced enough with men to imagine the muscles of his chest against her back so perfectly, the swell of his bicep around her side, and the hard length of his erection against her buttocks. Especially the last part. Oh no, that was certainly not of her mind's conjuring.

The cocoon of heat coupled with the feel of so much of his skin touching hers made her want to stay in that moment forever. But moving on to the next one had its advantages as well. She wiggled her buttocks back against him more firmly, delighting in the feel of his erection moving against her seemingly of its own accord. It was horribly wicked, but she couldn't help it. He felt so amazing, and she had longed for him for months now.

She went still as his hand moved down to her hip slowly, as if luxuriating in the feel of her curves, and gripped it firmly. Heat flushed not only between her legs but to her cheeks as well. He was awake! Mortification should have been her first response, she knew, but excitement coursed through her instead.

"If yah don't stop movin' like that, angel, you'll undo the last thread of my control," he whispered against her ear.

Both the feather-soft touch of his breath and the husky tone of his voice made her want to do exactly that. And the way he called her "angel" scattered the last bits of any need she may have had to maintain propriety. Head arching back so his lips touched her neck, she wiggled her buttocks against him again. Sean groaned, the sound coming out against her neck in a wonderful vibration.

"Lettin' go of your control does not mean lettin' go of your honor," she whispered to him.

She turned her head so she could see him. His heavy-lidded eyes were brown pools of desire shot through with copper. White teeth gripped his bottom lip as if in an attempt to hold back words or something far more physical.

"Honor isn't colored by whether or not you lie with a woman, but what you do afterward," she pressed.

Neck arching to bring her closer, her tongue darted out and traced a line along his lower lip. Suddenly his hand was cradling one of her nearly bare breasts and his lips were molding to hers. Overloaded by the amazing sensation of his fingers kneading her breast through her thin silken chemise, she allowed his tongue free reign of her mouth.

For so long she had wanted this so badly that she couldn't believe it was actually happening. To have him finally letting go of his strict beliefs in propriety felt almost as good as the things his hands and tongue were doing. Her tongue followed his back into the warmth of his mouth, and he let it. Fingers gently squeezed her nipple, drawing a moan from her that flowed into his mouth. Heat flushed from her breast all the way down between her legs, slickening the folds of her labia. A cry of protest almost escaped her as his hand slid from her breast and began to follow the curve of her hip. It turned into another sound entirely as he worked under the edge of her chemise and his fingertips pushed under the band of her drawers, touching her bare stomach. Her breathing quickened and she began to shiver with the force of her need.

Footsteps splashed in muddy water outside the tent, tearing her forcibly from her near-delirious state of joy. Sean's hand froze at her pubic hairline, making her want to scream. Silently, she begged for the footsteps to continue on, but they didn't.

"Miss O'Brian, I have come to check on why you have not reported for work this morning. Are you all right?" came Doctor Taylor's nasally voice.

The sound was like a bucket of ice water pouring over her desire. In the midst of her broiling anger she couldn't find her voice.

"Miss O'Brian? Are you in there?"

She looked at Sean, seeing the same toxic mixture of desire and anger building in his coppery eyes like a storm.

"Do you need medical attention, Miss O'Brian?" Fingers brushed against canvas and the tent flap moved a bit.

The bastard was actually going to come in!

"No, Doctor Taylor! I am fine. I was out late seeing to the soldiers and have overslept. I will be along shortly," she called out quickly.

"Are you sure you did not get any frostbite? I can check if you would like." The suggestive tone of his voice made her gorge rise.

Sean went rigid as stone beside her, the rest of his body suddenly as hard and unyielding as his erection.

"I am fine. And of course not. It would not be proper for you to enter my tent. I will be along shortly. Off with you!"

Another set of footsteps approached, these quick and short. "Dat isn't necessary, Doctor Taylor. I shall see to Miss O'Brian." Tension eased from Ashlinn at the sound of Abigail's voice.

"I am afraid I have to insist. If she was out late, chances are good that she has frostbite. I must check on her myself."

The tent flap moved, outlining a backside as if someone had leaned against it. "Ya most surely won't. Ain't proper, as de lady said. De new General Burnside would send ya packin' if ya tried," Abigail said.

Ashlinn wanted to hug the woman for her tenacity. While she wasn't so sure herself about how much the new general cared about the nurses' treatment, she loved that Abigail put that fear into Taylor.

Teeth gnashed, punctuated by a low growl. Water splashed, followed by a very unmanly yelp. Ashlinn hadn't even realized Cliste was outside until then.

"Fine then. If you are well enough, Miss O'Brian, there is work to be done and you need to get to it," Taylor snapped. Thankfully, his harsh words were followed by the splash of retreating steps.

Soft laughter sounded. "Good dog." After a few moments Abigail's whisper carried through the canvas. "Ya take ya time, Miss Ashlinn. Ain't no one else out here, just in case someone in der might wanna leave without bein' seen."

A long breath eased from Ashlinn. Sean's hand retreated from her drawers. He rolled over and sat up, facing away from her. Dread filled her as she realized he was reaching for his clothes. Sitting up beside him, she put a hand on his arm to stop him.

"Do not let that bastard ruin what we started," she whispered.

When he looked at her the regret in his eyes chilled her more than last night's frost had. Her reaction must have shown because his eyes softened and he cupped her cheek with one hand.

"If he'd caught us, you'd be labeled ruined, regardless of my intentions after the fact. I can't bear the idea of anyone thinkin' ill of you because o' me."

She leaned into his palm and trapped his hand against her face with her own. "Your opinion is the only one that matters to me. Truly." What else could she do to make him understand that?

Head turning away, Sean cast his gaze to the ground. "I'm not worth such an honor, literally. I'm practically penniless and can only get into society functions if I'm playin' the violin at them."

Rising to her feet, she walked around in front of him and lifted his face so he would look up at her. "After all I have seen and done in this war I cannot possibly imagine puttin' up with 'proper society' functions. Livin' is what matters, not parties and society ladies hangin' off my every word."

A thoughtful look entered his eyes. Knowing she had his attention now, she went on. "Those ladies only ever did so because of the coin my family possessed. Behind my back they talked about me, the woman who played at bein' doctor. They would never truly accept me, and I do not want them to."

He closed his eyes as if he could no longer look at her.

"Is it your pride that will not allow you to live off my family's fortune? Because that would be a foolish reason to keep us apart." She regretted the words as soon as they spilled from her lips, and yet she didn't. It needed to be said.

Shaking his head, he rose, arms going around her. "No, 'tis not that. I would not allow such a petty thing to keep us apart, though of course I do wish I could afford to give you the life you deserve of my own accord."

She relaxed against him, reveling in the feel of his skin against hers, even if the touch would only be brief. "What is it then?"

"If I ruin you, word will get around. And if I die…" He paused and swallowed hard before giving her a direct look that sent chills across her. "Then few will have you. It would destroy me to be the reason your choices diminished."

Sadness made her smile feel false. "Has it not occurred to you that I would not want any other?"

White surrounded his eyes as they grew wide. His mouth opened and moved, but no words came out. To relieve him of his torture, Ashlinn rose up on the balls of her feet and covered his open mouth with hers. As he returned her kiss with fervor, lips working against hers in a way nothing short of magical, she knew she had gotten through to him.

"I's sorry, Miss Ashlinn, but de sun is comin' up. De camp will be awake soon." Abigail's quiet voice came from outside the tent.

Letting out a reluctant groan, Ashlinn drew back. "You had better go. I do not want word of you stayin' here gettin' back to your commandin' officer," she said.

Not caring what others thought was one thing, but allowing her desires to get Sean in trouble was another entirely. That she would not do. Echoing her groan, he stepped back and picked up his clothing. She took great pleasure in drinking in the sight of his toned, naked chest in the dim light, the swell of his erection pushing against his thin drawers. The last thing in the world she wanted to do was let him walk out of this tent, but she had to, for his sake.

One leg in his breeches, he paused. "You have to promise me one thing."

"O' course."

His expression became so serious it was almost stern. "Don't go out alone, especially at night. 'Tisn't safe for a woman."

The words made her bristle with indignation at the idea of a woman not having the same freedom a man did. But as much as she wanted to, she couldn't argue. It was true. Eyes going automatically to the folded blanket on the floor where Cliste slept, she took a deep breath.

"I wouldn't be alone. Cliste would be with me."

He leveled a hard look at her. "She wasn't exactly capable of carrying you back. Which brings to mind, what were the two of you doing all the way out there?"

She sighed. "At each new camp Cliste searches for my brother's hound. She usually doesn't go that far..." She couldn't finish, couldn't tell him how she had become desperate with hope that Cliste's wanderings would lead her to Michael.

Kneeling down on the floor beside the cot, Sean took her face in his hands. "Please promise me you won't do it again. You could have died."

The agony in his voice tugged at something deep inside her and she slowly nodded. He had risked his own life to save hers. She couldn't deny him, or put him in danger again. And besides, they hadn't found Michael despite searching for hours in the woods.

Satisfied, Sean flew into a flurry of action. In between each bit of clothing he donned, he came back and planted a quick kiss on her lips. By the time he was pulling his boots on she was delirious with joy from his attentions. One button of his coat done up and rifle slung over his shoulder, he pulled her into an embrace, his tongue finding hers again. Step by step, he backed up to the tent opening, holding her close and exploring her mouth all the while. Finally, Ashlinn drew back and did up the last few buttons on his coat.

"Is it clear, Abigail?" she whispered.

"Yes, ma'am" came her deep whisper.

Fixing Sean with a hard stare, Ashlinn placed her hands on his chest. "This is not over."

He grinned like a young lad. "'Course not."

Satisfied, she returned the smile, spun him around, and pushed him out the tent flap. Letting him walk out was possibly the hardest thing she had ever done. Yet knowing what they had started would continue gave her the strength to do it.

Chapter 21

The last of his dried meat and hardtack downed, Sean sat in the relative seclusion of his tent and cleaned his rifle. Pale light just began to seep through the canvas walls when he heard the telltale sounds of tents being taken down and equipment loaded up nearby. Pulling his boots back onto his aching—though thankfully blister-free—feet, he steadied himself for what he would discover.

Not a bit of frost remained on the soggy ground. Last night's freeze must have been a fluke. Still, the bite in the air suggested it couldn't be more than ten degrees or so above freezing. Slinging his clean rifle over his shoulder, he started through the misty light of dawn toward the sounds. Through the rows of tents he could see the next company over from his rapidly breaking camp. He approached a burly man with stripes on his coat sleeves.

"Leavin' so soon, Sarge?" he asked the man.

The man nodded to him as he continued to tie his tent to the top of his knapsack. "That we are, and you'll no doubt be following us soon."

Though his heart sank, he did his best to keep his expression neutral. "On our way to put down more of the Rebs?" he asked with mock enthusiasm.

He wanted to win this war, he truly did, but his men needed rest before they could be at their best. Without it, they would die as easily from exhaustion as from a Rebel bullet. The other sergeant stood and leaned close to Sean.

"The new general is sending us to march on Fredericksburg. President Lincoln just sent word of his blessing. I imagine the general will send your Fighting Irish on a special route."

Sean forced a grin and clapped the man on the shoulder. "You know the 69th, *Fàg An Bealach*. We'll get it done for you."

Clear the way. It was what his regiment did, so much so that it had become their battle cry. The English among the other regiments didn't much appreciate it, but they respected what the 69th did for them.

The sergeant returned the grin with such fervor that his dimples pushed back his sideburns. "You always do. A fine group of fellas you lot are." He clapped Sean on the shoulder in return, hefted his knapsack onto his shoulder, tipped his cap, and turned to give orders to his men.

Heart heavy, Sean returned to his camp. He went from tent to tent, spreading the news to clean their weapons, eat, and rest up, because they would be on the march again soon. Knowing tongues were prone to wagging, he left out the details but made it clear that the matter was pressing. Though they groaned and protested, his men did as he bid. Green eyes narrowing as he coaxed the coals of last night's fire back to life, Fergusson shook his head when Sean gave him the news.

"One general refuses to run us into the ground, so they remove him and assign us another," he grumbled.

Eyebrow rising, Sean shook his head at the man. "Careful now. Talk like that will get you pulled up on charges."

Fergusson waved a hand dismissively and threw a few pieces of wood onto the burgeoning flames. "No worries. I wouldn't say that to anyone but you." The man's short-trimmed beard moved as his cheeks pulled up into a grin. "Found that lass of yours last night, did yah?"

Heat scorched Sean's cheeks before he could stop it, revealing more than he would ever say, even to Fergusson. The over-muscled corporal laughed deep and hearty. "So yah did! I take it she's right as rain then?"

"Aye, but just barely. I found her collapsed out in the woods. She had gone lookin' for that hound o' hers."

He wouldn't have revealed so much to any other man in fear of him using the information to entice Ashlinn away from camp. Not that any of his men would do such a thing, or any of the 69th for that matter. But he couldn't speak for those of the other brigades and he had heard stories.

Concern furrowed Fergusson's brow. "'Tis a dangerous thing for a woman to be out alone." He echoed Sean's thoughts.

"Aye, I told her as much."

"Did she find Cliste?" Fergusson asked

Sean rolled his eyes and nodded. "Cliste is the one that led me to Ashlinn."

"Right smart dog, that one."

As they talked the camp began to awaken around them. Men from their company made their way out to sit by the fire and either clean their weapons or warm their breakfast. The moment they seemed idle, Sean took those that were well enough out to a nearby field and began to run them through reloading drills. It was the easiest drill he could think of, one that would keep them off their sore feet for the most part. While he wanted them rested, he also needed to keep their minds sharp and their skills even sharper. That, and he didn't want their new general getting word that his company was being lax. The 69th hadn't earned the name of the Fighting Irish by being lax. His lads were the best in the regiment as far as he was concerned, and he didn't want anyone thinking otherwise.

The day passed by at an agonizing pace with no sign of Ashlinn. Thankfully, the orders to march never came, either. Sean struggled to remain focused on readying his men for battle yet again, but all he could think of was Ashlinn's soft skin beneath his fingers, her warm body pressed up against his. In a way, these thoughts confirmed his lieutenant's fears, but he hoped his dedication to drills and readiness cancelled them out. The last thing he needed was to be busted back down to private if the man thought he was getting distracted.

Set up at the southern border of the encampment as they were, he also saw to it that a few of his men ran picket duty along the tree line. No one had required it of them, but Sean figured it was better to be safe than sorry. The perpetually gray sky began to swallow the sun but the clouds choked out all color that the sunset tried to cast. At first the silhouette striding toward him at a pace that could barely be called a walk, outlined by the fading light, looked like a man. But as the coat flapped with the breeze it revealed shapely hips and a bust that no man Sean had ever known possessed. The figure drew closer, moving with a light-footed gait he knew all too well. Hair all done up beneath her cap, Ashlinn's flushed face with its high cheekbones, blue eyes, and milky skin were all woman. Her full lips reminded him of how they had started the morning and sent blood rushing to his groin. The too-wide eyes belied a concern that cooled his desire.

"What 'tis the matter?" he asked when she reached him.

"'Tis Cliste. I cannot find her anywhere. Have you seen her?"

Sean thought back. "No." He turned to Fergusson. "Have you?"

Fergusson shook his head.

"'Tis odd, she always visits us durin' the day," Sean pondered aloud.

Brow furrowing deeper, Ashlinn turned toward the trees. "For days she has been disappearing for longer periods of time than normal, and now, this 'tis the second day she has not come back to me at all."

By the direction of her gaze and the look of desperation on her face, he knew what she was thinking. "I'll help you look for her," he said.

"As will I," Fergusson piped in.

Sean clapped him on the shoulder. "Thank you, my friend. But I need you here to ready the men if the word to march comes."

Much more lay behind his reasoning than that, but he couldn't say so aloud. To do so would harm Fergusson's ego. The man's feet were still healing and Sean wouldn't risk him injuring them worse, not with a pending march looming on the horizon.

Fergusson winked and gave him a knowing look. "You can count on me, Sarge."

Nodding to his friend, Sean walked with Ashlinn toward the edge of the tree line, having to lengthen his stride to keep up.

"I did as you asked and did not venture anywhere alone. But when I could not find her, I began to get desperate," Ashlinn said as they walked, though truly the pace was almost a jog.

"I can see that. You think we'll find her in the forest again?" He asked the obvious question, for she was leading him there after all.

Once they had left the tents behind, the clean, damp air became easier to breath. But Sean didn't dare relax. Enough poplars and birch trees choked the monstrous white oaks to hide the entire Rebel army. Orange, yellow, and red leaves littered the forest floor, but the trunks and branches were numerous enough that a careful soldier could easily conceal himself behind them. The thought made him reach back to touch the stock of the rifle slung over his shoulder.

"Aye," Ashlinn mumbled in response as she marched into the forest without hesitation.

Red oak leaves disturbed by her boots flipped up around her feet, looking like blood splashing on the other fallen leaves. A shudder went through him at the thought. He grabbed her arm and stopped her.

"Careful now. Rebel scouts could be anywhere out here," he said softly.

Her eyes opened wide as she turned toward him. "Then she is in even more danger."

She tried to pull away but he held her fast, reaching out to grip her other arm as well. "We'll find her, don't fret. But we must be careful."

Whether it was his soft voice or pleading tone, he wasn't sure, but something made the desperation in her eyes fade a bit and he was grateful for it. Swallowing hard and blinking back tears, she nodded. His hand slid down the length of her arm and he wove his fingers through hers. As daring and intimate as the gesture was, he surprised himself by doing so without hesitation or even second-guessing the act. Her palm felt warm and wonderful against his. The state she was in made him feel bad for taking pleasure in her touch at such a moment, until he saw a look of calm come over her.

With a great amount of effort, he tore his eyes from her magnetic gaze and scanned the forest around them. His keen gaze fell across only the varying shades of brown and white tree trunks. The occasional late bird that hadn't been driven off by the cooler weather sang from the skeletal treetops. It all looked and sounded harmless enough, but since his time in this war he had learned that nothing was as harmless as it seemed.

He leaned close to Ashlinn's ear. "Don't call for her, 'tis too dangerous. Besides, you won't need to. She'll hear our footsteps and smell us."

The crease in her brow and downward turn of her lips told him she disagreed, but she nodded anyway. Hand in hand, they crept deeper into the woods, losing light by the minute. As a violinist, the only things Sean knew about tracking was what the war had taught him. Perhaps he should have brought Fergusson along after all. The man had eyes as good as dog's nose or better. After nearly half an hour of searching he began to feel quite useless, and quite worried about the shadows of twilight crawling across the forest floor. At the edge of one such shadow, something caught his eye.

Something pale, slightly square in shape, flat, and about the size of a playing card lay atop a bed of red and orange leaves. He bent to inspect it and recognized it immediately. A cracker. The scent it gave off told him it wasn't just any cracker, but a sweet cracker like the one he had at the ball months ago.

"What would that be doing out here?" Ashlinn whispered.

While part of him wanted to believe it was from soldiers on picket duty, he knew better. Sweet crackers like this were a rare treat and if a soldier were lucky enough to have one, he certainly wouldn't have dropped it and left it behind. Another, darker suspicion began to surface, one that made a lot more sense.

"I'm afraid someone might be usin' them to lure Cliste out here."

Ashlinn shook her head. "But why? Who?"

He waited, knowing she would figure it out. Her brow smoothed and her eyes went as cold as a New York winter. "Taylor, that son of a bitch."

Shocked, and a little impressed, Sean almost smiled. He shared her sentiment, and then some. If that man was luring Cliste out here, it was likely to get her away from Ashlinn so he could approach her unchallenged when Sean wasn't around. Sean wanted to kill him for it. The force of that desire scared him, considering he didn't even want to kill Rebel soldiers until they were trying to kill him. But they threatened *him*; this man threatened something far more precious than Sean's own life.

Leaves crunched at a quick pace coming toward them from the left. Rifle swinging around, Sean stepped between Ashlinn and the sound. She pressed up against his back, hands on his shoulders. Was it two people? No, the cadence was wrong. An animal moving swiftly on all fours from the sound of the footfalls. His hammering heart slowed and his finger moved away from the trigger as a huge gray shape bound through the tree trunks toward them.

Moving around him, Ashlinn went to a knee. "Cliste!" To his relief she said it so softly the name was almost a whisper.

Tail wagging as if nothing were wrong in her world, Cliste bounded to Ashlinn and promptly licked her face. Ashlinn endured it with a smile, scratching behind the hound's ears vigorously. Their greeting complete, Ashlinn drew back and shook a finger at Cliste. The hound's ears lay down and she ducked her head as if ashamed.

"You have got to stop runnin' off, girl. We are in the middle of a war here," she chastised quietly.

A crawling sensation began to work its way up Sean's spine. Rather than turn his head and look around them, he smiled at the pair as if nothing were amiss and tried to see out of his peripheral vision. No movement nor even a sound revealed itself, but the feeling remained. He had come to trust that feeling, a soldier's intuition some of the men called it, and he wasn't about to discount it now. Feigning ignorance, he went to scratch Cliste, whose eyes were now darting about.

"Let's go, girl. Time to get back," he said, hoping she took the hint to be discreet, if dogs could do such a thing.

She bounded in the direction of the camp at an easy pace that would quickly outdistance them, considering the length of her gangly legs. Trying to scan the area as casually as possible, he took Ashlinn's hand and started after Cliste. The smile he pasted on wasn't all for show. He was glad they had found the hound before whoever was making the skin along the back of his neck prickle did.

"We'd best keep up with her," he said with a laugh that he hoped sounded genuine.

The gleam of happiness left Ashlinn's eyes and the corners of her smile wilted, but only a little. She accepted his arm with an enthusiasm that he could only tell was faked because he knew her so well. Her head remained pointed in the direction they traveled, but her gaze darted from side to side.

"We should indeed. We do not want to lose her again," she said with false cheer.

Her hip brushed his as she pulled him closer than was necessary and picked up a brisk pace that had him lengthening his stride to keep up with. Bumps rose along the exposed skin of her arm and he had a suspicion it wasn't because of the dropping temperature. Clearly, she had either felt the presence of someone else in the forest as well or had picked up on the fact that he had. He loved that rare quality about her, that intelligence that had no doubt kept her alive so long during this war.

As they quickly left the forest behind and started across the open field, he couldn't help but shiver as the skin of his back prickled with warning. Several agonizingly long moments later, they finally entered the safety of the tents. He would be having a very serious conversation with Taylor on the morrow. For now, he only wanted to get Ashlinn somewhere safe and warm.

Chapter 22

The bad feeling that came over Ashlinn in the woods only grew worse upon waking and discovering the regiment was packing up and marching yet again. Word among the nurses and doctors was that they were headed to Culpepper, a blessedly short distance away. In her breeches and wool coat, hair wound into a bun tucked beneath her cap, she prepared for her trek.

When she had loaded her trunk and tent onto the supply wagon, Abigail had asked her to join the other nurses there, but she had politely refused. It wasn't because some would look upon her unfavorably for riding with the Negro nurses; she couldn't care less about what others thought. Walking helped keep her blood flowing, kept her warm. More importantly right now, though, it allowed her to keep a better eye on Cliste. She wasn't about to let the wayward hound out of her sight. And it didn't hurt that she might get a chance to see Sean's company marching in the distance.

The temperature felt barely above freezing, but the longer she walked, the more she warmed up. Clouds threatened rain but never quite unleashed it, as if they were waiting for the perfect moment. Marching pace was a bit slower than she wanted to go right now, but she kept back alongside the nurse's wagon as best she could. Not knowing what they were walking into, she wanted to stay close to both her friend and her medical supplies. She was happy to leave Falmouth behind, regardless of their short stay. The only thing she regretted was not having had the chance to confront Dr. Taylor about luring Cliste into the woods. Once the march was over, she planned to make that her first task.

They had nearly reached Culpepper when the regiment veered south and kept marching. Ashlinn watched the steeple of a church poking up through the bare trees as it faded away in the distance. For a while, she clung to the hope that they were merely marching toward a suitable camp, but that hope faded with each minute that passed. Much to her relief, they came across no resistance. Hours later, as the sun darkened the evening sky, they crested a small hill and the whole of the Union army stretched out before them like white moths across a cream and brown landscape. So many tents...just beyond them wound the bank of the Rappahannock River.

Across that murky brown water she could just make out the first buildings on the outskirts of what one soldier told her was Fredericksburg. Apparently, the general had either changed his mind or had taken them purposefully on a detour. Either way, relief made her knees weak as the first lines of the 69th regiment began to set up camp. It had been a short march, but she was still exhausted from the grueling one they had finished only a few days ago. Which meant the soldiers, who had no wagon in which to rest, were no doubt in worse shape. After helping set up Abigail's tent and then her own, she took up her medical bag and went to check on the men with Cliste in tow.

Being one of the last regiments to arrive, the 69th was setting up camp farther back from the river. Normally Ashlinn liked being close to bodies of water so she had easier access for cooking, cleaning, and bathing. But the amount of soldiers here—numbering in the tens of thousands—gave her a bad feeling. The way the tents faced the river and the sheer amount of soldiers on picket duty along it made her suspect the river had a key part to play in what was going to unfold.

The urge to rush to find Sean wasn't as strong as it usually was, but then, this was one of the shortest marches they had been on so far. And it didn't hurt that they had seen no resistance. She took her time seeing to the men of the 69th, ensuring they were all properly cleaning their wounds and had poultice for their blisters. So many of the faces were new to her that she couldn't immediately recall all of their names. They died so quickly it was hard to keep up with the new recruits. But despite the cap and breeches, most knew her on sight. Those few survivors that did remain were quick to teach the new ones to respect her for all she did for them. They were good Irish lads, every one of them.

As they listened to her instructions intently, laughed, and played with Cliste, her mind kept picturing them dead and dismembered. This place had such a bad feel to it that she couldn't stop such morbid fears from manifesting. Their kindness touched her so deeply that it threatened to choke her up, but she soldiered through it. Such loyalty instilled a deep sense of pride within her, making her want to be strong for them.

"There's the best doc the 69th has ever seen" came Fergusson's voice from behind her.

She turned to see both Fergusson and Sean striding toward her. Almost too late, she remembered to tone down her smile so she didn't look like a smitten fool. Thankfully, Cliste bound toward the men, drawing attention from her.

"And there is the most flattering corporal the 69th has ever seen," she answered.

Laughing deeply, Fergusson bowed his head to her. "Guilty as charged."

One hand perched upon her hip; she narrowed her gaze at him. "Mmmhmm. Guilty, no doubt. Have you been caring for those blisters as I instructed?"

Fergusson straightened and drew a cross in the air above his heart. "O' course, Doc O'Brian. I'm a good patient, remember?"

"Well, you had best be getting off your feet soon or you will prove that statement wrong. I want you to rest those feet before"—she gestured around them—"all this comes to a head."

His short mustache drooped a bit as his smile faded, but he recovered quickly enough with another bow. "As you instruct."

He strode over to a group of soldiers outside of a tent and sat down on one of the vacant logs among them. Her gaze shifted back to Sean, who began to rise from where he'd been crouched to scratch Cliste. From beneath too-long brown hair, his eyes regarded her with sadness. She pretended not to see it as he offered her his arm.

"May I escort you on your rounds?" he asked.

She shook her head but accepted his arm. "I am finished with my rounds, but you may escort me safely back to my tent."

As he bowed his head, tipping his face in her direction, she saw a sexy smile that was meant for her eyes only. "That would be wise, as there are a lot of other regiments here and not all of them may treat a lady as honorably as the 69th would."

Much as she hated to, she gently extracted her arm from his as they began to walk. "True, but 'tis best not to betray my disguise."

He cocked his head. "So there is a drawback to you in those breeches."

Eyes widening, she gave him a coy look. "Are you insinuating that there are advantages other than those I am aware of?"

Though he kept walking, his eyes closed for a moment as if in indulgence. "Insinuating. How can you make a word sound so delicious?"

She smacked him in the chest, trying to ignore how the hard feel of his chest made muscles in her lower abdomen tighten. He laughed, the sound having nearly the same effect on her.

"Oh aye, there are definitely advantages aplenty," he said.

Out of habit, they walked toward the outskirts of the encampment, gravitating toward somewhere more private. The light of a cloud-filtered afternoon sun gave the encampment a false softness that Ashlinn found very ironic.

When they were away from curious ears, she finally asked the question that had been burning within her since they'd veered away from Culpepper. "Why is the entire army here?"

Sean sighed long and deep. "To take Richmond, but first we have to get through the forces at Fredericksburg."

The shock nearly stilled Ashlinn's feet. She had to force herself to keep walking. "But 'tis a town filled with innocents, not just soldiers."

Pain flashed across Sean's face as his features pinched. "Aye, I know. But taking it will give us a tactical advantage that General Burnside thinks will help lead us to a major victory." From the forced sound of his words, it was clear he did not agree.

Ashlinn wanted to touch him, hold his hand, show her support for him in some way, but she didn't dare, not with so many strangers around. The expression on his face told her he didn't want to harm the citizens of the town any more than she did.

"Perhaps the townsfolk will evacuate," she suggested.

He nodded, leading them a bit farther away from the last line of tents toward a massive willow tree. "Some of the men on picket duty report seein' people leavin' the town, but as they leave, Reb soldiers move in on the other side of the river." Words halting, he looked deeply into her eyes, as if contemplating how much more to say.

"Anything you tell me will not be repeated, Sean, have no worries," she coaxed gently.

The smile he gave her said he figured as much. "There are only forty thousand or so Rebs on the other side. If we can cross soon, chances are they may not even resist."

Hope blossomed in her chest, a warm, dangerous thing. "How wonderful would it be if the final battle of this war was won without a single shot?"

Fast as a water snake, his hand darted out, grabbed her arm, and pulled her behind the willow tree. Grinning like a misbehaving lad, he pressed her against the tree trunk and placed his hands to either side of her head.

"Almost as wonderful as this," he whispered as he leaned closer.

His soft lips covered hers and suddenly the war melted away. Nothing mattered but his body pressing against hers, the heat of his flesh finding its way through all their layers of clothing, even their wool coats. That warmth caused her nipples to harden when even the cold hadn't. Her reaction to him made her curious, excited, and intrigued. Sighing into his mouth, she wrapped her arms around his waist, pulling him as close as she could. She wanted to experience more of him and these wondrous sensations, but he drew away all too soon.

Thunder rumbled overhead, shaking the ground ever so slightly. Had he sensed the thunder? Was that why he drew away? Eyes still half closed, breath coming too fast, she tried to gather her senses. Oddly, Sean wasn't looking at her; his head was turned and his gaze cast out. Following his eyes, she saw the distant gray shape of Cliste bounding through the tree-dotted field away from them.

"Cliste, come here, girl," Sean called in a somewhat hushed voice.

The hound's head lifted from the dead, frost-brittle grass, ears perking up as much as her bent-over ears could.

"Come, Cliste!" Ashlinn commanded in a voice no louder than the one Sean had used.

Tail wagging as if she hadn't a care in the world, the hound came bounding toward them. With those long legs of hers, she was at their side in a matter of moments, tongue lapping at their hands. Again thunder rumbled, causing Cliste to cower down, dropping her head below the level of her shoulders.

"Good girl," Ashlinn said as she petted her head, calming her.

The warmth of Sean's body retreated from hers, drawing a reluctant sound from her throat. His smile warmed her sufficiently. "Best keep a close eye on her while we're here."

Ashlinn nodded in answer.

They ducked out from beneath the scraggly, leafless branches of the dormant willow and started back toward camp. Dark gray clouds roiled overhead, pressing down upon them as if the sky itself wanted to wash this war away. In the short time they had been hidden beneath the willow tree, the temperature had dropped low enough to raise bumps along the exposed flesh of her neck. Storm or no, the memory of that kiss would keep her core warm well into the night.

Chapter 23

In the early morning light, Sean made his way across a half-frozen landscape dotted with more tents than trees. Frosty mud crunched beneath his boots as he approached the hospital tent. He longed for the weight of his rifle, having had to leave it back at his tent. On one hand, it wasn't prudent to walk about camp without it; on the other, if he had brought it, he feared he'd be tempted to use it.

Knowing the doctor's tent would be around the back, he skirted around, thankful that he was the only soul out and about in this part of camp. The slightly larger tent with its chair and table out front was impossible to miss. Pulling his gloved hand from his wool coat, he paused to take a breath before rapping on the tent. He had to keep his head about him, for if he lost his temper, he had no idea what he would do to the doctor.

"Taylor, I would speak with you. Step out this instant," he called loud enough to stir the man.

Rustling came from within. Several moments later Taylor threw the tent flap open and glared at Sean from beneath his bushy brows. With a blanket clutched around him and untied boots upon his feet, he looked more fool than menace.

"What do you want?" he demanded.

"To know why you lured Ashlinn's hound into the woods."

The man didn't even have the decency to look shocked. Instead his eyes narrowed and he half-smiled. "It is no fault of mine if Miss O'Brian loses track of that despicable animal."

Fury burned through Sean's common sense. His hand darted out and grabbed hold of the blanket around Taylor. He yanked him closer. "If you do anythin' to hurt either her or her hound, God help me but I will—"

The pressure of something cold and hard against his throat halted his words. A slight movement caused a sharp pain as a blade sliced through the first few layers of his skin. He froze. Taylor's sneering face leaned closer until Sean could see the flecks of tobacco between his bottom teeth and smell his rank breath.

"You will do what, mick?"

Darkness framed the edges of Sean's vision as his control over his temper dissolved. Faster than the doctor could ever hope to be, Sean snatched the man's hand and pulled it down, away from his throat. In one easy move, he twisted Taylor's wrist at an odd angle until the scalpel in it clattered to the table beside them. Holding on to his wrist, Sean used it as leverage to pull Taylor into him as he thrust his fist into the man's face. Whimpering, Taylor scrambled backward, stopping when he got tangled in the tent flap. Wide, fearful eyes stared at Sean.

"Or I will kill you. Do not doubt it for a moment," Sean said in a voice colder than the December air.

Disgusted, and not trusting himself to keep up his restraint, he turned from the sight of the cowering man and stormed off. Taylor didn't even have the bollocks to call out a tart response. Sean hoped, for the doctor's sake, he had the wisdom to heed the warning.

* * * *

Days passed as they waited for the pontoons to arrive that would help them build a bridge across the Rappahannock. The soldier's itch for action began to plague Sean's company on the third day. Snow began to fall on the fourth. Considering the pontoons were supposed to be coming from the same direction the weather was, it came as no surprise that they were late. To keep his men busy and warm, Sean had them running drills whenever they weren't assigned to picket duty. The constant watch of his superiors made visiting Ashlinn difficult. He had to be content with proper conversation when she did her rounds to check on the health of the men in his company. That, and of course the letters they shared through Cliste.

It was for the best, or so he told himself when he couldn't sleep at night from missing her touch. But her words from that morning when they had nearly crossed the point of no return rang in his memory like bells trying to wipe away his doubt. Honor lay in what he did after he bed her, if he did. He wanted to believe with every fiber of his being that such a thing was true. She believed it was true. Slowly he was coming to realize that might be all that mattered.

Boredom made the other regiments all too observant of his interactions with her. He couldn't have them thinking she was anything less than a lady, else they may think they could take advantage of her. So he waited and cooled his desire with exercise and the frigid air that wrapped around everything. The one good thing about waiting was that his men healed and caught up on their rest. They became sharper, more focused, finishing drills with precision and in record time.

At night he rewarded them with the occasional concert to lift their spirits, and to soothe his own. Ashlinn, Abigail, and a few of the other nurses often made it to these, but they sat separate from the soldiers and mingled with them very little. At least he was able to watch her across the firelight, and even entice her to sing once in a while. Abigail surprised them all by having a lovely, soulful singing voice as well, and she was easier to entice to sing.

Days ticked by. The number of Rebel troops across the river doubled. Now instead of outnumbering them by at least three times, the Potomac army less than doubled their enemy's numbers. Two weeks later, during a night while Abigail sang a mournful song that had moisture shining in many of the men's eyes, word came that the pontoons were arriving. For a few moments the men were elated, and hope spread through them like wildfire, driving away the cold and their impatience.

After two more days of heavy snowfall and still not being able to build the bridges, that hope began to wane. Day after day, snow continued to fall with a fury that seemed determined to stop the crossing. It melted quickly, but that only made a muddy, frosty mess. Patience all but gone, Sean's company hardly responded when word came on December 10th that they were to prepare to cross. But the next night, when the engineers began constructing three bridges under the light of the moon, their hope for action was at last renewed.

Staring out across the frosty landscape broken by the dark ribbon on the Rappahannock where the Union engineers labored, Sean couldn't share in his men's hope. Some eighty thousand Rebels awaited them on the opposite shore now. There would be no getting out of this without a bloody confrontation as they had first hoped. At over fifty thousand more men than the Rebels, they were almost assured a victory, but it would not be without a high cost. One good thing had come from the weather delaying them. The citizens of the city of Fredericksburg had been given time by nature to evacuate. But as sure as he knew his own sense of honor, Sean knew not all of the citizens had left. He wouldn't have, were it his home, or his business that was threatened. That meant there would be more than eighty thousand resisting them.

"Such heavy thoughts on the eve of battle?" Ashlinn's voice came out of the dark like a dream.

Paws padded across the frozen ground toward him. A moment later a canine head pushed beneath his hand. Turning, he scratched Cliste behind the ears. Clothed all in dark blue wool, walking with the light-footedness of a doe, she moved out of the shadows toward him. The breeches she wore tonight were a bit large, and that combined with their dark wool conspired to hide her form from him. While it disappointed him, he was also relieved that anyone else who saw her wouldn't immediately recognize her womanly shape. Had she not spoken, he may not have noticed her approach.

"You could have been quite the thief, lass," he said as his gaze traveled across her.

She gave him a coy smile as she leaned against the large trunk of the skeletal deciduous tree beside him. He had chosen this copse of trees for its location far back from the shore and away from the army a bit. Not because he had been expecting her—that was a welcome surprise—but because he didn't want to be shot at, or disturbed by other soldiers.

"I may have missed my callin' then," Ashlinn said in a voice so sweet he could almost taste it.

He leaned against the tree beside her, close enough that their arms touched. The scents of soap, crisp snow, and the tang of iodine mingled about her in a pleasant concoction. Only she would be able to find soap in the midst of a war.

"Most certainly not. You were meant to be a doctor."

Pink flushed her cheeks, adding to her beauty. "Surely you mean a nurse."

Reaching out, he cupped one pink cheek in his hand. "*Níl*, I don't."

She leaned into him, and by her rapt expression, he had a feeling it wasn't because his hand was warmer than her cheek. After a moment, she pulled away, glanced around, then relaxed back against the tree again. For a long moment she was quiet, her lips pursed as if the words that she wanted to say tasted foul.

"You can say anythin' to me, you know that," Sean urged.

In a rush, both her breath and her words left her. "I do not want you to go across that river. I know you have to, but I don't want you to."

The words seared him to his soul both with desire and pain. A quick glance around ensured Sean that they were alone in the shadows cast by the copse of leafless trees. Everyone was focused either on the construction of the bridges or watching the far shore for any sign that the enemy had detected what they were up to. But to him, having something to live for seemed more important than having something to die for. He didn't want to cross that bridge and leave her either, but he had to, for honor's sake, and more importantly, for the sake of his men.

Sliding closer, he took her in his arms. "I wish I didn't have to. But maybe this battle will finally help bring an end to this war. Then we can be together."

It wasn't hard to sound hopeful; he truly felt that way. The only problem was the additional troops that had gathered across the river. Those were just the ones they could see. There could be more. But he refused to allow those doubts to surface, especially now with her looking so vulnerable.

Out in this cold her body gave off little heat, but it still felt good against his. Too good. The curve of her hips beneath his arms, the swell of her breasts against his chest, they drove him to a wonderful distraction. Wonderful, and horrible. He didn't dare spoil her on the eve of what could be the worst battle of this war, one in which he could die. It was best that her maidenhood and honor remain intact, just in case.

For a while, they stood holding one another, molding as closely as they could. Soon her hands began to work inside his coat, then along the waistband of his breeches. It wasn't so much the cold touch that made him jump. He took her hands in his and pressed them against his chest inside his coat.

"That will lead us somewhere I fear I won't be able to turn back from."

Lips parted in a delicious smile, she kissed his chin. "Good, I do not want to turn back."

He steeled himself, reaching deep for his control. "Nor I, but I can hardly strip you down in this cold, and we cannot go back to our tents and risk bein' seen."

A groan of protest from her worked at his restraint. "If only I had worn a dress, you could lift my skirts and join the fire that burns within me."

The image her words conjured was enough to ignite a fire all his own within him, and make him so hard he feared for the crotch of his breeches. Eyes going skyward, he leaned his head back against the tree and fought to regain his control. Words both explicit and urgent spoken in Gaelic left his lips. Ashlinn leaned against him, her pelvis pressing against his erection in a way that made him dizzy.

"I want you, Sean. I *need* you."

Finding his control, he wrapped his arms around her and met her longing gaze. "And I you. After this battle I promise you that we shall find a secluded place and I will let you ravish me all you want, my angel." What he didn't voice was his doubt over surviving the coming battle. It was the true reason he didn't dare take her virtue tonight. But she didn't need to hear that. She needed encouragement so she could make it through the hell that lay before them.

"Do you now?"

Eyes closing as he pictured her naked, he nodded. "I do."

She drew away, leaving him chilled and more than a little wanting. The hooded look she cast him over her shoulder, the way she chewed her bottom lip, both nearly undid him. "In that case, will you escort me back to my tent so I may get to sleep and get this night over with? I am lookin' forward to the next one ever so much."

Her voice was all sugar and spice, pouring over him like the most delectable of treats. Hands in their pockets, they walked back to the encampment, so close together their elbows overlapped. It was best that she was dressed as a man so he couldn't offer her his arm. Being that close would have certainly shattered his resistance as if it were brittle glass. Reluctant though he was for the next day to dawn, at least he had something to look forward to at the end of it. If he survived.

Chapter 24

The first light of dawn that brightened the dim interior of her tent came with a terrible drawback: the distant sound of gunfire. All the excitement and desire she had felt with Sean last night suddenly became eclipsed by fear for him. Him and her brother. At this large encampment, filled with so many other regiments, she had hoped to at last come across Michael, or at least word of him. All the prior day she had scoured the tents, asking troops about him, looking for him. No one had seen or heard of him. But a new day could bring new possibilities.

She went through her morning routine as quickly as she could, dressed in men's clothing, bound and hid her hair beneath a cap, and gathered up her medical bag. Almost as an afterthought, she paused at the tent opening, grabbed a few cotton balls, and stuffed them into her ears. She had a bad feeling she was going to be in the thick of it today.

Gun smoke wafted on the air, carried by a cold breeze that blew up from the river. Head hung low, Cliste trotted alongside her as she made her way across the half-frozen ground. Once they left the rows of tents for the open space between the encampment and the riverbank, the stench of death reached Ashlinn. Doing her best to breathe through her mouth and not think about how the smell coated her tongue, she allowed the cries of the wounded to draw her in. Looking around, she realized she was one of the first nurses to arrive.

Soldiers in blue lined their side of the ice-edged river, all crouched low or lying prone as they shot at the Rebels across the way. Amidst the chaos, engineers labored over three pontoon bridges, struggling to continue building them under fire. Behind the line of soldiers, Ashlinn spotted a wounded man closest to her location. Crouching low, she went to him.

Blood covered the front of his uniform but his hands clamped so tightly over his midsection that she couldn't see the damage. She tried to speak to him but the sound of gunfire was too great. His wild eyes refused to focus, meaning he likely wouldn't have responded anyway.

Ashlinn snapped her fingers and pointed at the man's shoulder. Cliste shot in, grabbed hold of the man's coat just above his shoulders as carefully as if taking a treat from a child, then began to pull him back. The man struggled at first, but once he realized he was moving away from the fighting, he went limp save for his hands clutching his middle. Ashlinn strode straight to a small group of trees a few feet back. Cliste followed with the soldier in tow. Thin though the trees were, she and the other nurses had piled sandbags between them up to chest height the week prior. That, combined with the old blankets they had strung between them to keep out the wind, had turned the copse into a battlefield triage.

Skirts clutched in one hand, the end of a canvas stretcher in the other, Abigail strode from the encampment toward her. Three other nurses, two of whom were Negros, walked with her, one holding the other end of the stretcher's poles. Unable to speak and be heard, Ashlinn smiled her thanks to them as they helped her load the man onto the stretcher. When they reached the hospital, the soldier had passed out. Ashlinn's heart sank as she moved his hands away from his midsection. A gaping hole in his stomach revealed shiny innards. Knowing there was nothing she could do for him, she turned him over to the hospital doctors.

Cliste in tow, she and the other three nurses set out immediately for the battlefield again. Working as a team, the women brought the wounded to the makeshift triage at the small gathering of trees. Throughout the morning they treated those they could on the spot, taking the more seriously wounded to the hospital in most cases. When time allowed it, Ashlinn insisted on treating even the serious ones, knowing handing them over to Taylor and his team would surely end in either their death or dismemberment.

One of the lieutenants of the 69th stopped by sometime after the first hour of dawn. Wrist-deep in a man's stomach, searching for a bullet, Ashlinn didn't have much of a chance to look at the man, let alone talk to him.

"Sorry, Lieutenant, sir, but Miss O'Brian is diggin' out a bullet. What can we do for ya?" Abigail asked on her behalf.

"I want to thank you ladies for all that you're doing for the men, and I'd like to let you know that we've erected a smaller hospital tent much closer for you."

Interest piqued, Ashlinn looked at the man while she continued to dig around for the bullet inside the unconscious soldier. "Thank you,

Lieutenant, that is most appreciated." Heartfelt though her sentiment was her tone remained reserved. She couldn't help it—having Taylor closer to where she worked was the last thing she wanted.

As if reading her mind, Abigail asked, "Excuse me for askin', sir, but which doctor will be workin' dis new hospital?"

The man smiled at Ashlinn, and she inclined her head as if to say she too wanted to know. To his credit, he looked at Abigail when he answered.

"I'm afraid we haven't got a doctor to spare, but word is you ladies are doing so fine that you'll be all right. I hope that is truly the case."

Fingers wrapped around the misshapen bullet, Ashlinn smiled. "It is indeed. Thank you, Lieutenant. We will work better that way, more efficient. If there is any patient we cannot handle we will take him to the big hospital." The small lie rolled easily off her tongue. She was used to downplaying her abilities in the medical field when speaking to men.

He smiled back. Inclining his head slightly, he began to back away. "If you'll excuse me, I must see to the placement of the cannons."

Before either she or Abigail could question him, he turned and strode away. Ashlinn's smile wilted as she dropped the bullet onto a table beside the cot and held her hands up. Bucket of warm water in hand, Abigail was at her side in a flash, ready to help her wash. For the first time in hours, Ashlinn looked out over the battlefield as she scrubbed her hands together. Soldiers worked diligently along the bank, moving huge cannons into position, pointing them at the town of Fredericksburg. Still no sign of Sean, or her brother. Heart sinking and hands shaking, Ashlinn picked up the sterilized needle and thread.

* * * *

After hours of cannon fire, not even the cotton in Ashlinn's ears helped anymore. The wounded kept her attention off the destruction that no doubt lay across the river and for that she was grateful. When the muted light of the cloudy day darkened into early evening, the cannon fire finally stopped. Between patients Ashlinn stepped out of the hospital, looking for the 69th regiment. They were easy to distinguish by the sprigs of bright green boxwood tucked into their caps, and thankfully she located them quickly.

Several companies began running across the bridges, but Sean's—or any of the other companies of the 69th—weren't among them. A breath close to a sob tore from her. It was foolish, she knew, but she hoped the battle could be won before his regiment moved in. Duty called in the form of a groaning soldier, drawing her back into the hospital.

Gunfire sounded all throughout the night, making sleep nearly impossible, but she tried when she could. After all the surgeries were complete, she and the other nurses at her small hospital tent took turns doing rounds and napping on two cots tucked at the back of the tent. All the while Cliste clung close to Ashlinn's side, watching her every move with a protective eye. In the rare moment she actually fell asleep, Ashlinn did so with one hand hanging off the cot, touching the hound. She had to make sure she didn't run off, especially now with the confrontation right outside.

Like a diver surfacing, she clawed her way from the deepest sleep she had ever experienced. Big brown eyes amidst a canine face stared at her from the edge of her pillow. A tail began to thump on packed dirt. Muscles protested as she lifted a tired arm and patted the hound on the head. Something crinkled when Cliste lifted her head. A folded piece of paper tied with a strip of bark like a present lay on her pillow with a bright green sprig of boxwood tucked into the bark. Her hands shook from more than the chill in the air as she sat up and opened the letter.

My Dearest Angel,
We are off to the battle, but have no fear, neither heaven nor hell shall make me miss our appointment tonight. There is something I have been meaning to ask you and I can think of no better time to do so than tonight.
Forever yours,
Sean MacBranain

Hot moisture stung her eyes as she clutched the letter to her chest. He had been here, and she had missed him. To add fuel to the fire of her regret, gunfire sounded in the distance. Not a lot of it, thank goodness, but any was too much for her ears. A wet tongue brushed across the back of her hand. She looked down to find Cliste turning her head, exposing the small cylinder on her collar as if something awaited within it.

Could Sean have left another letter? One even more private perhaps? The thought of words more private than those he had left on her pillow sent heat rushing through her. She made quick work of opening the cylinder and fishing out the paper within. The words on it stopped her heart for sure, but not in a good way.

Go home, little sister.

The inelegant scratch was certainly not Sean's. But she recognized it, oh yes, she recognized it. Her eyes slammed closed against burning tears and she sucked in hard for a breath that offered her no relief. He was here, he was really here. But where? And was it as a soldier, or a deserter hiding nearby? No one had seen or heard of him, which did not bode well. She dare not say a word to anyone in case it was the latter.

Light footsteps made her open her eyes. Abigail approached down the narrow aisle between the two rows of cots. "Ah, Miss Ashlinn, ya's awake. Dat's good, Private O'Keefe's complain' of pain in his side. Thought ya might wanna know."

Folding the letter back up, Ashlinn put it, along with Sean's letter and the sprig of boxwood, in the pocket of her breeches as she stood. No matter how much she wanted to run from the tent and scream for her long-lost brother to reveal himself, she couldn't. Not only would it endanger the fool, but people were relying on her. People who hadn't abandoned their army like a coward. For surely he had, else she would have seen or heard of him among all these troops.

Putting aside such thoughts, she stretched to get her blood flowing to sore muscles and help set her mind to the monumental tasks the day would no doubt ask of her. Her brother had waited this long; he would have to wait a little longer. The important thing was that he was alive. That fact brought her enough strength to get through just about anything.

All throughout the day she was forced to remain in the hospital, handling case after urgent case. She lost count of how many bullets she had removed and wounds she had stitched up. In a few cases, arms or legs had been so badly damaged that she had been forced to remove limbs, but damn it all, she was smart about it, unlike Taylor. She knew many of the soldiers she treated because they insisted on being brought to her and her alone. The cots filled with those who had major injuries and soldiers with more minor injuries lined up outside the tent to wait for treatment. Blood, muscle, bone, and tissue filled her day, keeping her mind distracted from that which it desperately did not—could not—think about.

The day came to an end and still the 69th hadn't returned. One of the soldiers from Sean's company who came through with minor wounds told her they were waiting to launch an assault on Marye's Heights. The meaning of that kept Ashlinn up much later into the night than her patients, or even thoughts of her brother. If they were attacking the Rebels on a place called "Heights," that likely meant the Rebels were entrenched in the high ground. Greater numbers or not, she feared terribly for the Union troops because she had come to know that tactical position was everything to a victory.

With Cliste at her side, she wandered the dark camp that night in search of Michael but still could not find him. Having done a full sweep of the huge encampment and come back around to where the 69th had set up, she collapsed into her tent, exhausted and frustrated.

The next morning fog shrouded the ruined town of Fredericksburg from which smoke curled up. Chills crawled through Ashlinn more from the sight than from the frigid morning temperature. Death hung heavy on the air that blew across the river from the town. The bad feeling that had gripped her days ago grew so much that it nauseated her. She skipped breakfast and did her rounds instead. All the while, she prayed that the 13th of December would be a lucky day for the Fighting Irish. After her rounds, she scoured the entire encampment once again for any sign of Michael. She found nothing. Near sunset, she learned the day had been anything but lucky for the Fighting Irish.

Breath coming in great gasps, Abigail came running into the hospital with her skirts gathered in one hand. "Miss Ashlinn, ya must come quick," she gasped out between breaths.

Fear closed icy giant's fingers around Ashlinn's throat. "Is it Sean?" she somehow managed to get out.

A cry of relief nearly tore from her when Abigail shook her head. "No. Deys callin' for volunteers to help de wounded in de field. Dey say it's mighty bad."

Fear crept back over her, but it lacked the grip it had previously had. Sean and her brother were out there. She had to go. She put a remarkably steady hand on Abigail's shoulder. "Can you stay here and see to the hospital for me?"

Nodding her head, Abigail stepped out of the way, offering Ashlinn an open aisle to the hospital exit. Fingers that now shook worked to tuck stray bits of her hair back up beneath her cap as she strode for the open tent flap. The golden light of early evening that lay over the land came as a shock to her. Where had the day gone?

Men in filthy, torn uniforms hustled about with nurses under the direction of a doctor, gathering stretchers and blankets. To Ashlinn's relief, the doctor wasn't Taylor. Of course it wasn't. The coward would never volunteer to go into an active field of battle. Realizing she forgot her medical bag, she turned back to the hospital, only to find Abigail standing at the entrance with it in hand. Full lips drawn into a tight smile, her friend handed her the bag.

"Ya be careful now, Miss Ashlinn."

Ashlinn covered the woman's hands with her own and held on for a moment before taking the bag. She hoped the look she gave her conveyed her thanks and the depth of gratitude she felt toward the woman.

"I will. You do the same," she said before turning away.

She hadn't even turned around completely when a soldier took one look at her bag and approached her. "Right this way, doctor...uh, nurse?" The last bit turned into a question as his eyes fell upon her face.

"'Tis safer to enter a battlefield full of men in disguise," she said, ignoring his question.

He nodded. "Right." Sweeping a hand toward the half a dozen or so other volunteers, he picked up a bag of supplies and marched in their direction.

Clutching her own worn leather bag to her, she followed. The crisp evening air heavy with the tang of rain to come filled her lungs, driving away the stuffy feel of the hospital tent. Looking around at the battered banks of the river, she marveled over how she could have spent all day inside and not even realized it. The urge to run for the nearest pontoon bridge seized her so strongly that the muscles in her legs twitched. Sean was over there somewhere, in the thick of battle no doubt, in danger. This was why she hadn't stepped outside. She knew she wouldn't be able to resist the pull to go to him. But now she didn't have to. She was going to find Sean and Michael and bring them back if she had to walk into the mouth of hell itself.

Chapter 25

Ashlinn had no trouble keeping up with the long stride of the soldiers who flanked her as they marched toward the closest bridge. The others in the medical group seemed far less eager, lagging behind several paces until the soldiers in the rear called for them to pick up the pace. That could have been due in part to the huge hound trotting alongside Ashlinn, keeping the others at bay. Though Ashlinn both saw and heard all this happening around her, she remained singularly focused on that bridge. It was all she could do not to break into a run and pass the soldier in the lead. But she didn't dare. Not only would it be disrespectful, but the knife she carried in her boot was hardly a match for the enemy's rifles.

The planks of the bridge made a hollow click beneath her boot heels and the entire structure dipped and swayed ever so slightly with each step. There was room for Cliste to walk beside her, but just barely. Ahead of and behind her walked soldiers, free hands held out in case she needed to be stopped from stumbling into the freezing, muddy brown water. That only made the sight of the sludgy mess a little less daunting. Falling into such water would result in hypothermia and frostbite within minutes, if one was fetched out. If one wasn't… Shaking the thought away, she forced her eyes forward, to the waiting bank and the city of Fredericksburg beyond it. Though it felt like forever, they reached the other side in only moments.

A corporal to her right helped her through the half-frozen, half-muddy mess that was left of the bank. Truly, he seemed to need more help than she did. The frozen ground held for her for the most part but he sank time and time again. To Ashlinn's relief, no bodies lay upon the shore, but the crimson evidence of their prior existence was enough to make her heart ache. Likely, it was the blood of the enemy, she knew, but still, their lives had meaning. Sights like this always made her think this whole mess could have been solved with words rather than weapons.

At last, they were through the muck of the bank and onto the slight hill that led up to the town. Her eyes fell upon what she had been trying to avoid seeing. Many of the buildings lay in ruins, having been peppered with cannon balls. Walls of both wood and brick were torn away, their materials scattered like a child's building blocks into the streets. The devastation went on and on, seeming to have spared very little. Bodies dotted the ruins and the streets, not as many as she had feared, but even one was more than she wanted to see. Each that caught her eye wore gray, but then, that could also be a combination of frost and dust from the rubble.

She turned to the corporal who had helped her ashore. "Have we gathered all our dead from the city?"

He nodded. "Aye, as best we can tell. We're headed to the wall where the lads are entrenched."

No one spoke again as they wove their way through the streets of the ruined town, going around and even over rubble in some areas. The soldiers flanked them at all times, weapons at the ready, rising at every sound. Of all the horrors Ashlinn had seen over the past two years, this eclipsed them all. People's homes and businesses lay in ruins, slave owners who were in the wrong for certain, but still people who would have been Americans and members of the Union by the time this was over. How could their country ever recover from such a thing?

Tears stung her eyes and she repeatedly had to blink them away. One of the nurses behind her sniffled; another wept openly. Part of her wished she could let her pain out like they did, but she didn't dare. She had to stay strong. The other women needed her to keep them together; the men of the 69th needed her. Sean, and possibly even Michael, needed her. Standing a bit straighter, she let those thoughts surround her like armor, hasten her steps, and give her courage.

The battered city passed by in a blur, not because of tears this time, but because of her focus. In moments it seemed, they had reached an open field that sloped up to a hill. The cloying, horrible stench of death was so thick upon the air that it clung to Ashlinn's tongue when she breathed in. A stone wall ran along the crest of the hill and though it was too far away to see clearly, she knew with a horrible certainty that the Rebel army lay behind it. Upon a frosty, red ground, thousands of dead and dying men lay strewn across the field as if they were no more than broken, discarded dolls. Their wails assaulted her ears, stirring the urge to cover them. But she didn't dare. These men deserved to be heard, remembered.

Considering hundreds of dead and wounded had been pouring into camp since the battle began, the number here suggested the toll was unbearably high. The force of such knowledge made Ashlinn stagger and nearly go to a knee. A hand covered in a blue glove shot out and caught her arm, holding her upright. Mournful whining sounded from Cliste as she rubbed against Ashlinn's side. Cries of disbelief sounded from the other nurses behind her.

"'Tis not a sight for a lady. I'm sorry, miss," the corporal said in a hushed tone filled with pain.

Ashlinn swallowed her fear and pushed aside the horror gripping her. Unless she saw Sean's body, she was going to assume he was alive. She had to.

"'Tis not a sight for this earth, Corporal," she answered in a flat, level tone that sounded as hollow as she felt.

"So we've lost the battle then," another of the nurses said in a voice thick with tears.

"Regardless of who claims victory, no one won on this field today," Ashlinn said grimly.

Movement upon the field drew her attention. Soldiers had begun carrying the wounded down the rise, toward what looked like a small river that stood between them and the medical team. No, not a river, she realized, but a millrace. She started toward it, leaving their escorts hurrying to catch up. By the time she reached the water, soldiers had begun to cross the five-foot span on makeshift bridges made from planks and what looked like remnants of wagons. She searched the faces of the dozen or so men coming down the hill that were close enough to see but didn't find Sean among them.

One soldier carried another on his back across a plank barely wide enough for his feet. Head ducked low from the burden, cap pulled down, she couldn't see his face. He didn't teeter once while walking over the water, but the moment his feet touched the ground he stumbled and fell to his knees. She was at his side before his second knee hit the hard ground. Grabbing one of the man's arms who lay across his back, she lifted the man, easing the other's burden enough that he was able to rise. A shortly trimmed beard framed an all-too-familiar handsome face, one that was pinched in pain. Green eyes rolled as if struggling to keep open.

"Fergusson!"

Ashlinn laid him down upon the ground. She needed to check his injuries before she moved him any further. The soldier who had born him across his back knelt on his other side. Slowly, Ashlinn's eyes dragged up along the man's filthy, blood-splattered uniform. Coppery brown eyes gaped out at her from a face as haunted as a banshee's. Cliste bounded to the man's side and began to lick his cheek with great enthusiasm despite the soot, dirt, and blood covering him.

"Are you real?" Sean asked as he pulled Cliste's head down and scratched almost absently behind her ears.

Leaning across Fergusson, Ashlinn took Sean's face in her hand and pressed her forehead against his. He sucked in a breath and his eyes fluttered shut, moisture dampening their lashes. Tears slid down her cheeks; she no longer could hold them in.

"Quite real," she whispered.

Between them, Fergusson groaned. "Hate to interrupt your tender moment, but, soldier bleedin' out here."

Throat tightening with panic despite his playful tone, Ashlinn's gaze dropped to Fergusson. Dark blood stained his uniform near his left collarbone. With hands that shook as much from relief as from cold and stress, she peeled away his coat and tore his shirt open.

"I see why you like her," Fergusson teased Sean.

Ashlinn wasn't sure if his teasing was a good sign or not. She didn't know the man well enough to know if he still teased when he was in pain or under duress. Her searching fingers soon found the source of all the blood. A small bullet hole sat just below his collarbone.

"We have to turn him so I can see if the bullet went through," she said.

Giving his friend an encouraging nod, Sean grabbed Fergusson's belt and left arm and pulled. Though he groaned through gritted teeth and cursed quite colorfully in Gaelic, Fergusson didn't cry out. More cursing ensued as she pulled his coat and uniform down to get a good look at his back. Amidst all the blood, she found a slightly larger hole.

"This is good."

She beckoned for the two soldiers holding the canvas stretcher to bring it to her. Once she laid it out beneath Fergusson, she nodded to Sean, who eased him back onto it. One of Fergusson's brows lifted, as well as one side of his trimmed mustache—which covered his lips enough that she couldn't quite tell if he was smiling or not.

"Another hole in me body is a good thing?"

She smiled at him, letting her relief show through. "In this case, yes. It means the bullet went clean through, which means I don't have to dig around inside you."

He laid his head back onto the stretcher. "In that case, that 'tis good news."

Sean clapped him on his good shoulder, which still made him flinch and groan. "Good news indeed, my friend. Under her care you'll live to harass more lasses, have no fear."

Ashlinn produced a corked bottle from within her medical bag. "The sooner we get this cleaned out, the better. Will you hold him down, Sean?"

She met Sean's gaze again, mostly because she couldn't stop looking at him to make sure he didn't disappear.

"Ha! Hold me down. She's a funny little thing. No worries, little thing. I can take whatever you can dish out," Fergusson said.

Raising an eyebrow, Sean shrugged at her. The hard look Ashlinn gave him had him moving quickly to kneel on Fergusson's chest when she moved around to his shoulder.

"Hey..."

She nodded to Sean, who leaned weight onto Fergusson's chest at the same moment she poured iodine into his wound. The big, muscle-bound soldier screamed, thrashed, and cursed for all he was worth. Sean nearly went flying off of him twice, but somehow kept the bigger man down. When he finally stopped struggling all the humor had gone out of Fergusson's green eyes. She removed a clean bit of gauze from her bag and pressed it to his wound.

"Bloody hell, lass, did you have to do that? It hurt worse than the damn shot," he grumbled.

Expression solemn so he wouldn't see the humor bubbling beneath, Ashlinn nodded. "Aye, I did. That will help keep the wound from gettin' infected, which will keep you from dyin'." She gently patted his arm. "You rest now. I have done all I can for now. I will sew you up when we get you back to the hospital. Here, Sean, hold this." She took Sean's hand and pressed it to the gauze over Fergusson's wound. Meeting his gaze, she let her hand linger atop his far longer than was appropriate. "I am goin' to see if I can help any of the others."

Sean grabbed her with his free hand as she stood. Looking up at her with beseeching eyes, he said, "Don't go too far."

"Do not worry. I will not let you out of my sight," she promised.

With the other nurses in tow, she moved among the hundreds of wounded being carried across the makeshift bridges spanning the millrun. Those that she could help, she did; those that she couldn't she gave precious drops of laudanum and then opium when the first ran out. Much to her dismay, there were far more who wouldn't make it than who would, and even more who were already dead. Worse, Michael wasn't among them. But then, deep down, she'd had a feeling he wouldn't be. That he was somewhere close she had no doubt. More and more, though, she began to fear he was avoiding battle. Whether or not that meant he had deserted and merely been hiding in this area, she wasn't ready to face.

True to her word, she never let Sean out of her sight, to the point of having patients brought to her when possible. Thankfully, more nurses and even a few more doctors from other regiments arrived to help. Despite their assistance, Ashlinn did her best to see to every soldier who wore a sprig of boxwood in their caps, not because they were Irish, but because they were of the 69th; they were family.

Less than an hour later, they began carrying the wounded back to camp. Ashlinn took up one corner of Fergusson's stretcher, while Sean and two more soldiers took up the other corners.

"You sure you can carry this brute?" one of the soldiers at Fergusson's feet asked.

She smiled back at him. "All of him, certainly not. A quarter of him shan't be a problem, though."

Drunk on the bit of laudanum she had given him, Fergusson rolled his head her direction and grinned like a fool. "This lass could probably carry the general's horse back to camp," he said, voice slurring more than a little.

His banter lifted her spirits, and with them her guilt as well. That she could be even a little happy surrounded by so much death seemed terribly wrong. Yet she couldn't help be glad that both Sean and Fergusson had survived. They marched in silence, leaving the ghastly site of the corpse-strewn hill behind only to trade it for the ruined city dotted with bodies. Were it not for Sean's survival and presence with her now, Ashlinn might have feared she'd ventured into hell.

By the time they reached the pontoon bridges that spanned the Rappahannock, her arms ached, but considering her burden, it was an ache she welcomed. Due to the narrow bridge, Sean and one of the soldiers carrying the end of Fergusson's stretcher took over to get across. When she offered to take up a corner again Sean shook his head.

"I've got him. You lead the way."

Her arms shook too badly for her to put up much of a protest, so she simply nodded and did as he bid. She led him to the small hospital she had been working at, only to find dozens of soldiers waiting outside. Arms loaded down with blankets so high her chin could barely fit over the top of them, Abigail emerged from the hospital tent. Upon seeing her, the woman's full lips turned up into a huge grin.

"Miss Ashlinn, ya's a'right, thank de saints! And de sergeant, too!"

Ashlinn relieved her of half the load of blankets and together they passed them out to the soldiers waiting. "I take it we are out of cots inside?"

"Yes'm."

Steeling herself with a deep breath, she pressed a hand to her stomach, mostly to keep Abigail from seeing how badly she shook. "Due to the number of casualties, there will be plenty of tents for these men in the area. Let's get them in out of the wind and the coming dark, whatever tents are closest will do. We will treat them once we get them inside."

She turned to give Sean and the soldiers carrying Fergusson directions to carry him to the nearest empty tent.

"You'll be along soon to do my stitches, won't you, Doc?" Fergusson asked.

"Of course," she promised.

Once they were on their way she had Abigail brief her about the wounded, instructed her to move anyone who wasn't serious out of the hospital and into one of the nearby tents, and asked her to gather any medicinal supplies she could. She looked to the men waiting, some standing and some sitting, others lying down on the cold ground.

"If you are able to get into one of the nearby empty tents on your own, do so. If not, one of the nurses will be out to help you. We shall get to each of you, I promise." With that she spun and marched off to the tent they had taken Fergusson to.

The anxiety building in her dissipated the moment she stepped inside and saw Sean lighting a candle. She nodded to the other soldier who had helped carry him in.

"Thank you, Private."

He stood up taller. "You're welcome, ma'am. Is there anythin' else I can do for you?"

"I need boiling water."

Sean sat the candle down on a small log covered in wax and met the man's gaze. "Ask Abigail, the nurse who had the blankets. She'll have some. Then build a fire close by and put another pot of water on to boil. I have a feelin' Miss O'Brian is goin' to need a lot of it tonight."

Hand shooting up for a sharp salute, the man straightened, heels clicking together, and then darted out of the tent.

Together she and Sean removed Fergusson's coat and shirt, all the while exchanging long looks and finding excuses to touch one another's hands or arms. Were Fergusson not between them, Ashlinn would have thrown herself into Sean's arms, propriety be damned. Both the private with the water and Abigail with an armload of medicinal supplies arrived at nearly the same time. Head propped up on the foot of Fergusson's cot, Cliste sat patiently, her tail thumping away at the packed dirt. With Abigail's assistance, Ashlinn had Fergusson's wounds cleaned, stitched, and wrapped in clean gauze in no time at all.

She rose from where she'd been kneeling beside the cot and met Sean's magnetic gaze. "I understand if you want to stay with him, but I must check on the rest of the men."

Sean rose from where he had been sitting, resting with his back against one of the tent poles. "You should have an escort. The camp is in chaos, a mixture of regiments, and many of the men are...out of sorts. I'll go with you."

Tension drained from her as surely as if she had stepped into a warm bath. "Thank you, that would be much appreciated." She turned to Abigail. "Are you able to accompany us?"

Abigail picked up her own medical bag and quickly stood. "Yes, ma'am."

With Cliste in tow, they hurried out of Fergusson's tent and started toward the next closest one.

The night was a blur of wounds, sutures, and blood. Having both Abigail and Sean by her side gave Ashlinn the strength to see to every man that the other nurses and doctors were unable to get to, which was a lot. For every person with even the slightest amount of medical ability, there were a hundred or more wounded. After she had seen to the last man, Sean finally carried her to her tent, but it was only because she couldn't walk anymore. Heavy head sinking into her hard pillow, she watched him sit down at the tent's entrance and stretch out. She wanted to protest, tell him to come join her, but sleep stole over her before she could open her mouth.

Chapter 26

Hundreds of reluctant voices combined with the sounds of tents being taken down finally pulled Sean from a deep, dreamless sleep. They were sounds he knew all too well. Camp was breaking. How long this had been going on, he had no idea. The constant patter of rain on canvas last night had drowned out all other sound until now. Looking over at Ashlinn sleeping so peacefully, not a line of worry on her pretty face, he found himself reluctant to leave.

Yet duty—and nature—called. He tossed the blanket he had thrown over himself aside and rose stiffly from the hard ground. One look down at his filthy, bloody uniform and guilt burned through him. He wished he had at least cleaned up before using her blanket. Fetching his knapsack, he dug out one of the last sheets of music he had left, wrote her a quick note and placed it upon her pillow. He also dug out the fresh pair of socks he had and put them, his boots, and coat on.

Left with no other reason to linger, he still stood over the cot, staring down at her sleeping form. The light that seeped through the thick canvas of the tent illuminated her, making her golden hair glow softly and the features of her lovely face seem all the more gentle. Despite fighting it, his feelings grew stronger for her every day. And now, they were powerful enough to override even his fear of being a disappointment to her. Even though the battle was behind him with a river between it and them, he still didn't want to let her out of his sight. But he had to, at least for a moment. Grabbing up his knapsack and his rifle, he forced himself from the tent.

In the chaos of camp breaking up no one really noticed him leaving a nurse's tent. Soldiers dashed here and there, packing things up and loading wagons with the wounded. Already men were breaking down the small hospital tent not far away. Rain drizzled down over it all, giving the air an oppressive feel as if it carried the weight of their defeat with it. Sean's eyes went immediately for the tent they had left Fergusson in only to find it gone. He grabbed the nearest soldier, a man from another regiment that he didn't recognize.

"Where are we off to?" he asked.

"Back to Falmouth."

"Do you know a Corporal Fergusson? Do you know where they've taken him?" Sean asked. "His tent was right there."

The soldier looked where he pointed but shook his head. "Can't say that I do. Sorry, Sergeant."

Sean let him go and the man dashed off. Looking for a familiar face in the bustling crowd, Sean moved on. He found a few of his men, but none of them knew where Fergusson had gone.

"Sergeant, Sergeant" came a feminine voice heavy with a slave's accent.

Sean turned to find Abigail reaching toward him hesitantly as if not sure she should touch him or not. He took her hand in his and gave her a warm smile.

"Abigail, I'm so happy you're all right," he said.

White teeth beamed as she gave him a shy smile in return. "Thank ya, Sergeant. I's glad to see ya's a'right, too. Fergusson is in one of the wagons. I saw to it myself he was loaded up safely."

The threat of panic left him like a receding tide. "Thank you, Abigail."

"'Course, Sarge. I best see to wakin' Miss Ashlinn now."

He nodded. "Would you let her know I'm checkin' on my men, and I'll be along shortly?"

Dimples formed in Abigail's cheeks she smiled so big. "'Course I will."

After seeing to his morning routine, Sean set out to check on those of his men he knew had survived the battle. All the wounded of the 69th who couldn't walk, his regiment and the others, were within wagons. Talk among the soldiers was that the 69th deserved to ride within wagons as they had carried the army on their backs the previous day. Such a grand gesture choked Sean up, and he agreed. They had fought valiantly, with both honor and fearlessness. Not all sergeants could say their men had performed in such a manner and he was beyond proud that he could. The Fighting Irish had more than lived up to their name. Sadly, many of them were dead because of it.

Sometime later, while helping a private with his arm in a sling fold his tent up, Sean spotted Ashlinn redressing a soldier's wound. The man sat upon a boulder, listening raptly to her instructions with a look of worship in his eyes. He knew how the man felt. Giving her time to finish, he worked his way over to her slowly. So caught up was she in her work that she didn't see him coming until he was nearly upon them. Her lovely smile lit her face up, but she kept talking, focusing on her work like a true professional. He loved that about her, the confidence with which she gave her patients instructions, and the way she treated each of them as if they were the most important part of her day.

Finished, she patted the man on his good shoulder, and started walking toward Sean. Somehow she had found time to wash, brush her hair, and put on a fresh shirt and breeches. He suddenly felt quite self-conscious about the current state of his own attire. Water dripped from his cap as he dipped his head to her. At least the pouring rain had cleaned him up a bit. His tongue burned with a question that he had just recently decided to ask her. Like a coin newly acquired, this question begged to be released. Yet this wasn't the place.

Ashlinn paused and looked around. Her back straightened and her shoulders went stiff.

"Cliste?" she called out.

A sinking sensation pulled at Sean's stomach. He turned to look about them. The hound was nowhere to be seen. Ashlinn continued to call the hound's name, and still she did not come bounding back. Ashlinn's voice began to take on a desperate sound. Sean grabbed her hand.

"'Tis all right. She likely just wandered off to beg from the soldiers. Come on, we'll find her," he said.

Though she allowed him to lead her along, she shook her head. "I do not think it is a squirrel," she said in a quiet voice.

Hand in hand, they started toward the nearest wagon.

"Miss Ashlinn, Miss Ashlinn!" came a breathless voice.

The woman ran toward them, her skirt gathered in one hand, black hair a cloud of chaos about a face pinched with concern. "Ya must come quick. Corporal Fergusson needs ya!"

Alarm shot through Sean like a Minie ball. "What happened?"

Gasping for breath, Abigail shook her head as she came to a stop before them. "Don't rightly know. All's I know is Doctor Taylor said de corporal was having a seizure and won't let no one tend to him save Miss Ashlinn."

Conflict broiled in Ashlinn's eyes as she met his gaze. "Will you find Cliste for me?"

He patted the back of her hand. "O' course. You go see to Fergusson."

Her eyes darted about the busy camp. He lifted her hand and pressed a kiss to the back of it. Those blue eyes of hers widened even more as they fixed on him. Pink flushed her cheeks.

"No worries. She and I will be back before you know it," he said.

She nodded. "All right. But be careful."

Before she could change her mind, he nodded, kissed her hand once more, and then dashed off into the dissolving encampment. Behind him he heard her ask Abigail to accompany her. It tortured Sean to run the other direction when his best friend was having issues. But he knew the man needed Ashlinn worse than he needed him, and Ashlinn wouldn't have gone without knowing he would be out searching for Cliste. Normally her patients came first no matter what, but something desperate in her eyes had told him that this time was different. There was something she wasn't telling him, something that made her even more fearful of Cliste's absence.

Sore and still exhausted from battle, it was all he could do to keep his pace at a jog, but he managed. Seeing how he knew Cliste's favorite haunts and the soldiers she would beg off of, it didn't take long to search the dissolving camp. With no sign of her, his eyes eventually turned to the tree line. It was the only other place she would have gone. Taking in a deep breath, he turned and jogged in that direction. Bare branches of birch and alder thrust through the frosty air, low and numerous enough to make it impossible to see very far. Deeper and deeper into the forest he went, calling out softly for the hound to return. Sean opened his mouth to call out again when he caught a glimpse of a gray tail swinging in the distance ahead.

"There you are!"

A dark, bulking figure hurtled at him from a birch tree directly to his right. One arm flew up to defend himself while the other reached back for the rifle he had left in the camp. Something solid collided with his arm and the shadowed figure bore him to the ground. He looked over the blade of a hatchet and up into the muddy-colored, bloodshot eyes of Taylor. The man's forearm had hit his, effectively blocking the hatchet he had tried to bury in Sean's skull. Sean tried to turn his hips and throw the man off, but exhausted as he still was from yesterday, he was unable to move the heavier man's bulk. Grinning so large it made him look a bit mad, Taylor raised the hatchet.

"Now I can kill two birds with one stone, and no one will be left standing between me and Ashlinn," he hissed through clenched teeth.

As the blow descended, Sean blocked it with one hand and drove his other fist into Taylor's stomach as hard as he could. A great breath of rank air blew from the man as he doubled over. Using the man's own momentum, Sean bucked his hips, raising one higher than the other to send Taylor up and over him. Pain shot through Sean's shoulder, making him pause halfway to his feet. Rather than try to stand, Taylor rolled over, sat up, and reared his arm back to throw the hatchet. Before that arm could even come forward, a huge gray shape barreled out of the trees and snatched a hold of Taylor's arm. The hatchet dropped to the ground and suddenly the furry gray shape was upon Taylor.

"Cliste," Sean called out, not caring so much what she did to Taylor as what Taylor might do to her.

However, his fears quickly proved unfounded. In moments Taylor went very still and blood began to flow onto the frozen leaves beneath him. Cliste released the man and trotted over to Sean's side. Her head dropped low but her guilt-filled eyes still met his.

"'Tis all right, girl. The man brought it on himself," he told her as he scratched her head.

Leaves crunched in the distance. Sean's head whipped in that direction. Through the white and black trunks of the trees he spotted Ashlinn running toward him. She collapsed on the ground next to him, one hand going to Cliste's scruff, the other to his right shoulder.

"What happened? Are you all right?"

He sighed and touched her hand where it rested on his shoulder. "Aye, just sore. Taylor attacked me. From what he said it seemed like he has been tryin' to lure Cliste out here to get to me."

She gasped and covered her mouth with the hand that had been buried in Cliste's scruff. Her gaze shifted from Sean to the now still form of Taylor and her expression went hard. "I am so sorry to have put you in danger, Sean."

"You, no—" He cupped her face in one hand and leaned his head against hers. "Don't ever think that."

Ashlinn opened her mouth to answer but a soft bark in the distance interrupted her. Cliste's head jerked up, her eyes going toward the sound. In a streak of gray, she was off like a shot, disappearing into the trees. With Ashlinn's help, Sean rose and together they broke into a run after the hound.

Chapter 27

Cliste led them on a merry chase deeper into the wood. She stopped time and again to look back at them, then bounded off again. No amount of calling, cajoling, or threatening could bring her back to them. Soon it became far too late to suggest they turn back. Not that Sean would without Cliste. But, at this distance from camp, they may as well catch the hound and meet up with army farther down the road. After a time they had to slow down to a walk so they could both catch their breath. Despite his suggestions, Ashlinn refused to stop, even once the rain began.

On and on they went and on and on Cliste led them. At this rate Sean began to fear they would reach Falmouth before the army, if they were still going in the right direction. He was no longer sure. Daylight began to wane, casting the long shadows of tree trunks across the damp forest floor. The air grew cooler to the point where Sean was uncomfortable in his wet clothing, which meant Ashlinn had to be cold. Her jaw quivered a bit but he wasn't sure if she was shivering or fighting the urge to cry.

Darkness began to set in and with it came the beginnings of frost. With no tent, no bedding, Sean had no idea what they were going to do. They could freeze to death if the temperature dropped as low as it had been in past nights. He had his knapsack, but a violin and two days or so of hardtack wouldn't exactly keep them warm. His plans for the day couldn't have gone more wrong.

A shape loomed in the shadows of the trees ahead, a building perhaps. Tugging Ashlinn to his side, Sean pointed to the building, then to his lips. She nodded. Careful to keep them hidden behind the trees, Sean slowly approached. The closer they came, the less he worried. The building was little more than a shack with a moss-covered roof and one filthy window to the right of a door that sat partly askew on its hinges. A hunting shack, most likely. The South was littered with them. Sitting before the door, as if waiting to be let in, was Cliste. She looked at them and gave a quiet woof.

Letting out a colorful curse in Gaelic, Ashlinn tried to rush toward the hound, but Sean held her back. He pointed to his eyes and made a circling motion toward the shack. To his surprise, she nodded. With a pointed look at her, he let go of her hand. As if she'd read his mind, she stuck close by him. They made their way slowly around the shack, keeping behind trees when they could, hurrying when they couldn't. Barely larger than a tent as it was, the trip around it was short. The small window beside the door was the only one.

Sean made his way up to the window, ignoring Cliste's tail thumping against the wooden step. He had to swipe grime and mold off the glass. Inside stood a wooden platform that could either be a bed, a table, or both, over which a few shelves filled with blankets were mounted. A trunk sat at the foot of the bed and a small cast iron wood stove sat to the right of it. Over everything lay a thick layer of dust.

Through the umbrella of evergreen trees overhead, Sean searched. A canopy of thick clouds oozing rain covered the sky, obscuring the stars. But, Sean was fairly certain they weren't far out of Falmouth. Far enough, though, that they would need to camp for the night. This seemed as good a place as any.

Shaking his head, Sean patted Cliste on the head. "Whatever are you up to, hound?"

Tongue lolling out the side of her mouth, she seemed to smile at him. He hated it when she did that; it usually meant trouble of some kind. Still, she had at least led them to somewhere dry for the night. He worked on opening the door that was only half-attached to hinges while Ashlinn scolded the hound thoroughly. Darkness settled its full weight over them, making it hard to see. Thunder boomed overhead, shaking the step beneath his feet. The pitter-patter of rain that had persisted all day suddenly increased tenfold and became hard little balls of ice. Cliste whined and pressed against his legs while Ashlinn pressed against his back.

Gently pushing them both back, he opened the door and ushered them inside. Unable to see, he had to feel his way along the wall so he didn't smack into anything. Stopping just inside, he removed his knapsack and dug inside until he found his small box of lucifers and the snub of a candle he had left. He struck a lucifer against the rough wood of the wall and lit the candle. For such a small thing, it managed to pour an adequate amount of light into the room. Sean carried it over to the trunk.

Inside he found more candles, a collection of skinning and carving knives, and a few corked bottles of what he suspected were moonshine.

"What is this place?" Ashlinn whispered.

"A huntin' cabin. One that hasn't been used in a while from the looks o' it."

Ashlinn began to pull down the blankets and shake them out. "We should not stay long. Just enough to rest."

Her voice was so quiet it was hard to hear over the pounding of rain upon the roof. The fear in her tone caught his attention. He sat the candle down on the top of the trunk and went to her. Taking her in his arms, he became alarmed at how much she shivered.

"We aren't far from Falmouth. We'll be safe enough for the night. I'm going to see if there is any wood outside we can use to start a fire," he said.

Her eyes widened. "Do you think that is a good idea? Someone could see the smoke."

Rubbing her arms, he pressed close to her for a moment. "Not in this storm, they won't. Besides, if we don't get dry and warm, frostbite could set in. No worries, I'll be right back."

She swallowed hard and nodded.

Careful not to let the door fall off the hinges, he went back out into the wet darkness. When they had walked around the shack he had seen a small lean-to on one side that had wood piled beneath it. One hand on the wall of the shack to guide him, he walked around to that side. Beneath the cover of the lean-to, he dug back into the woodpile until he reached dry pieces. Gathering as many as he could, he returned to the shack. No light filtered through the window, making him wonder if the candle had gone out. Then he realized a blanket covered the window. That was his Ashlinn, always thinking. The moment he tried to open the door she was there, helping.

The thanks on his tongue froze the instant he stepped within the candlelit room and laid eyes on her. Gone were her coat, boots, and cap. Her damp tunic clung to her body like a second skin, revealing the outline of her corset and her plump breasts that rested above it. The points of her nipples pushed against the white cotton fabric, making his knees and his will weak. Long, wet strands of her hair rested over her shoulders and down the sides of both breasts, outlining them. Just like that, he became hard as a lad glimpsing his first naked woman through a peep hole.

Finally, shamefully, his eyes made their way up to her face. Pink colored her cheeks, but she made no move to cover herself. Bottom lip pulled in between her teeth, eyes locking with his, she prowled toward him. That was the only way he could think of the way she moved, as a prowl. It was quite possibly the sexiest thing he had ever seen. Digging up all his willpower, he looked away. The timing, the place, none of it was right. She deserved to be treated with more respect than this.

He dropped the wood near the fireplace and slowly walked to meet her. She peeled his coat from him and let it drop to the ground. Her hands splayed across his wet shirt, sliding even lower. They passed his waistline and brushed his erection, making it press harder against his breeches. Moaning, she worked her way back up to his belt. The sound made his eyes roll back into his head. When she started to unbuckle his belt the last of his resistance washed away and he was at her mercy. That's when he realized, timing and place could be dammed, *she* was right and that was all that mattered.

Chapter 28

She was aware of what the male anatomy looked like from her medical work, but never had she seen it in such a manner. Looking upon it for the first time—aroused no less—she felt as ignorant as any maid would. Rather than strike concern or uncertainty into her, it kindled curiosity and need.

"Oh my," she murmured in an appreciative tone.

She hadn't even realized she had spoken aloud until Sean laughed, a warm sound that resonated deep with desire. Hoping her hands weren't too chilled, she took hold of his erection, stroking the surprisingly silky skin. That it could be both silky soft and hard as a rod at the same time was a marvel to her. The moan that slid from him chased away the chill clinging to her, sending a lightning bolt of heat straight to her midsection. Seeing him with his head thrown back, muttering in Gaelic, only served to stoke the growing fire within her.

The almost painful looking mixture of passion and restraint that filled his eyes when he looked down at her made her heart skip. His fingers slowly pulled her tunic free from her breeches but he paused before lifting it.

"I will cherish and respect you just as much tomorrow as I do tonight. It is not my intent to dishonor you, however. If you are not sure about this…"

Shaking her head, she pressed a finger to his lips. With her other hand she relinquished his erection only to pull him close and press it against her lower stomach. "I am more sure of this than I have ever been of anythin' in my life. Too long I have hidden away who I really am and done what society deemed proper, what my parents wanted me to do, what my brothers wanted me to do. Tonight I do what I want to do." Each word filled her with courage and determination, like sips of wine from an endless goblet. Only it wasn't spirits giving her this fearlessness, it was desire and need.

For all her boldness learning and practicing medicine when society deemed it most improper, she had never felt so bold as she did tonight. Pressed up against Sean, his body mostly naked against her wet clothing, she both saw and felt how much he wanted her. He stroked her cheek.

"How can I argue with an angel?"

Laughing, she pushed back from him just enough to peel her wet tunic off and toss it aside. Cool air tickled across her bare breasts, tightening the skin of her areolas as her nipples hardened. It felt deliciously wicked when Sean's gaze dropped to take her in. His rough hands covered her breasts, cupping them as if they were precious orbs made of glass. She leaned into his touch, pulling his body tighter against hers at the same time.

"Tonight I am more devil than angel," she whispered.

Soft lips covered hers, gently pushing them apart to allow his tongue access to her mouth. His exploration was reluctant, slow, as if he awaited her permission with each flick. Using her own tongue like a lure, she drew his into her mouth deeper, swept under and across the top of it, sucked gently. At that his erection jumped against her stomach, making her realize she wanted more of him inside her, sooner rather than later. The wait had already been excruciatingly long. She drew back from him, pulling her breasts from his needing hands, and turned.

"Will you help me with my corset?" Her words were scarcely more than a breathy plea. The blasted thing was nearly impossible to get off by herself when wet. She didn't want a stitch of clothing between them.

His fingers worked at the laces until finally he had them loose enough that she was able to push it down over her hips and step out of it. Arms wrapping around her, he unbuttoned her breeches and slid them off her as well, going slow over the curve of her buttocks as if savoring the view from behind. Hands trailing back up her legs, over her hips, and around to the front of her stomach, he slowly stood back up. She leaned against him. The planes of his chest blazed hot against her back, the swell of his erection pulsed against her buttocks.

One of his hands trailed up to cup her left breast while the other moved down to toy with the edge of her pubic hair. The ache, the need for him to touch more soon had her gasping for breath. Instead of begging like she so desperately wanted to, she reached up to grasp the back of his neck and pull him down for another kiss. His tongue delved into her mouth at the same moment his hand brushed lower over her mound of hair. A single finger slid between her wet folds, tearing a moan from her that he swallowed eagerly. That finger pushed down lower, dipping inside her channel. Slowly and gently, his finger began to move in and out of her, making her knees weak. The sensation was amazing, like a million points of pleasure being rubbed all at once. She wanted to return the favor, she *had* to return the favor.

The bed that she had made up with the nearly half a dozen blankets she had found in the place began to look all the more inviting. Cold, packed dirt beneath her feet helped ground her and bring her back to herself as she stepped toward the bed. Tonight would not be all about pleasuring her; she wouldn't allow it. This was about them both. One of his hands grasped hers as she walked away and she clung tight to it, pulling him along with her.

Sometime during her disrobing, he had stepped out of his breeches and now stood completely naked before her. Fit and trim as only a half-starved soldier could be, he still managed to be so handsome he was breathtaking, scars and all. He walked closer but he did so slowly, as if giving her a chance to change her mind.

"You're sure of this?" he asked.

A grin worked its way across her lips. She leaned back onto her elbows, loving how his gaze raked across her naked body with a barely contained need. "Careful, you will make me feel as if I am the one ravishin' you if you keep hesitatin'."

Laughter slid from him, free and easy, the likes of which she hadn't heard in a long time. He strode across the last few paces between them, climbed onto the bed, lifted her by the waist, and scooted her back onto the blankets. His knees settled between hers, his erection pressing at her opening in a line of delicious heat. Copper eyes bore into her very soul, a quirky grin teasing beneath them.

"Angel, you can ravish me anytime you'd like," he said in a husky voice that drove away the last chill in the air she could feel.

Arms wrapping around him, she grinned all the wider. "Watch what you say. I will take you up on that."

Legs spreading and lifting, she wrapped them around his waist. She slid her hand down between the two of them, grasped his erection, and guided it inside her. They both gasped at the same time. His copper eyes slammed shut as his hips moved, slowly pushing his erection deeper into her until he filled her. After only a pinch of pain, the sensation of him inside her, filling her, was exquisite. Never had she felt anything so amazing, until he began to move in and out in a tantalizing slow rhythm and her world exploded with pleasure like the New York sky on the Fourth of July.

Chapter 29

The faint light of dawn mixed with the glow of firelight pouring from the stove allowed Sean to see the tiny branches of boxwood he worked into a braid. Every now and then he checked on Ashlinn but she remained fast asleep, blankets pulled up to her chin. She hadn't even awoken when he'd rose to start the fire or opened the door to let Cliste out for nature's call. But then, after their enthusiastic lovemaking, it didn't surprise him. Finally, he finished braiding the branches into a small ring, one that would precisely fit her left finger. He held it up in the flickering light to inspect it.

To make it easier to work with, he had stripped the bright green leaves from the tiny branches, leaving it unadorned. While it wasn't made from a precious metal and didn't possess a beautiful gem, it held a significance that he hoped she would cherish. No soldier of the 69th would go into battle without a sprig of boxwood tucked into their cap or uniform. Not only did they need a bit of green to represent their mother country, the boxwood meant luck and good fortune to each of them. Which was precisely why Sean chose it for this purpose.

Two deep breaths brought him the confidence to turn on the bed and gently shake her awake. Long lashes fluttered over her blue eyes a few times before her eyelids fully opened. The adoration that filled those lovely eyes brought a foolishly large grin to his lips, but he didn't care if he looked the fool. So long as he could look upon her, that was all that mattered. With blond hair tousled about an impishly lovely face, she looked like a creature from the legends he had heard as a lad. Only he had never pictured fairies quite so sexy.

"'Twasn't a dream," she said in a pleased tone.

He brushed a lock of hair from her face, allowing his fingers to trail along her cheek and down to her jaw. Warmth like that of a hearth fire—full of promise and sustainability—gushed through him when she leaned into his hand and closed her eyes.

"No, not a dream."

She made a sound like a purr. It touched him on a deep level, both physically and emotionally.

While her eyes were still closed, he slid from the bed, knelt beside it, and held up the ring of boxwood branches. A moment later her eyes opened, fixed upon the ring, and grew so wide more white than blue showed. The smallest twinge of regret pinched his heart at having such a meager ring to offer, but her slowly growing smile helped him ignore it. He had guessed right. The emotion shining in her eyes proved she was more sentimental than materialistic.

Before he could lose his nerve, he asked, "Miss Ashlinn O'Brian, my angel, will you do me the honor of marryin' me?"

The blankets fell from her as she sat bolt upright and scooted to the edge of the bed. Not even the swell of her wonderful breasts could draw his gaze from her face right now, not until she answered.

"Now, Sean, you had better not be askin' me this merely out of a sense of honor, 'cause I merely meant that honor lies in not sneakin' away while a lady is sleepin', nor ignorin' her after you've had your way with her. You do not have to marry me simply because we had sex," she said.

He shook his head. "'Tis not about honor, I swear. You make me happier than anyone ever has, or ever will. I want to spend the rest of my life with you. I love you with all my soul." And it was true. For the first time in his life, he was doing something because he wanted to, not because he felt like he had to make up for his parents' lack of honor.

Fear crept up around his heart like tendrils of ice as her mouth worked but no words came out. Then moisture filled her eyes. "Yes! Yes, Mr. Sean MacBranain, I will most certainly marry you!" she exclaimed as she flew into his arms.

He held her close, burying his nose in her hair, not caring a bit that she smelled of musty blankets. The swell of her breasts against his bare chest, the tickle of her pubic hair against his stomach, wonderful as it all felt, it paled in comparison to the euphoria her words caused. She knew about his family, and still she wanted to be his. That knowledge set him free in a way he hadn't even realized he'd been chained.

Giggling, she pulled back and held out her ring finger. He slid the makeshift ring onto it, having to push a bit to get it over the knuckle. She flew into his arms, lips seeking his. They kissed until he had to come up for breath. To his delight, she giggled again, held the ring up into the light to admire it, and draped her other arm around his shoulders.

Slowly, her smile faded and her eyes shifted from the ring to the stove. "You built a fire." Her voice was heavy with worry.

Concern began to gnaw at him when her eyes scanned the room. "'Tis all right. With the rain comin' down so hard and the army marchin' this direction, we're safe. There are no Rebels out this way to worry about." The thought had crossed his mind before building the fire. Enemy soldiers seeing the smoke of a fire was always a concern during war. But there truly were no Rebels in these parts, at least not in any force large enough to worry about. The army had cleared them out.

Head turning from side to side so slowly he wouldn't quite call it shaking, she rose from the bed and grabbed her breeches. "Where is Cliste?"

Rising, he followed her to the door and pointed out the small window. "Nature called so I let her out for just a moment. No worries, though. I've kept her in sight the whole time. See, there she is."

The big gray hound loped toward the shack, nose down in the low fog that covered the half-frozen ground. Without a word, Ashlinn stepped into her breeches, went back to the bed, and picked up the rest of her clothing. Puzzled by her level of concern, Sean slid his belt into the loops of his breeches, stepped into his boots, and opened the door. The hound's head perked up at the sound of the creaking hinges, but she didn't approach. He called softly to her, patting his leg. Her head dropped a bit, along with her ears. Afraid she was going to dash off again, Sean descended the step and called to her with a bit more enthusiasm, still keeping his voice low. At last, she began to slink his direction, slow and deliberate, as if she were afraid she were in trouble.

"'Tis all right, girl, no worries," he encouraged.

She began to move faster, but her head did not rise, and her ears did not lift. Only a few steps from him, Sean realized her lips were pulled up to reveal wickedly curved canines. Were Cliste's teeth really that long? He wasn't sure. She had never bared them at him before.

"Whoa, girl. What's the matter?"

A deep growl rumbled from the hound. It picked up its pace, coming straight for him.

"Get back, Sean. 'Tis not Cliste!" Ashlinn snapped as she dashed out.

In a flash of blond hair she was suddenly between him and the hound, hand held out toward it, palm out. "*Scáth, stad*!" she hollered in Gaelic.

Back straight as a rod, face set in a scowl, he had never seen her look so fierce nor imagined she could.

The hound stopped in midleap. Ashlinn snapped her fingers and pointed to the ground. "*Suigh*." It sat, head hanging low as if ashamed. Red lips still quivered over sharp teeth and the warning in its eyes remained. Now that the hound sat so close, Sean realized it was bigger than Cliste and a few shades darker, with different markings surrounding its eyes. Irish wolfhounds were quite rare in America, but he did recall Ashlinn mentioning Cliste had a mate once.

"Could that be your brother's dog?" he asked, voice quiet so as not to launch the thing into action.

"Yes." The cold, angry tone of her voice struck him as odd.

He put a hand on her back, preparing to grab her and pull her back if need be. "'Tis been wanderin' around all this time alone. Careful, it could be feral by now."

Moisture shown in her eyes when she looked at him. "He hasn't been wanderin'. Sean, there is somethin' I have to tell you."

The desperation behind her tears sent prickles of warning across his skin. Those prickles exploded into a scream for action when he heard footsteps crunching in the leaves both to the left and right of them. In only his breeches and boots, he suddenly felt quite naked. His hands itched for his rifle, but he had left it back at camp. To their right, a mountain of a man with ebony skin stepped out from around the edge of the shack. The worn dark breeches and threadbare coat he wore suggested he wasn't a soldier, but the rifle in his hands belied that. Sean's eyes flicked to the left, where he had heard the other steps. Another dark man, this one only slightly smaller, stood with another rifle.

Even if he could get past the rifles, chances were slim that he could take these men down with his limited boxing capabilities. He held his hands up, palms out to show he was unarmed. "Easy there, friends, we're fightin' on the same side. I'm Sergeant MacBranain with the 69th regiment of the Union army."

To his dismay, Scáth rose and trotted over to stand beside the biggest man, who gave Sean a sad look. "Afraid we's not fightin' on de same side, Sarge. Ya need to come wit' us."

Sean shook his head, not understanding. "But, sir, if you join the Union you will be a free man, fightin' for the freedom of all your people."

Something flashed in the man's eyes, hope maybe, but it was quickly shadowed by fear. "Free men hang in dese parts. We've no desire to hang."

He knew there were those that still lived in fear of their masters, or worse, the Rebels that found and hanged freed slaves. But that didn't make meeting one any easier. He wanted to convince the man that he'd have the protection of the Union army, but after yesterday's defeat, Sean wasn't sure what that protection was worth.

"All right, I'll go with you. Just let me get my coat."

The man to the left lifted his rifle, leveling it at Sean, which put Ashlinn right in the line of it. Sean gently tugged her back behind him.

"No. Ya will get ya rifle and try to kill us," the second man said.

Sean shook his head. "'Course I won't. I'm fightin' to free your people. I wouldn't kill you." He would if they posed a threat to Ashlinn, but he hoped the man couldn't see that in his guarded expression.

"No. Sampson's right. Ya come now, both of ya," the biggest man said.

His grip on Ashlinn tightened. "Surely you only need me."

The man shook his bald head. "De master would want us to bring ya both. Come now." He motioned with his rifle. To Sean's relief the man's finger was outside of the trigger guard, but by the way it lay alongside it, poised and ready, he had a bad feeling the man knew how to use the weapon. The knowledge made his hope sink for more reasons than one. A master that allowed their slaves to become adept with firearms was one who had complete control over them.

Gripping Ashlinn's hand tight, he stepped down from the shack and they started toward the biggest man. Keeping his eyes on them, the man motioned toward the shack with a lift of his chin.

"Get der gear," he said.

A groan of protest sounded from Sampson. "Shouldn't leave ya alone wit' 'em."

"Do it."

Sampson stomped toward the shack, leaves and frosty ground crunching beneath his big boots. "Fine, Ezekiel, but if dey kill ya, I ain't takin' 'em back."

The bigger man shot him a scowl before turning a serious look upon Sean. "We be fine. De Sarge won't try nothin'."

Sean fought the temptation to ask the man to be careful with his violin. Better not to show that he had any emotional attachment to it.

Ezekiel motioned with his rifle again, indicating the direction he wanted them to walk. Glad for his boots, even if they weren't tied, Sean went where he was directed. The crisp morning air, so near to freezing, tiptoed over his skin like a fairy wearing King Henry's football cleats. Sean pulled Ashlinn close and wrapped an arm around her, partially to offer her whatever warmth he could and partially to keep her close just in case. A few paces behind them and to the left, Ezekiel walked, quiet as only a man who has worked all his life to be invisible can walk.

Sean leaned close to whisper in Ashlinn's ear. "Will Scáth obey you?"

Ashlinn's eyes narrowed as her gaze shot to the huge beast trotting beside Ezekiel. "Barely," she whispered, eyes flicking to where the two hounds followed on their right.

In his peripheral vision, Sean saw the muzzle of Ezekiel's rifle swing in their direction. "No plottin'. Don't wanna have to hurt ya."

"We're not plottin', sir. Me lass here is just cold. How far have we got to go?" Sean asked, trying to redirect the man's focus.

The barrel remained pointed in their direction, encouraging Sean to pick up his pace. Beneath his arm, Ashlinn began to shiver. He would have thought it for show if it weren't for how cold to the touch her skin was.

"Not far" was all Ezekiel would say.

They marched on through the forest, their breath marking the air in plumes of white. Moments turned into minutes. Tremors so powerful they rattled her teeth resonated from Ashlinn and into him. Perhaps they both shook; he could no longer tell. Watching Cliste rub along Scáth as she walked made him wonder how much help the hound would be if they needed her. Soft, large footsteps soon sounded behind them, the distance between each suggesting the person was running. Ezekiel made some kind of motion with his head. What it was exactly, Sean couldn't tell out of the corner of his eye. A moment later Sampson strolled up alongside him and handed him both his and Ashlinn's coats.

Accepting them, Sean gave the man a smile. "Thank you, sir. We're much obliged."

Dark brows furrowing together, Sampson shook his head and dropped back behind them. That he wasn't used to such kindness did not bode well for the character of his master. While that came as no surprise to Sean, it concerned him. Again, he considered the two rifles, and the muscle-bound men behind them. Were it just him, he would take them on in a heartbeat, but with Ashlinn to worry about, he couldn't chance a bullet going astray. The gray beast of a hound trotting alongside Ezekiel, glaring a hole through Sean, didn't help matters, either. No, he would have to wait for a better opportunity.

He helped Ashlinn into her coat before putting his own on. Though the wool was scratchy against his bare chest, he more than welcomed it for the way it blocked the morning chill. While Ashlinn readily returned to his side and clung tightly to his arm, the hesitant look in her eyes and the way she avoided his gaze struck worry into his heart. Something more was going on here than a lost dog who had found his way to a group of slaves, he could feel it. He just didn't know what it could be.

In the few minutes it took to reach the cluster of bare-limbed alder and oak trees, through which he could see a sprawling Victorian mansion, the opportunity to escape didn't come. Approaching the backside of the property as they were, Sean got a good look at any possible routes of escape. Wooden fences, many of which were down in several places and housed no livestock of any kind that he could see, offered no obstacle. A backdoor crouched within the shadows of a wraparound porch badly in need of painting. Brush and briars choked what once could have been flower beds and landscaped areas. Leafless, they wouldn't offer much in the way of concealment should the need arise.

Far off to the right of the house the roofs of several tiny shacks poked through the trees here and there. Slave quarters. Just in case they were all as fearful as these two of their master, Sean made a mental note not to run that direction.

"Go get Miss Collins, Sampson, I keep dem here," Ezekiel said as they stopped just before the back porch.

Boot heals clicking on the loose boards, Sampson trotted up the porch steps and entered the back door.

"Don't do this, Ezekiel, please. At least let the lady go." Sean made one last attempt.

The man's brows pulled together and he looked as though he were considering it, but then he shook his head. "I's sorry, Sarge, but if she gets away, Miss Collins will take it out on Sampson's little 'uns."

Shaking her head, Ashlinn gripped Sean's arm with both hands. "Then I will not go."

Those furrowed brows lifted as Sampson's eyes filled with surprise, then flicked quickly to the house. "Thank ya." The words were choked, forced, but they sealed her fate, and his.

Kind or not, Sean would take Ezekiel out if he had to so they could get away. He truly hoped he didn't have to.

Footsteps pounded within the house. A moment later the back door burst open and a man flew out of it at a run. He caught one of the beams that held the roof up and yanked himself to a stop, wide eyes drinking them in. Tingles like the brush of stinging nettles worked their way across Sean's skin. Softness to the man's features suggested he was around twenty. Blond hair framed a face with familiar blue eyes and high cheekbones. Gray tail wagging, Scáth jogged to the man's side.

"Ashlinn, is that really you?" the young man said. Even his voice had a similar timber to hers.

Sean's gaze moved slowly to Ashlinn. It struck him as sure and hard as a slap that she had been hiding something from him. How could he not have seen this? But then, what did he expect. Deserters were hanged, without exception. If she had told him about her brother being alive, it would have been as good as tying the noose herself. How could he blame her for that?

The cold expression on her face showed no signs of surprise, or happiness. "Yes, brother. It is me."

At the sound of her wintery tone, the young man's smile wilted and his eyes narrowed. "'Tisn't what you think. I was wounded. The lady of the house here found me and nursed me back to health. I was going to come back to the army as soon as I was able, but things changed."

Stiff as a board beside Sean, Ashlinn grunted. "You look quite healthy now. If that were the case, you would have come to me yourself rather than have Scáth find Cliste and me."

From her pinched expression he feared she had come to the same conclusion he had. Her brother had deserted. No wonder she had hid it from him. But still...

"Now, big sis, don't be that way. I warned you to leave, knowing how I would disappoint you." Anger flashed across the man's face.

Red darkened Ashlinn's face, spreading like a port wine stain up from her neck. "You are my baby brother. I could not leave without you. Besides, I signed up to serve as a nurse to the 69th and I would not abandon that responsibility." She flung a hand toward Scáth. "You had to know Cliste would find him and lead me to you."

Michael shook his head. "If you had left when you received my letter, that never would have happened. You and I differ greatly, dear sister. Survival is paramount to me as honor is to you. That is something you have never come to accept." A tightness remained around his eyes as they flicked behind Ashlinn to where Ezekiel stood. "Bring them inside, Ezekiel. 'Tis freezing out here."

With that, he spun and practically pranced back into the house. That the man hadn't so much as acknowledged Sean's presence with even a glance ratcheted up his suspicion. Angry as he was at Ashlinn for keeping this from him, he still wanted to pummel the man for speaking to her that way.

"How long have you known he was alive?" Sean demanded in a harsh whisper as Ezekiel urged them forward with a grunt.

The hurt in Ashlinn's eyes made him regret his harshness, but only partially. How could he trust her if she wasn't honest with him? "Only for a few days."

She tried to pull her hand free as she started up the stairs, but he held fast to it. Only a few days didn't seem all that bad. It was barely enough time for one to process such a revelation. "'Tis all right. We'll figure this out," he said.

Her lips twitched upward but the smile couldn't quite reach them. Fingers with more strength than those her size should possess gripped his hand tighter. Using his longer legs to his advantage, he lengthened his stride to go through the door before her. Brother or not, he didn't trust this man and wouldn't allow her to go into harm's way first. They stepped into a sunroom, just off the back of the kitchen by the scent of baking bread. Plush chairs, a fainting couch, and a long coffee table sprawled across the space to their right. To the left a small hallway led to several doors.

In one of those doorways stood a woman in a blue dress that swelled out like a bell. Long brown hair wound in an elaborate bun atop her head, ringlets framing a lovely face that had likely never seen a day of work in the sun. Harsh brown eyes narrowed at them as if they had wronged her in some way. Waving a hand in the woman's direction, Ashlinn's brother put on a tight smile.

"Marylou Collinsworth, meet my sister, Ashlinn O'Brian."

Inclining her head slightly, Marylou took up the sides of her skirts and curtsied. Her eyes maintained their hard look of suspicion as they moved from Ashlinn to Sean. "I would say it's a pleasure to meet you, but it most certainly isn't considering you are Yanks." Sweet as she looked, her words stung like drops of acid.

Ashlinn's brother shot the woman a vicious look. "Watch your tongue, woman. That is my sister you are talking to."

Eyes widening with fear, Marylou shrank away from him a bit as she shook her head and covered her heart with her hand. "You said so yourself, Michael." Her soft voice and hunched demeanor suggested something Sean didn't want to think of Ashlinn's brother. But then, this day was revealing many things he hadn't wanted to think about her brother.

"Yes, well, this is my sister we are talking about," Michael snapped.

Hands smoothing her perfect dress, Marylou's gaze shot to Sean again. "And she is with a Yankee," she nearly whispered.

Finally, Michael's gaze fell upon Sean, turning calculating as it did so. "Yes, he does present a problem."

Nails scratching at his chin, Michael walked over to the fainting couch, scooped up a blanket, and approached them. Moving with deliberate slowness, he draped it around Ashlinn's shoulders, hugging her a bit awkwardly as he did so. "Please, come, sit. We have much to discuss."

Ashlinn shrugged his hands off. "Playin' the Southern gentleman now, are you?"

His eyes narrowed to slits and his hand closed around her wrist. "Careful, sister. This is a delicate situation."

The fury in Ashlinn's eyes suggested she was about to be anything but careful.

"Delicate? You desertin' the Union army is anythin' but delicate, Michael. What exactly do you plan to do? Hide out here until the war is over?" The deadly calm of her voice even gave Sean chills.

Michael's false cheer drained away. "I am going to California. Mark, Ryan, and I, we bought some land down there ripe for planting. The sun shines three hundred days out of the year there they say. You will come with us, o' course."

Sean did not like how the man hadn't let go of her arm.

"Mark and Ryan are dead."

The skin around his eyes pinched and he looked down for a quick moment. "I know that. I meant you could come with Marylou and I."

Ashlinn lifted her chin and looked down her nose at her brother, who was scarcely taller than she was. "You are a married man, Michael O'Brian."

Michael spat on the polished wooden floor. "To a wench I cannot stand the sight of, and forced into it at that."

In one swift movement, Ashlinn twisted her wrist free of her brother and slapped him so hard across the face his head whipped back. "You took Catarina's virtue, you impetuous, selfish little brat!"

Too fast for Sean to react, the man backhanded Ashlinn. The resounding smack burned deep into Sean's ears, igniting fury within him like oil reaching a flame. Were it not for Sean having hold of her arm, she would have fallen.

"She took my future. 'Twas not exactly a good trade-off!" Michael bellowed. Loud though his voice was, it sounded far away, as if coming from a tunnel.

Sean knew it was the rage burning every sound and sensation in its path, but he couldn't stop it any more than he could a wildfire. He launched at the man, fist swinging. The blow caught Michael full on, just below the red mark that Ashlinn had left on his cheek not a moment before. Eyes wide, Michael raised his hand to his face. But his raging eyes didn't fall upon Sean; they went to the man behind him. Too late, Sean remembered Ezekiel and turned toward him. The butt of a rifle slammed into the side of his head, turning the world black.

Chapter 30

The butt of the rifle rose again, but Ezekiel hesitated, looking to Michael. Still holding the side of a face contorted with rage, Michael nodded. Ashlinn dove, covering Sean's prone body with her own, putting her head in the way of his. Bright red blood shone in his hair only inches from her face. She braced for impact.

"No, Ezekiel, please!" she begged.

The impact didn't come. Eventually, she let out a slow breath but didn't move away from Sean.

"Ezekiel, you do not answer to this Yankee bitch. Do as Michael told you!" Marylou's high-pitched voice snapped.

Footsteps pounded out a rapid, angry rhythm against the hardwood floor. Ashlinn watched, helpless, as Michael backhanded Marylou so hard she went to a knee. "Shut up, Marylou! That is my sister, regardless of her foolishness."

Sobbing, Marylou scrambled backwards like a terrified animal and disappeared into the doorway. A moment later Ashlinn heard the woman's heeled boots clomping up stairs.

Appalled, Ashlinn looked up at her brother. "We will leave and not tell a soul. You have my word, Michael. Just please do not harm Sean."

Fair brow furrowing, amusement filled Michael's eyes in contrast. "You love this man?"

Her gaze shifted back to Sean. Though his clean-shaven features were slack, his chest rose and fell steadily, suggesting he was only unconscious. Along with the relief came a flood of something else.

"Yes, I love him."

Joyless laughter burst from Michael. "The Ice Princess is in love. I wouldn't have thought it possible."

One hard glare from her at Ezekiel had the slave backing up several steps. Once he was far enough away for her liking, she rose to her feet and faced her brother. "I do not know what happened to you, and whatever it is, I am truly sorry. But do not allow it to turn you cruel, Michael, please."

The hardness in his blue eyes flickered for a moment, like a candle flame about to go out. "Come with us. You are the last family I have," he said.

Ashlinn swallowed down her anger, taking a moment to answer so she didn't scream. "No, I am not. Catarina is waiting for you back in New York."

Michael threw his hands up in the air and began to pace. "I can never go back to New York, to my barren wife. Do you really think they will just overlook the fact that I deserted?"

From the speed of his pacing she knew he didn't want an answer, wouldn't hear it, so she waited. After only a few steps, he ranted on. "I tried, I really did. First Mark died, and then Ryan. What chance did I stand when they both fell? I knew it was only a matter of time, and mine was runnin' out. Then I got lost durin' a battle, wandered around until I was so tired I became ill. When Marylou found me and saved me, I knew what I had to do." At this last part he stopped before her and took her hands in his.

She didn't want to let him touch her, not with her anger so piqued, but he was her baby brother, the sibling she had spent her life protecting and making excuses for. Another part of her wanted desperately to embrace him. But it was a small part. The sting of her cheek kept her wits sharp, reminding her that this was not the little brother she remembered from before the war.

"I am sorry I could not protect you better," she whispered.

A short, tolerant sounding laugh came from him. "I am a man, have been for some time now. You have not had to protect me since we were children."

She had to clench her jaw against a reply that would no doubt stir his considerable temper. If he only knew half of the things she had done to protect him over the years: paying off gambling debts, squelching vicious rumors among high society, crediting him for acts of benevolence and charity that she herself had done...

"Come with me to California." His eyes flicked about the room. Voice dropping, he said, "We will send for Catarina to join us."

Claws clicked on hardwood, the sound carrying to her from a hallway to the right. Ears perked up, head held high, Cliste trotted from the hall. Her ears wilted a bit as she dashed straight for Ashlinn. Knowing the hound would go to Sean since he was down, Ashlinn bent and swept her into a hug to stop her. Michael had always been a jealous person, and if he saw Cliste go to Sean it would turn his mood worse for certain.

"Cliste and Scáth will come with us, o' course," Michael said, as if they were children and he were tempting her with a sweet.

Ashlinn couldn't do it. She wouldn't go with him. Dead though their family was, she still had friends in New York. And the family practice. True, she would have to take it over in the guise of a nurse or a midwife, but people would still come to her, regardless of what she called herself. They had been for years already. But the hopeful, almost desperate look in her brother's eyes made it clear she couldn't tell him that. She would have to lie to get both her and Sean out of this alive.

"All right," she said through a sigh.

His eyes widened and a smile banished his concern in one fail swoop. "Truly?"

Gaze going to the doorway Marylou had gone through, she nodded. "Yes." She leaned in closer to him. "But what about your Southern lady?" She finished in a conspiratorial tone.

A quiet groan behind her told her Sean was regaining consciousness. It was all she could do not to turn around or let her relief show on her face. Michael was like a cornered fox. If she moved too quickly, or gave him any reason to doubt her conviction, he would either attack or skitter away. That part of him hadn't changed a bit. The ruthlessness she saw in his eyes, the way he had commanded Ezekiel to strike Sean, all of that was new to her. She had a bad feeling he wouldn't hesitate to do worse if it came to protecting himself.

He laughed, covering his mouth like he had when he was a little boy. The sight pinched at her heart, especially since she was about to deceive him and likely never see him again. "I never really intended to take her with me. Besides, she has this entire plantation."

She resisted the temptation to close the distance between them, grab him, and shake some sense into him. Instead, she forced a smile and nodded. The lie she had concocted flowed a little too easily from her lips. "It won't be safe for us to go now. We need to wait for the Union to pull back further. I can get information on their movements, return with it, and we can decide on the best route to avoid them."

His eyes widened, filling with the light pouring through the many windows. "That's brilliant! You were always good with plans like that. But will you be safe returning to them?"

She looked pointedly down at Sean. "O' course, I will be returning one of their wounded to them. They won't suspect a thing."

Chin thrusting in Sean's direction, Michael narrowed his eyes. "You trust him not to tell them about us?"

Watching Sean's closed lids and relaxed face, she realized he was no longer unconscious at all, merely faking it. She nodded. "I trust him with my life."

"And mine?" Michael asked a little too quickly.

Her eyes remained on Sean. She couldn't look her brother straight in the eye and lie to him. "He will protect us both. He is just as tired of this war as you are." It was true for the most part. She believed Sean would do what he could to protect them both, and he was tired of the war. But she also knew Sean was a loyal soldier with a deep sense of honor, one that would never allow him to take part in the plot of a deserter. Nor would she, but her brother needed to believe they both would.

"What of your Southern lady?" she asked again.

With a shake of his head and a dismissive gesture, he revealed his lack of dedication to the woman. "She has her land here. Once the Union pulls out she'll be fine."

The urge to slap him again made her clutch her hands together before her. Petulant and selfish were two traits her little brother had always possessed, just not to this blatant level, at least not that she had ever seen. Sean's right cheek twitched and his body went tense, a subtle sign of movement that she wouldn't have noticed if she hadn't been staring at him.

The hammer of a rifle clicked back, the sound echoing in the big room. "Oh, I will definitely be all right, because I'm going to California. I told you not to hit me ever again, you bastard" came Marylou's high-pitched voice from the doorway she had vacated minutes ago.

Darkness flashed before Ashlinn. Something clattered to the floor as footsteps brushed across it. Suddenly Ezekiel stood between the three of them and Marylou, hands held out to his sides as if to shield them better. His rifle lay upon the floor, not far from Sean.

"Ya don't wanna do this, Miss Collins. Ya love master O'Brian, and dese good people. Dey mean us no harm," Ezekiel pleaded.

Nostrils flaring, Marylou tried to glare a hole through the man. "Get out the way right now, Ezekiel, or I will have you whipped until there is no skin left on your back!"

Anger so hot it burned like her father's Irish whiskey scorched its way up from Ashlinn's stomach. "You horrible witch," she hissed.

Marylou's eyes slid to her. The rifle barrel moved up and to the left, past Ezekiel.

"I will take everything you promised me, Michael," she said.

A shot rang out like a massive drumbeat that reverberated all through Ashlinn. Blood sprayed across the flower-patterned fainting couch a moment before her brother fell back onto it. Screams tore from Ashlinn's throat, some wordless, others bearing her brother's name. She lunged in his direction just as Sean launched to his feet, rifle in hand. Blood bubbled from a gaping wound in her brother's chest, pouring out and soaking his clothes in the moments it took her to kneel beside him. Putting all her weight behind them, she pressed her hands against the wound.

Claws clicked on hardwood, skidding as they rounded a corner. Scáth entered the room, fangs bared, and eyes boring into Marylou as he stalked toward her. Gray flashed as Cliste joined him. In the chaos Ashlinn froze, not knowing what else she could do. Useless words of comfort flowed from her as her eyes went to Sean. He stood before Ezekiel, blocking both him and Michael from another shot. She could not save them both. Hell, she may not be able to save either of them.

Marylou sneered at him. "You would give your life for livestock?"

Never had Ashlinn wanted to hurt anyone in her life, until now.

Sean's expression remained calm, sad even, as he leveled the rifle upon her. "Ezekiel is a man, same as myself, same as Michael."

Horrible, cackling laughter hiccupped from Marylou. "That is the problem with you Yanks. Thinking I would allow my slaves to carry a loaded rifle."

The rifle barrel lowered. Just as Ashlinn was drawing in a relieved breath, Marylou pulled a pistol from her dress pocket and aimed at Sean. With one hand, Ashlinn snatched a vase off the coffee table and flung it at Marylou, striking the barrel of the gun a moment before another boom assaulted her eardrums. Sean fell back. Big arms caught him and eased him to the ground.

"Sean!" she screamed.

Every muscle in her body commanded her to go to him, but she couldn't. If she let go of the wound on her brother's chest, it would become a fountain. Even after all he had done, she couldn't just let him die. The pressure of the blood building beneath her hands assured that was exactly what would happen if she let go. Sean didn't answer, and Ezekiel's hulking form blocked her view of him, but she saw his legs move. The snarls of hounds erupted and suddenly Marylou was born to the ground by gray fur. Horrible, pain-filled screams pierced the air, echoing through the room. Light flashed off the steel of the bayonet on the end of the rifle as the woman raised it. Growling turned into a sharp yelp of pain and one of the gray hounds went still, but so did Marylou.

"Sean?" Ashlinn called again, nearly ready to let go of Michael and run to Sean.

"Ashlinn? Are you hurt? Is she hurt?" His voice faded with each word, growing softer.

Relief tore a sob from her. He was alive, at least for now. Fingers brushed against Ashlinn's arm, pulling her attention back to Michael. Blood covered him as well as her hands, and his face had grown terribly pale. Despite it, he smiled as he held out a piece of paper to her.

"Take it, go to California. You deserve a fresh start. I am so sorry, for all that I have done..." His words halted, turning into a cough.

The hand holding the paper dropped as if it were too heavy for him to hold up any longer. The paper fell to the floor. "I will, Mikey, I will," she lied.

His smile grew and he relaxed back onto the couch. Blood began to run down onto the fabric, making the flowers look as though they floated in a macabre sea. No matter how hard she pushed, she couldn't stop the flow. Tears dripped down, splashing atop her crimson hands. Nothing in her medical bag could fix what was wrong with him. From the amount and color of the blood, it was clear the bullet had nicked his heart.

His eyes fluttered. "They aren't all like Marylou. I met several who were kind...made it hard to kill them after that."

Keeping one hand on his chest, she brushed his hair back with the other. "I know, brother, I know."

Tension eased from him and he nodded slowly. His eyes slid closed, as did hers. The breath eased from him and his chest did not rise beneath her hand again. Not long after a rough tongue began to lick the side of Ashlinn's face. She opened her eyes. Ears down, brown eyes wide, Cliste regarded her with concern. Tears spilled over with relief that Cliste hadn't been the one to catch the end of the bayonet. Guilt immediately followed the relief, but it was a guilt she could live with. Ashlinn sniffled and the hound launched into action, trotting to where Ezekiel crouched over Sean. Lifting her bloodied hands from her dead brother, Ashlinn forced her legs beneath her, rose, and followed her hound.

One of Ezekiel's big, dark hands covered the left side of Sean's face. Panic rose in her, making her grab the big man's shoulder and pull back as if it wouldn't take a mountain to move him. She could not lose them both. Her heart could not handle it. His head turned toward her. The look of anguish on his face pierced through her panic and made her realize he wasn't hurting Sean—he was covering a wound.

"I's tryin' to hold back de blood," he said in a choked voice.

She knelt on Sean's other side and nodded to Ezekiel. Sean's chest rose and his eyes moved behind his eyelids. Even devastated as she was, seeing him breathe allowed her to breathe. Her medical training kicked in, helping her put aside her grief for now. Were it anyone else other than Sean, she wasn't sure she would have been able to.

"Thank you. But I need you to remove your hand so I can see how bad it 'tis."

Without a word, Ezekiel pulled his hand away. Blood drained steadily from a long gash along the side of his Sean's face. Laughter mingled with a sob.

"I's sorry, ma'am, I's so sorry. I didn't want de Sarge to get hurt," Ezekiel said.

Ashlinn shook her head and looked up at the huge man. "He will be all right. The bullet only grazed him, knocked him out." The deep gash oozed blood, a lot of it, but she could close it. He would be fine with the proper care.

Moans that struggled to become words made her look down. Copper flashed as Sean's eyes fluttered open. Ashlinn held his head still and gripped one of his hands in hers. "'Tis all right. You lie still. The bullet only grazed you, but I will need to stitch you up."

Silent as a shadow, Ezekiel leapt to his feet. "I go get your pack, ma'am. I saw it had medicine in it."

"Thank you, Ezekiel. I could also use some boiling water," she called after him.

He dashed from the room, calling out a woman's name. Ashlinn hoped he didn't have a change of heart and betray her. It wasn't likely anyone besides Marylou remained of the Collinsworth family. Taking up with a woman who had complications such as children wasn't Michael's way. The thought caused a lump to rise in her throat the size of which she feared may choke the life right from her. She couldn't afford to let herself get emotional right now, not when Sean needed her help. The way his eyelids kept fluttering suggested he may have a concussion and be fighting to stay conscious.

"I'm sorry..." came Sean's weak voice, the words thick and forced.

She cradled his head in her lap, not caring about the blood. "For what, my love?"

His brow furrowed and he winced as if the small movement caused him great pain. "That I didn't save your brother."

Shaking her head, she stroked his dark hair back on the side without the wound. "Do not be. I should have learned long ago that my brother could not be saved from himself." She wanted to say more, but emotion choked the words off.

Two figures rushed into the room, one hulking, and the other dainty. Ashlinn knew she should reach for a weapon in case she had to protect herself and Sean, but she couldn't bring herself to. As if sensing her tension, Cliste began to growl. The hair on the hound's spine stood on end as she faced down Ezekiel and the dark-skinned woman that entered the room with him. In his big hands, Ezekiel held a large pot of water that he slowly lowered to the ground. The woman with him looked to the ground as she held out Ashlinn's bag.

"Thank you. Do you have any clean rags?" Ashlinn asked.

The woman nodded, turned, and dashed from the room without ever looking up. Part of Ashlinn wanted to tell the woman it was all right, that she would be free now. But she knew if she spoke too much she would break down. Allowing instinct to take over, she opened her medical bag and set to work saving the man she loved.

* * * *

The weight of even half of Sean's body was enough to make her arms shake, but Ashlinn insisted on helping Ezekiel load him into the hay cart. The house servants had laid enough blankets atop the straw that Sean would hopefully feel very little of the jostling. When she, Ezekiel, and Sampson laid him down upon the blankets, his eyes fluttered open. Within their cloudy, copper depths she could still see the hazy effects of the laudanum she had given him, but just barely. The cart moved as Cliste leapt into it and lay down beside Sean, placing her head across his stomach.

He petted her head as his eyes went from Ashlinn to the cloudy sky overhead. "How long have I been out?"

"A few hours," she said, not quite wanting to admit that it had really been half the day.

It had taken shaving his hair and putting in fifteen stitches along the side of his head to close the wound up properly. But that hadn't been the worst part. Cleaning it had made him black out twice. The second time she had dipped her finger in laudanum and stuck it in his mouth, unable to take his pain any longer and desperately needing him to hold still.

"You're a terrible liar, angel," he said as he lay his head back onto the rolled-up blanket.

She almost smiled as she pulled another blanket up to his chest. After tucking it around him and Cliste, she leaned down and gently kissed his forehead. When she rose he took hold of her hand, his fingers playing with the boxwood branch ring on her ring finger.

"Me proposal to you is still open, if you'll still have me," he said in a soft voice that was heavy with the need for sleep.

Careful not to move him, she bent down and touched her lips to his, taking comfort in the way they moved against hers. "O' course I will. You had best not think you can get rid of a guardian angel after one little head wound."

He laughed, but the sound cut short as his features pinched into a wince of pain.

"Easy now, you rest. We'll be back at camp by sundown," she said.

He gave one brief nod and let his eyes slide closed. For a moment longer she watched just to ensure herself that his chest rose and fell. The injury wasn't anything that would cost him his life, so long as it didn't get infected, but she still couldn't bring herself to stop checking on him. Paper crinkled inside her jacket pocket as she rose, reminding her of what she was leaving behind, and what she was taking with her. She wouldn't go to California. Her home was in New York. But she was determined to ensure Michael's widow got the deed to the land there.

At the back of the cart Ezekiel waited to help her down.

"Thank you."

He nodded and stepped back but didn't turn to leave. "I wish I could pay you for the cart and horse," she said.

The big man shook his head. "No, ma'am. Wouldn't be right if ya did. Dey aren't ours."

Ashlinn swallowed hard, gaze traveling across the overgrown grounds. Several of the servants, both men and women, stood upon the back porch, watching them with a mixture of curiosity and caution. Among them stood three children, all barefoot and wearing little more than rags. The sight of the people tugged at Ashlinn's grief-stricken heart. Ezekiel had told her that Marylou hadn't had the decency to free them even after the Union army had come through months ago and taken all their livestock and most of their food. Many had run off, but most of them had stayed, fearing the hangmen in the woods far more than Marylou.

"You are free now, all of you. You understand that, do you not?" She had already told him and the house servant girl this when they were helping her with Sean, but they hadn't said anything in response.

Ezekiel's big, dark hands with their pink palms wrung one another like sheets on washing day. He stared down at them as if they captivated him. "Yes, ma'am, we do. I's hopin' to talk to de Sarge 'bout dat."

"You can ask me anything. I will be honest with you," she said.

Slowly, his bald head rose and he met her gaze. "Me and some of de boys would like to join de army, fight with those who's fightin' for us."

The light of pride shown upon the shadows of grief that choked her soul, pride for this man who could show so much courage after all he had been through. She reached out and touched his arm. His eyes widened as if startled, but he didn't pull away.

"Sean will welcome you, and the Union army will welcome you and any who want to join. And if the women want to help, we can always use more nurses," she told him.

Dimples formed in his cheeks as his grin grew. "We'd like that, ma'am."

Motioning for him to follow, she walked to the front of the cart. "In that case, would you mind driving? The horse knows you and I think she will respond better to you."

"I'd be honored, ma'am."

He offered her a hand up, which she gladly accepted. After today, her legs barely held her up and she wasn't about to let her pride get in the way. Before climbing up after her, Ezekiel motioned to the group of freed men and women standing on the porch. One of the women and two of the men approached, while the others set off in the direction of the shacks that had been their homes. The tang of smoke stung Ashlinn's nose. In the distance, great tongues of orange and yellow flames worked at devouring the slaves' shacks. Wherever they were going, it was toward something new.

One arm across the wooden backrest, Ashlinn turned to look upon the freshly turned dirt of her brother's grave. Ezekiel and Sampson had been kind enough to bury him in the garden out back. She couldn't very well take his body back with them; it would leave far too much to explain. No, it was best to allow him to remain missing according to the army. At least that way it would save his honor and his widow's. Part of Ashlinn had gone into that ground with him, but it was a part she thought might have died a long time ago.

Chapter 31

Ignoring his protests, Fergusson gave Sean a hand up into the wagon, steadying him with another on his back. The world swayed so much that his friend's hands and his own iron grip on the wagon seat were all that kept Sean upright. From the ground, Ashlinn gave him an encouraging smile and placed a hand upon his hip to steady him. With her and Fergusson's help, he made it into the wagon with hardly any effort at all. The world swayed a bit, not stopping until a few moments after he sat down. A tail thumped against wood. Cliste gazed up at him from where she lay taking up over half of the bench seat.

"The disorientation will pass. 'Tis only a side effect of the concussion," Ashlinn assured him.

Had his concern shown that badly on his face? The sight of her smile banished his unease and warmed him all the way to his core. She moved away from the steps to embrace Abigail, and he turned his attention to Fergusson, whose great height caused Sean to barely have to look down from the wagon seat.

"Be safe, my friend. I expect to see you in New York soon," Sean told him.

Fergusson's cropped beard moved up into a huge grin and white teeth flashed. "Oh, you will. And I expect to see a few wee ones tuggin' at that one's skirts by then." He shot a wink at Ashlinn.

To her credit, she recovered swiftly and shot him a devious look. "Oh, there will be wee ones all right, they'll just be gray and fluffy," she said over her shoulder.

Eyes going wide, Fergusson cocked his head at her. "Cliste's goin' to have pups?"

"Aye, that she is."

"I would love to talk you out of one of those," he said.

"You come visit us as soon as you can and one of them is yours."

He inclined his head. "You have yourself a deal, Miss O'Brian. But by that time I at least expect to see you sportin' a swollen belly."

Through the wisps of blond bangs that had come free of her bun, Sean caught sight of the beautiful blush that turned her cheeks pink. "Well, we'll get to work on that right after the weddin'," Sean said through a huge grin.

Laughter sounded from Fergusson as he slapped Sean on the shoulder. "Yeah, *after* the weddin'. Now get on up there and recruit me some new men. I trust you to do a better job at it than the brass they're sendin' up to do the job." With that he stepped away from the wagon.

The head wound, along with his concussion, had made Sean's lieutenant recommend he be sent along to New York with the rest of the brass to recruit more troops. It hadn't taken much to convince him to add Ashlinn as one of the few medical personnel going along to care for the returning wounded. An honorable discharge for a soldier who had served his country well, they called it. His country. Those words still resonated through him. As much as it pained Sean to leave the men of the 69th, he had to keep Ashlinn safe, and his men would be in good hands. Besides, the freed men from Marylou's plantation had helped swell the Union's numbers a bit.

The white stripes on his friend's shoulders drew Sean's eye. He knew the promotion wouldn't keep Fergusson any safer, but he was glad for it nevertheless. Fergusson was as good a soldier as Sean had ever known. He deserved to be a Sergeant. More than that, he deserved to survive this war, and Sean would do all in his power to send him exactly what he needed to do just that.

Ashlinn and Abigail were clutching hands and sniffling, each clearly reluctant to let go of the other. "De other nurses and I shall carry on ya work, Miss Ashlinn. Have no fear," Abigail promised her.

With a deep sigh that shook her chest, Ashlinn pulled her friend in for another brief hug. She pulled away and turned to hug Fergusson. Her lack of propriety made Sean smile. Their friends were more important than what others thought, and he would not fault her for acting on that.

"Take care of this one for us, will you, Abigail? He tends to land right in the middle of trouble," Ashlinn said.

"I surely will," she promised.

Taking her arm, Fergusson assisted Ashlinn into the wagon. The warmth of her thigh against Sean's burned away the lingering cold of the morning. He hid a smile as she snuggled closer to him. From the ground, Fergusson and Abigail waved and called out farewells.

The reins flicked and the horses hitched to the wagon began to plod forward. Sean and Ashlinn waved back at their friends until the wagon turned a bend in the road and they disappeared from sight. Though his chest tightened with worry, Sean's heart swelled with the promise of seeing New York's shores once again. This time they held even more promise than they had the first time he'd laid eyes on them from the deck of the ship. This time they meant not only a new home, but a family. The thought made him look to Ashlinn. Early morning light softened her lovely features and highlighted her blond hair, reminding him of the first time he had seen her.

"I love you, Ashlinn O'Brian," he told her. Part of him suspected he had since that day.

Her eyes widened and filled with moisture even as a smile turned her radiant. "I love you, too, Sean MacBranain."

They leaned toward each other at the same time, as if of one mind. Her pliant lips moved beneath his, gentle yet insistent. Though his stitches pulled on the left side of his face, causing little stabs of pain, the pleasure of her lips was more than worth it. In them he found a love so pure it made him feel like a man born again, one with an honor none could take from him.

Keep reading for an excerpt from the next book in the Emerald Belles series

Courting the Corporal

May the road rise up to meet you . . .

The Civil War has ended, but for Corporal Patrick "Rick" Fergusson the battle rages on. Still haunted by what he witnessed on the battlefield, the earnest Irishman is heading west, seeking only to be free of the past. His services are in high demand; wealthy East Coasters in need of escort clamor to join him on the journey. But one client, a beautiful lady named Cat, disturbs Rick's newfound equilibrium.

High society widow Catriona O'Brian is anxious to get to California, even if it means traveling with the handsome corporal who seems to dislike her so. Cat no longer seeks marriage; she has pinned all her hopes on making it to the west coast and starting her own winery. Between the elements, wild animals, and hostile natives, however, everything seems to be conspiring against her. Time and again, Rick comes to her rescue. And soon, the independent lass discovers that her biggest obstacle may be the longing of her own traitorous heart . . .

Chapter 1

The whispers frayed at her last raw nerve. With careful precision, Catriona set the delicate crystal wineglass down on the marble table. The dark red liquid didn't so much as ripple. Such good wine was hard to come by; she didn't want to waste it. Her fingers closed into a fist, her overly long nails biting into her palm. But it was a good pain, the kind that helped bring focus and calm so she didn't do something foolish. As the founding board member of the organization, she couldn't very well fly off the handle every time someone spoke ill of her beneath their breath.

Gathered like a brood with their coiffed hairdos leaned together, half the board members cackled all manner of derogatory things about her. Their too-loud whispers about her being "new money" and "already out of mourning clothes" were clearly meant to be overheard. Over half the eyes in the packed tearoom rested on her because of it. Her skin crawled and her cheeks heated. The old Cat would have torn into them like a wildcat, but sadly, she hadn't been that woman for a long time now.

Beyond the women, muted sunlight filtering through the grapevine-framed window beckoned her. She wanted nothing more than for this meeting to be over so she could return to her garden where she could find a bit of serenity. A delicate hand came to rest on her shoulder just as a full skirt brushed against her own. Gentle though the touch was, it was all she could do not to flinch. The white lace glove could have belonged to anyone, but the almost hesitant hand within it could belong to only one person.

"You pay them awful women no mind now, Catriona. They are jealous is all," came a carefully measured feminine voice with just the barest hint of an African accent.

Brown eyes as gentle as her voice gazed out of a lovely face nearly the color of obsidian to bathe Catriona in sympathy. She managed to force a tight-lipped smile.

"Aye, but they are jealous for the wrong reasons," she all but whispered. "But thank you for your kindness, Sadie. You are a treasure." She patted the lady's hand where it rested on her arm.

Many of the ladies in the finely furnished sitting room shot frowns their way. Some likely because such familiarity with one's servants was frowned upon. But then, even allowing Sadie to attend was frowned upon by most in the room. While the North had been the first to free their slaves, they still believed in separatism. Not Catriona, though, and on that she stood up to these hens. Sadie was a widow of a soldier of the 69th infantry, which gave her every right to attend these meetings. Besides, she was Catriona's friend and for her, Catriona would withstand all the evil glares those hens could dish out.

Lovely dark brows drawing together, Sadie waved a dismissive hand at the group of women. "The hens wouldn't believe the truth if it slapped them upside their pampered backsides," she said.

At that image, a genuine smile turned up the corners of Catriona's lips. However, the sight of a black-haired woman with skin the color of porcelain descending on the group of board members like a storm wiped the smile away. Trouble flowed around the immaculately dressed young woman like a cloak of dark foreboding.

"Oh no," Catriona murmured.

Sadie laughed quietly. "Don't you worry. Our Miss Deirdre there is going to give those ladies a taste of what they've got coming," she said.

Catriona groaned. "That is precisely what I am worried about."

All those coiffed heads raised at once, sharp eyes darting to Deirdre as if they could pin her back with their glares alone. But Catriona knew it would take far more than icy looks to stop Deirdre. Perhaps a battalion of Rebel troops.

The pointed chin of her lovely, heart-shaped face lifted and her long lashes swept down over dark blue eyes that looked as black as her hair without the light hitting them. She focused the weight of her gaze upon the brood's ringleader: a tall woman with a prominent nose. "To speak ill of your founder is to speak ill of the very manner in which you spend your free time." Deirdre thrust that delicate-looking chin of hers in the direction of the double doors leading from the room. "The wind would most certainly be at your back should you choose to walk out that door."

All five women in the brood stiffened, eyes filling with disbelief as they widened. The worst of the lot stood her ground, angling her chin up so she could look down that prominent nose at Deirdre. "Our founder merely shocks us all by coming out of mourning so soon. Had any of us landed the catch of the century for a husband, we would have extended our mourning period," she huffed.

One of Deidre's hands went to her hip. Catriona couldn't help but notice it had curled into a fist.

"Would that you had, then it could have been you who felt the snap of 'the catch of the century's' jaws instead of my dear friend."

Gasps traveled through the brood. Gloved hands flung up to cover gaping mouths.

"What exactly are you implying?" their ringleader demanded.

Deirdre took a step forward. "That Michael O'Brian was a—"

"Enough, Deirdre!" Catriona found her nerve and her voice at last.

As much as she appreciated her friend defending her, the last thing she wanted was for these horrible women to know her darkest secrets. Deirdre's mouth snapped shut and she spun away from the women on what Catriona knew to be a scandalously high heel—though it was well hidden beneath the hoop of her burgundy gown. Head held high, she pranced like a prized, gaited mare to Catriona's side, spun back toward the women, and looped an arm through Catriona's. With her friends to either side of her, they stood as a unified front against the brood. All eyes in the room turned to watch the drama unfold.

Catriona took a deep, steadying breath before speaking. "After today's testimonies we are all a bit emotional. We need to keep focused on what we are here for, to support one another." A bit of her old strength and confidence helped her voice carry throughout her five-hundred-square-foot tearoom.

The head hen opened her mouth, but a door banged open, halting her words. Her friends' arms withdrew from hers, allowing Catriona to turn. Dread made her movements slow. Little on this green Earth could cause her help to throw a door open with such carelessness. The last time it had happened, news of her husband's death had followed. A young Irishwoman, her pale face flushed red, stood in the doorway, a hand clutched against her heart, her wide eyes seeking out Catriona.

"Mrs. O'Brian, please pardon the intrusion, but your sister-in-law, Mrs. MacBranain, is here," she gasped.

Stomach churning with a mixture of joy and dread, Catriona dipped her head to the servant girl. "Thank you, Emily. Please make her comfortable in the sitting room. I shall be along shortly." With that, she swallowed her emotions, ensured her expression was one of regret, and turned to face the waiting group of women.

"Ladies, I fear I must adjourn this meeting of the Widows of the 69th as I have pressing business to attend to. Thank you all for coming. My servants will bring your wraps and cloaks along post-haste," she announced.

Murmurs spread throughout the women with the speed and relentlessness of the pox. Many, like the hen and her brood, didn't even try to whisper their comments.

"Isn't that the former Miss O'Brian, Michael's sister?" one woman said.

"Yes, it is! I am sure of it. And she was so close to Michael. Whatever will she have to say about Catriona being out of mourning already?"

Grinding her teeth against scathing replies, Catriona ushered the women out of the room and into the hallway where her servants were already bringing their belongings. Warm as it was outside this June afternoon, most of them hadn't worn cloaks or shawls, but almost all had brought either a bag or a parasol along. Though she was near to exploding with anticipation, she played the good hostess and bid farewell to each woman as she departed, even the horrible brood. When the worst of them shot her a cold look, she had to remind herself that they had all lost husbands and many bad feelings were merely born from that. Still, women like her made Catriona wish she hadn't opened the organization to all widows of soldiers of the 69th without thinking what that meant.

A very unladylike snort came from Deirdre, who stepped up beside Catriona when the head hen—the last to leave, by no accident for sure—made a snappy remark. Flinging her long, black curls over her shoulder, Deirdre looked down her nose at the woman.

"Hasten your step through the doorway now, Mrs. MacNeil, else your bustle may get closed in it," Deirdre said in a wickedly sweet tone.

Powdered brows rising into her carefully arranged brown bangs, Mrs. MacNeil gasped almost comically loud and stormed out of the parlor. Sadie giggled behind her gloved hand and Catriona groaned as she covered her face with one hand.

"She'll be impossible now," Catriona said.

Another snort sounded from Deirdre. "Because she was completely congenial before."

Catriona slapped playfully at her friend's arm. "You know what I mean."

Looping an arm through hers, Deirdre walked with her and Sadie to the front door. "I do indeed. You take too much from those hens," Deirdre said.

Unable to argue, Catriona merely hugged her friends in turn as they waited for her servant to bring along Deirdre's parasol. "I shall escort

Deirdre home, stop by the market for ingredients for dinner, and return post-haste, unless you would like us to stay for moral support?" Sadie asked.

Catriona smiled as she grasped her friend's hand. "Thank you, but no. Ashlinn and I were friends, of a sort. I will be all right."

With a nod, Sadie stepped out onto the wide porch into the brilliant sunshine and opened her parasol. The clop of many hooves on cobblestones echoed into the house, accompanied by the din of voices that seemed constant in the heart of New York. What Catriona wouldn't give for the quiet of the country home she had grown up in. Days like these made her long for seclusion, if only she could take her friends with her.

Deirdre joined Sadie on the porch but turned back to give Catriona a stern look. "You send for us as soon as they are gone. I do not want you to be alone after such a visit."

She gave her a mirthless smile and nodded. "I shall. Now, off with you, so I can get this over with."

Waving, they descended the wide stairs leading up to Catriona's grand home and started north down the sidewalk. A deep breath steeled her enough that she was able to turn away from the sight of her retreating friends and nod to her servant girl to close the door. The click of the mechanism securing the door behind her stirred a burning anxiety within her chest. Her hands fumbled with her green skirt. Of all the things she could have worn today, this was perhaps her most cheerful dress. Never had she regretted being out of mourning clothes so much as she did in that moment. Hiding it as best she could, she strode to the parlor doors and pulled them open without hesitation.

Sky-blue dress arranged about her, Ashlinn sat on the edge of a plush couch, looking as though she may burst from anticipation. Blue. She wore blue, not black. Relief rushed through Catriona, passing her lips in a long breath. A man clothed in a fine gray suit stood beside Ashlinn, one hand resting on her shoulder. Short brown hair framed a handsome face with dimples that suggested a grin often graced his face. The smile soothed her fears enough to loosen her tongue.

"So this is the man who won my sister-in-law's heart," Catriona said as she stepped into the room.

The smile that spread across Ashlinn's lovely face as she laid eyes on Catriona eased a bit more of her anxiety, but only a bit. Golden hair floating about her like the cloak of an angel, Ashlinn flew to her feet and crossed the distance between them to embrace Catriona. She stiffened at first, but was quick to relax in Ashlinn's gentle arms. The woman's joy slowly began to dissolve Catriona's trepidation. Ashlinn drew back, took Catriona by the hand, and led her over to the couches.

"I am so sorry it took us so long to come visit. I wanted to come to you right away, but we got caught up in Chicago while Sean was recruitin' and then the riots made it impossible to travel to this side of the state from where we were. Still, 'tis a poor excuse for keepin' me from my sister-in-law," she said.

For a moment Catriona was struck speechless. Never had she heard Ashlinn allow her Irish brogue to slip through until now. She looked harder at her sister-in-law, surprised to see a woman filled with light and happiness, a woman very unlike the one who had followed her brothers into war.

"'Tis a fine reason, for which you have no cause to apologize," Catriona finally managed.

Ashlinn stopped beside the man, whom Catriona presumed was Sean.

"Mrs. Catriona O'Brian, 'tis my pleasure to introduce you to my husband, Sean MacBranain. My only regret is that you were unable to attend our wedding. I would so have loved to have had you there," Ashlinn said as she clutched Catriona's right hand.

The sincerity in her clear blue eyes touched Catriona, but the hint of shame in them confused her. Surely such emotion wasn't just from not being able to visit sooner.

Sean bent at the waist, bowing deeply to her. "'Tis a pleasure indeed to meet you, Mrs. O'Brian. I apologize that we were unable to bring you news of Michael's death in person, or to return his body to you."

She shook her head. "Please, there is no need to apologize for something outside of your control."

Out of habit, Catriona cast her gaze to the floor and nodded her head, effectively hiding the lack of an emotional reaction to the mention of her husband's death. She didn't want to give Ashlinn and her nice husband the wrong idea about her feelings, or worse, the right idea. Not noticing, Ashlinn took one of Catriona's hands in both of hers and pulled her down onto one of the couches beside her.

"We've much to discuss," Ashlinn said in a guarded tone that made the hair on the back of Catriona's neck stir.

It was what she had come to think of as the woman's "physician tone," the one she used when she removed herself emotionally from a situation. Catriona had witnessed her do so several times while working with patients in the family practice down the street. What could cause such detachment now, though, she had no idea. Behind her eyes, regret stirred.

"I could tell you that Michael died honorably, fighting to unify our country and end slavery. I *should* tell you that. But I won't lie to you," Ashlinn began.

Prickles of concern danced their way across Catriona's skin. While Ashlinn had always protected and doted on Michael, she had seemed ignorant of his true nature. No ignorance shone in the depths of her eyes now. Catriona wanted to ask her not to go on, but she couldn't find her voice.

"I am deeply sorry, Catriona, but Michael was a deserter who nearly got both myself and Sean killed with his foolishness. I do not tell you this to hurt you, or cause you shame, but because you deserve to know the truth," Ashlinn said softly.

Heart sinking, Catriona's mind began to race. This made her the disgraced widow of a deserter. If she left soon enough, before word spread, perhaps she wouldn't be stoned to death on her way out of town. A shiver went through her as she recalled the stories of such things happening. She had no family to go back to, the pox had seen to that. And there was no way she would even attempt to impose upon her friends. Awful as this news was, it didn't surprise her. Nothing horrible that came her way through her deceased husband surprised her anymore. A deep breath helped her straighten her back and swallow her emotions.

"I understand. I will gather my things and be gone by morning," she said.

She fought back the instinct to beg for time to leave before Ashlinn spread the word. The words hung heavy on the back of her tongue, but she bit them back. If Mrs. MacNeil from the Widows organization found out, she'd lead the stone throwing herself. The thought of giving that woman any reason to hate her more turned Catriona's stomach.

Ashlinn's eyes flew open, moisture gleaming in them. Her grip on Catriona's hand tightened. "No! You misunderstand. No one but you, Sean, and I will ever know about Michael's disgrace. I do not seek to disinherit you, or have your position in society threatened in any way. You are my sister as surely as if we had been born of the same mother. I will never allow harm to come to you, especially because of something my foolish brother did," Ashlinn swore.

Catriona's mouth moved, but she was unable to give voice to any words. Leaning toward her, a fervent light filling her eyes, it was Ashlinn who filled the silence.

"I saw something in my brother that day, something dark and terrible. I pray that it was a side of him you never had to see, but I fear maybe you did."

Tears scorched lines down Catriona's face. Though she dropped her head, her hair was bound back with pins and clips, offering no way to hide her shame. Not so much as a single scarlet strand hung free. A strangled curse thick with emotion came from Ashlinn.

"Oh God, you did. I am so sorry, Catriona." Ashlinn drew her into an embrace.

Silent sobs shook Catriona to her core. Tears streamed from her eyes to fall upon her sister-in-law's fine silk shawl. They sat like that for some time, with Ashlinn patting her back and murmuring comforting words into her ear. When her tears finally dried up, Ashlinn drew back and offered her a handkerchief. As she saw to pulling herself back together, Ashlinn pulled a large envelope out of her bag.

"My brothers purchased a plot of land in California. Michael gave me the deed before he died. I want you to have it. You deserve it after all that you have been through." She handed the envelope to Catriona.

Both excitement and trepidation shook her hands as she accepted the envelope. California, the land of sunshine and gold. More intriguingly, a place with at least a nine-month growing season. She had only ever heard stories of it, wondrous stories. It could be much worse. Ashlinn could be banishing her to Nebraska, or simply disinheriting her altogether.

Ashlinn touched her arm. "Do not misunderstand me, Catriona. You don't have to go if you don't want to. You may stay here in New York, in this very house, for the rest of your life if you so wish. I merely want you to have this land, this choice, because it is rightfully yours."

The tenderness in Ashlinn's eyes revealed the truth of her words. She had always been kind enough to Catriona, but this was completely unexpected.

Catriona shook her head. "No. Rightfully this belongs to your family, as does this fine house. You are too kind to me."

"You are part of this family, Catriona. Even if you decide to remarry in time, you will still be my sister. If you choose to go to California, this home, Michael's inheritance, all are still yours and always will be."

Had she any tears left, she would have wept again, but, thankfully, they were gone. A huge part of her, a part she had buried four years ago, wanted out of this city in a desperate way. But she had ties here now, friends, and from the look of devotion on Ashlinn's face, even family. Did she dare? Her fingers fumbled with the envelope until she finally managed to extract its contents. Smiling, Ashlinn helped her.

"To be honest with you, I was tempted myself when Michael gave me the deed. But somethin' told me it was meant for you," she said in a wistful tone.

As Catriona pored over the documents, she went on. "It is a total of four hundred and eighty acres, a lot, I know, but three plots really. My brothers wrote to a friend of theirs in California, paying him to put in for a plot under the Homestead Act while they were in the war. Unfortunately, that means it has already been two years, leaving you only three to make the required improvements on the land."

She heard every word, but it was background noise to the words on the pages before her. Sonoma Valley California, near San Francisco. Almost five hundred acres was hers if she built dwellings on the three plots and improved the land by 1867. *Hers*, by her own hand and hard work. She hadn't had anything like that in a long time.

"Three dwellings," she murmured.

The very idea of such a cost made it hard to swallow. Ashlinn leaned forward, pointing to a line lower on the page. "'Tisn't as bad as it sounds. They only have to be twelve by fourteen feet, a shack really. You could build a manor house on the prime plot and two small guest houses on the other two, and still have coin from Michael's inheritance left for cattle or whatever you choose to do with the land," she said.

Not an ounce of push tempered her tone. It was merely matter-of-fact, almost disinterested. "If you don't want it, don't worry, I can send along a cousin of ours to settle it. Take a few days to think it over. We can discuss it more over the week if you like."

Grinning, Catriona set the papers aside. "You will be staying awhile?" She tried not to sound too eager, but feared she failed terribly.

The few times she and Ashlinn had been able to visit with one another before the war had always been filled with interesting conversation and fun. Michael had always been happier when she was around, as if his sister brought out the best in him. It had made her visits the highlight of Catriona's married life. Now, with Michael gone, she longed to have her sister-in-law all to herself. Guilt stirred within her over feeling that way, but she pushed it down.

"Yes, we are staying in the hotel down on main street, and visiting whenever 'tis convenient for you," Ashlinn said.

Catriona shook her head. "A hotel, no. You must stay here. There are dozens of empty rooms in this house, and you and Sean are more than welcome."

Eager gaze going to Sean, Ashlinn inclined her head. He grinned and nodded.

"Only if you are sure we are not imposing. We did arrive unannounced, after all," Ashlinn said.

They clasped hands and grinned at one another like schoolgirls. "O' course not, you're family!" Catriona insisted.

After a bit of giggling and more hugging, Catriona called for her servants to ready the rooms and draw water for baths for both Ashlinn and Sean. She would see to it that her sister and new brother-in-law had every comfort she could provide. As they headed up to their rooms to retire for the evening, Catriona called for one of her servants. The head of the household help sent along a skinny young man who either hadn't filled his clothes out yet, or had just gone up a size due to a growth spurt. A shock of hair almost as red as her own peaked out from beneath his cap. Catriona handed him a letter.

"Please deliver this to Mrs. Deirdre Quinn," she told him.

Accepting the letter, he bowed deeply to her and hastened out the door, closing it carefully behind him. Catriona's heart began to beat a steadily increasing rhythm. Her heart wanted two different things, and her head another entirely. Right now, she needed desperately to speak to her friends.

Meet the Author

Heather McCorkle is an award-winning author of paranormal, steampunk, and historical fiction.

When she is not writing, editing, or designing book covers and websites, she can be found on the slopes, the hiking trails, or on horseback. As a native Oregonian, she enjoy the outdoors nearly as much as the worlds she creates on the pages. No need to travel to the Great Northwest though; connect to her instead on her blog and her many social networking sites. You can also find her the first Monday night of every month at 6:00 pm Pacific Time on the #WritersRoad chat on Twitter, which she co-created and moderates. Entertaining readers and uncovering stories and points of view that haven't been covered are two of her greatest passions. For more info please visit www.heathermccorkle.com.